Personal Target

By Kay Thomas

Personal Target
Hard Target

Personal Target

ELITE OPS—BOOK TWO

KAY THOMAS

AVONIMPULSE
An Imprint of HarperCollinsPublishers

Excerpt from *Hard Target* copyright © 2013 by Kay Thomas.

Excerpt from *White Collared Part One: Mercy* copyright © 2014 by Shelly Bell.

Excerpt from *Winning Miss Wakefield* copyright © 2014 by Vivienne Lorret.

Excerpt from *Intoxicated* copyright © 2014 by Monica Murphy.

Excerpt from *Once Upon a Highland Autumn* copyright © 2014 by Lecia Cotton Cornwall.

Excerpt from *The Gunslinger* copyright © 1999, 2014 by Jan Nowasky. A shorter version of this work was originally published under the title "Long Stretch of Lonesome" in the anthology *To Tame a Texan*.

EPub Edition JULY 2014 ISBN: 9780062290878

Print Edition ISBN: 9780062290885

JV 10 9 8 7 6 5 4 3 2

For Tom—thank you for making me laugh when life feels out of control, for loving me unconditionally, and for all the other things I can't mention here.

Prologue

November
Antón Lizardo, Mexico

"NICK DONOVAN, YOU'RE going to die!"

Nick felt the crushing impact, a burst of agony, and warm blood as bullets tore into his shoulder. More shouts echoed from down the hall.

He fought to catch his breath and think through the pain. *What the hell was going on?* He'd been sleeping after a back alley doctor patched him up, only to wake to this chaos.

A hulking shadow lumbering toward him registered at the exact moment Nick realized there was something in his own hand. He looked down and clenched his fingers. A huge sense of relief washed over him as his palm closed around the familiar handle of a Sig Sauer P226 9mm.

Thank God. Someone had left him a gun.

He couldn't see well enough to aim with much accuracy, but at the rate the shadowy figure was headed for him, aiming wouldn't be an issue for long. A deafening concussion rocked the room, and a fireball whooshed in from the hallway. Nick rolled off his gurney to escape the conflagration, crashing to the terrazzo tile. Pain blossomed in his stomach and shoulder. As an IV line gave way, medical tape ripped hairs from the back of his hand, spewing blood everywhere.

Still, Nick clung to the Sig.

A smoky silhouette thrashed about on the floor, a few feet to his left. Fire licked at the cool tiles under them both, and more shots blazed around Nick's head from the opposite direction. He crawled toward a massive stainless steel cabinet that had been toppled during the . . . *Jesus . . . the explosion?*

For a fleeting moment he wondered if this was some kind of hallucination brought on by the medication he was taking for his injuries sustained earlier at Rivera's compound, but the excruciating pain and the stench of burning chemicals told him this was all too real and happening right now.

Smoke continued to fill the room. He couldn't figure out where the shots were coming from. The body on the floor near him quit moving.

Shit, shit, shit. What in hell was going on? His right hand was going numb.

Where was everyone? Where was Marissa?

He had a vague memory of arriving at what looked like a veterinarian's clinic, complete with dog cages in the yard.

Bryan Fisher and Leland Hollis had been there. Someone must have carried him inside. After that everything went hazy and gray till he woke up alone in this insanity.

How long had he been out? Hours? Days?

He wasn't going to be able to do anything to help himself much longer. Another man moved through the thickening smoke—head down, running low. The murky apparition was fifteen feet away when Nick wrapped his left hand around his right and fired twice. His fingers, no longer working correctly, kept sliding off the trigger, which was sticky with blood.

Even through the haze he could see that the shadow was Cesar Vega, the enforcer for the most lethal drug cartel in Mexico. Nick knew he'd hit him at least once. No way he'd missed at this range, despite his impaired vision and dexterity.

Cesar continued racing toward him like a freight train, promising certain death with a booming voice that sounded like a concrete mixer. Between the threats, Nick could hear Cesar cursing in Spanish as he thundered through the doorway, heedless of the crackling flames. The dealer must be coked up and operating on adrenaline, even as he was bleeding out.

Nick tried to check the clip on the Sig, but his right hand was now completely numb, and he was never more grateful to be ambidextrous. Once he was able to switch hands with the gun and wrap his left index finger back around the trigger, he was out of ammo. *Perfect.*

Cesar's progress slowed, the freight train was finally running low on steam, but the dealer still had an AK-47 with plenty of bullets. He stumbled and tripped. When the man fell, he was practically on top of Nick, and the impact was like being hit by a Mack truck. The room shook. Cesar's assault rifle skittered across the floor.

This was Nick's chance, but he couldn't move. The stitches across his abdomen had torn when he rolled off the gurney. Blood seeped from new wounds at his shoulder. He and Cesar lay side-by-side; Nick's own blood mingled with the drug dealer's.

Cesar's lips were bloodstained as he whispered just loud enough for Nick to hear. "They're coming after yours, and you can't stop them."

The dying man laughed, his laughter changing to a cough as his damaged lungs filled with blood. Even so, he managed to rasp out one last threat. "It's personal now. Your family'll be dead in six weeks."

The shocking words were meant to taunt, a final insult. Cesar never would have spoken if he hadn't thought Nick was dying, too. Nick struggled to sit up, and Cesar's eyes widened in surprise. Obviously, he hadn't been expecting Nick to move.

Nick leaned close to the downed man's ear. "My family will be fine. I always see to it."

Cesar's eyes closed for the last time, and Nick heard another deep rumble starting farther back in the building. *Damn.* He recognized that sound. He glanced at the door, seemingly a thousand miles away. He'd never make it.

He looked back at Cesar, dead now in a puddle of blood. The dealer's dying threat galvanized him to action.

He rolled toward the wall, wrenching himself to his feet. His vision swam and blood seeped into his eyes, but he hung on and moved his ass.

Whatever happened, he was getting out. There was no other option. Nick Donovan took care of his family.

Chapter One

Mid-December, ten days to Christmas
Thursday evening
Dallas, Texas

DR. JENNIFER GRAYSON backed into the driveway and
turned off the ignition. Her day from hell was almost
over. She'd always enjoyed the last week before Christmas break, but not this year. Newly divorced and alone
in a town she hadn't lived in since college, Christmas felt
like something to be endured—not celebrated.

As a Southern Methodist University professor, this
week of final exams had been unmitigated insanity. Her
graduate students were bug nuts crazy, obsessing over
their final course grades and how they would affect internship opportunities. Lord, give her clueless college
freshmen partying their brains out any day.

Maybe part of her was just plain depressed. Her final

divorce papers had been in the mailbox earlier this week. Due to the financial strain dissolving a marriage induced, she'd had to cancel her sabbatical this spring for the Paleo-Niger Project and its fully intact Jobaria dinosaur. Withdrawing from the Russ Foundation's trip had cut deeper than the divorce itself.

That a philandering husband was less disappointing than a cancelled paleontology dig certainly testified to the state of her marriage to begin with, even before Collin's affair with his grad student and the bimbo's subsequent pregnancy.

That last bit had particularly burned. Practically everyone in her department had received the birth announcement today from Collin and his "baby mama." Jennifer slammed the car door a little harder than necessary.

Bah, this was crazy. It was almost Christmas. She stood in the driveway holding a bag of groceries and her huge handbag, waiting for the garage door to rise. Light from the full moon reflected off her windshield and illuminated the driveway. Breathing in the cool night air, she looked up at the stars through the bare limbs of a massive red oak.

Just because she was in a place where she hadn't lived for ten years was no reason to be maudlin. Her single mom had died when Jennifer was quite young, and she'd grown up with an older spinster aunt. It wasn't as if Christmas had ever been a huge treasure trove of happy holiday memories for her. Still, she vowed to start thinking of things to be thankful for this instant.

For starters, she was grateful to be house-sitting for

her best friend, where she could have a change of scenery from her own place with its busted hot water heater and flooded living room carpet. Angela Donovan and her family were on a Mediterranean cruise for the holiday, meeting up with her husband's brother Nick.

The lick of mind-numbing regret and lust hit Jennifer simultaneously. But since she was turning lemons into lemonade tonight, she focused on her thankfulness resolution and banished Nick Donovan—with his heart-stopping kisses and heart-breaking tendencies—from her thoughts. She refused to dwell on circumstances that could no longer be changed.

Thank God the salon trip from hell this afternoon could be remedied easier than those memories. The treat that was supposed to have cheered her up had been a bust. She should have known better. She didn't even want to look at her startlingly white blonde hair. What had happened to "Give me a few highlights. Nothing drastic."?

She looked like a bleached beach bunny gone bad, no offense to Angela, who had gorgeous platinum blonde locks. At least Jennifer could wear a hat until she got to another hairdresser who wasn't colorblind and slaphappy with the chemicals.

Right now she just wanted a glass of wine, a good book, and a long soaking bath with an unlimited supply of hot water. That was something to look forward to.

Juggling the groceries and her purse, Jennifer reached for the light switch on the wall. As the overhead bulb flashed on, an arm snaked out of nowhere and grabbed her around the waist, pulling her against a hard, pungent-smelling body. A wickedly serrated knife flashed in front of her eyes. She dropped everything. The bottle of wine she'd bought made a cracking *splat* sound on the floor.

"Don't move and don't scream. You won't be harmed." The voice held a heavy Hispanic accent.

Onions and body odor overwhelmed her senses, along with the sharp scent of cabernet sauvignon. Her knees wobbled, and her stomach lurched. She nodded her head, and the man's grip tightened.

"I said don't move!" The hand at her waist crept up her ribcage, and his fingers brushed the underside of her breasts. She tried not to shudder.

What was happening? Her mind raced to catch up. *This couldn't be possible.*

Another voice from across the room hissed. "No, she's not to be touched. It's only for show. That was a condition."

"Who's to know?" The hand continued to skate along her ribs and rub the front of her shirt. Fingers brushed across her chest once more rather brusquely. "She'll not tell."

The overhead light went out causing her to feel even more disoriented.

"Vega would find out. We don't want to risk it."

Jennifer looked up, but the man speaking was cloaked in shadow. Two silhouettes were outlined by a light from the microwave clock in the kitchen.

"Hosea, you take her. Tie her hands and feet, then strip her from the waist up. Snap the picture and get her out of here. We don't know when the rest of the family will be home."

The man Jennifer assumed was Hosea came and took her by the shoulders. He didn't smell as horrific as the other man, not that it meant anything. Criminals could shower like anyone else. She started to struggle before she remembered the knife and slipped a little in the spilled wine. Hosea just held on tighter and steered her through the kitchen toward the living room and fireplace.

She viewed the surreal scene and felt herself slip away. The Christmas tree was lit. Angela, Drew, and the children's stockings were all hanging in front of the cheerily decorated mantel.

"Sit here, Mrs. Donovan."

The courtesy was so out of place with what was happening that it took Jennifer a moment to realize the man was talking to her. *They think I'm Angela?*

Hosea pushed her into a chair in front of the tree and began tying her feet as the hygiene-challenged man who'd been touching her earlier stepped back to watch. Jennifer could feel his malevolent gaze on her, even in the dim light.

"Excuse me." Hosea bound her hands behind her back and stepped in front of her. Before she knew what he was doing, he'd grabbed the sides of her blouse and ripped.

Pearl buttons bounced on the carpet, and she heard one ping off the brick hearth behind her. She was so shocked she couldn't speak, not even to protest. She tried to suck in air as she sat in her torn silk shirt and Victoria's Secret bra. It was the sexy red-and-black one she'd bought last spring in an effort to rekindle Collin's interest in sex, in her, and in their marriage—like that had turned out so well.

Full-blown panic welled up inside, and her detachment was gone. It was impossible to breathe. Tears gathered at the edges of her eyes, and Jennifer fought to keep them in check, knowing she'd be lost if she started to cry.

Oh, God. She wanted to cover herself, but with her hands tied there was nothing she could do. The men viewed her dispassionately.

"It's not enough," said the third voice from the shadows.

"I agree," said Hosea. "She needs marks."

"Just one though. No more," said the shadow voice.

"Yes." Hosea put his hand on onion man's chest to stop him from coming forward. "No, I'll do it," Hosea insisted and without warning lifted his hand, striking her with his open palm.

Her head flew back with the force of the blow, and she bit her lip. Tears of shock and pain burst their dam as she began to weep in earnest. She hung her head, and blood ran down the corner of her mouth.

The man who'd copped a feel stepped forward, grabbed her chin, and tilted it up to study her face for a moment. His foul breath wafted over her, and bile rose in the back of her throat. He nodded and smiled cruelly. "Good."

The other man hidden in the darkness said, "She's ready."

Hosea propped a newspaper in front of her stomach, balancing it just under her satin-and-lace-clad breasts. "Hold your head up and look into the camera," he instructed. He never looked at her body but stared only into her eyes. "It's not personal, Mrs. Donovan."

The third man in the shadows began snapping pictures with the flash going off like a strobe light. But Jennifer knew Hosea was lying. Everything about this was as personal as it got.

JENNIFER WOKE SLOWLY with a pressing need for a bathroom. Her mouth felt like it had a wad of cotton dipped in sawdust stuffed inside. There was a gag tied loosely across her lips. She couldn't work up any kind of moisture on her tongue. At first she couldn't remember where she was or why her arms were aching so. When she realized her hands were tied behind her, everything rushed back with stunning clarity.

She'd been at Angela and Drew's, men had grabbed her, tied her up, stripped and hit her, then photographed her. When they were done with the pictures, Hosea had tied her shirt together in the front and stuck a needle in her arm. She'd known nothing else until now.

She tried moving her shoulders to work some of the circulation back into her throbbing arms and hands, but the effort made her whimper. She lay on a bed in what looked like a fairly nice hotel room.

She caught movement out of the corner of her eye.

"Ah, you're awake. I am glad."

She recognized the voice from Angela and Drew's house. It was Hosea, the man who'd been so oddly polite before slapping her across the face. She shut her eyes. "I know you're awake, Mrs. Donovan. There's no use pretending."

They still thought she was Angela. She wouldn't have told them otherwise, even if they'd taken the gag off.

"Your family would like to have you back in one piece, no?"

Drew would pay lots of money to get Angela back. But Jennifer's only family, her aunt, had died the year before she married. Jennifer had no one to speak of other than a philandering ex-husband. She doubted Collin would pay anything to get her back. In fact, he'd be glad not to ever see Jennifer again.

She opened one eye. Hosea was standing over her.

"If you promise not to scream, I will take the gag off and untie you so you may use the bathroom. If you scream, I will simply cut your tongue out."

Jennifer felt her eyes widen, but she nodded.

Hosea came forward and cut the ties on her wrists and ankles. As blood rushed back to her extremities, she found it difficult not to cry all over again. The pain in her fingers was excruciating.

She moved to the bathroom where she dealt with the most immediate need first, then washed her face and hands, taking an extra moment to slurp cool water from the faucet.

What was going to happen? If they thought she was Angela, she'd better not disabuse them of that notion. Who knew what this man would do when he found they'd made a mistake? Kill her and dump the body? She'd prefer to wait and find out, rather than tell him now.

She spied a tube of unopened toothpaste and gave her

teeth a cursory brushing with her finger. Feeling remarkably better, considering her circumstances, she walked out of the bathroom.

They were taking fairly good care of her, she supposed, for a kidnap victim. She hated that word, *victim*. She didn't want to think of herself that way.

For now, she was Angela Donovan. Until someone told her differently.

Chapter Two

NICK DONOVAN LAY back on the lounge chair and tried to ignore the vacationing beachgoers around him. He should be relaxing, dammit. He'd earned this. Hell, he'd almost died getting here.

He glanced at his flat belly and rubbed his aching shoulder. Both places had had multiple stitches removed yesterday. His doctor would pitch a fit if he knew his patient had boarded a plane and flown six hours after the appointment, but Nick was sitting on the beach and couldn't have cared less. He'd been stuck at home for weeks.

Two days ago he was so bored, he'd been reduced to going through a box of old papers in the bottom of his closet—documents from his parents' estate and his father's law firm he hadn't touched in ten years, other than to move them from place to place. After that depressingly low point, he'd gone online and bought a ticket to the islands. Following the surgeon's appointment, he'd boarded a plane last night for the Caribbean. His one concession to his recovery was that he was sitting under an umbrella instead of in the full sun.

He could have argued with the doctor that watching waves crash endlessly against the shore was good for his soul. That is, if he still had one. The work Nick had done for the government didn't allow you to retain your scruples or your conscience. Still, the Caymans were gorgeous as always with taut, tanned, uncovered bodies as far as the eye could see and water so blue it would make your head hurt—if it wasn't aching already from viewing those taut, tanned bodies.

But Nick didn't see any of that. His mind's eye was playing an endless video loop of a small room filled with leaping flames. The noises became louder with each repeated playback, and the flames grew hotter, but he wasn't bothered by nightmares over the incident. You didn't do the kind of work he had done and not give up some parts of yourself, the parts you could afford to lose—or chose to. He'd grown used to his own cold-bloodedness and lack of empathy that were both necessary for his job. Nick was ancient compared to other thirty-three-year-olds.

It was the unanswered question about what had gone wrong that disturbed him. How had Cesar known where to find him? What had really happened inside that clinic?

And it was what had come later that was making this all so damn hard to turn off—what Cesar Vega had whispered as he lay dying. Nick didn't even have to close his eyes anymore to see Cesar's blood-stained lips moving.

They're coming after yours, and you can't stop them.

As it was, those words had galvanized Nick to crawl out of the clinic and drag himself to safety before the place was blown to hell, along with a man who was on the DEA's "most wanted" list. People living in that poor Mexican neighborhood had found Nick in the rubble. He'd almost bled to death before they'd gotten him to a hospital, but his boss had shown up and saved his ass.

So here he sat on vacation until his doctor said he could go back to work and back to his family, what there was of it. His brother Drew was out of town, thank God, on a three-week cruise in the Mediterranean with his wife Angela and their preschool-aged children. Nick had had to do some fast-talking, but he'd convinced Drew to take everyone and just go. They'd discussed this possibility once before—half in jest, half in dead seriousness. Nick's work for the government made his brother's family vulnerable.

That had been the larger part of Nick's reservations about taking the CIA's National Clandestine Service position: his family's exposure and the nature of what he was going to be doing himself—paramilitary operations, the ultimate in black ops.

The work had been extraordinarily exciting and soul-sucking at the same time. While the adrenaline was amazing, the things he'd had to do—the methods required, the lives affected—had ultimately driven Nick to quit.

Still, someone had to do the job. He knew men who loved the business and who thrived on it. Nick had not been one of those men, even though he was seemingly the perfect candidate: single, SEAL-trained, parents deceased, with only a brother, sister-in-law, niece, and nephew to know he existed.

He'd struggled with that because, yes, the world was a precarious place, and the work was necessary. But the job, the lifestyle, had changed him dramatically on the inside and not for the better.

He'd become hardened to others' feelings—hardened to their pain, to their happiness, and to their fears. It had been necessary for his work to be an iceman, but with his family, he didn't want that.

Sitting with his brother and the kids on a rare visit home last year, he'd realized how bad it was when his niece fell out of a tree and broke her arm. It had been chaotic—as that kind of scene usually is—with a hysterical child in pain and hysterical parents in panic mode, but Nick had felt nothing. The lack of emotion he'd experienced had frightened him more than anything had in a while because he no longer recognized himself.

Realizing he was on the verge of a serious burnout, he'd quit and gone to work at a specialized security agency for Gavin Bartholomew. He and Gavin had worked together on a corruption case several years before, when Gavin had still been with the DEA. Nick had taken the job with AEGIS, Armored Extraction Guards and Investigative Security, because he was so damn tired of that desolation inside: of not feeling anything anymore, of constantly looking over his shoulder, of terminating targets he wasn't sure deserved it.

The relief of quitting the NCS had been surprisingly underwhelming. He'd expected to feel better, to feel . . . something. But he hadn't. That desolate emptiness continued, and—if anything—it had grown deeper.

Nick still worried about Drew, Angela, and the kids being at risk because of choices he'd made. That thought kept him up nights, as much as questioning if he was like his father and capable of living the lie Reese Donovan had.

Just before he'd quit working for the government, Nick had started wondering if someone would put a bullet in the back of his head while he was out for a morning run or having a cup of coffee in a café. By the end of his tenure with the CIA, that possibility hadn't bothered him nearly as much as it should have.

Working for AEGIS was better for him, even if he'd had no idea when he took the job that it would be a threat to his family as well. But for now, Nick's family was safe. He was safe, and he'd join them soon for Christmas in Venice.

The Vegas and Riveras wouldn't be able to do anything to them on a Mediterranean cruise line, not on this short notice. Ernesto or Tomas would have to find them first. Nick lay back and gazed out across the tanned bodies once more. Things could be looking up.

"Mr. Taylor?" A waiter stood over him, his face shadowed by the sun. "This was left for you at the front desk with instructions that it be delivered immediately." He handed Nick a manila envelope with the words *For Nick Donovan* written in block letters on the front.

Nick felt the hair on the back of his neck stand up as he took the envelope. No one here was supposed to know his real name. He was registered at the resort as "Matthew Taylor." He never left the country as Nick Donovan anymore. Old habits died hard.

The waiter continued to hover. "May I get you anything, sir?"

"Did you see who delivered this?" Nick heard the intensity in his own voice and knew the package held bad news. The envelope was plain enough, but he found himself loath to open it.

"No, sir. Clarissa at the front desk brought it to me to be delivered. I can ask her. Is everything all right, sir?" The waiter was beginning to look concerned.

Nick forced a nonchalant grin. "Everything is fine, thank you. But I would like to speak to Clarissa. Where can I find her?" He smiled again. "I'd really like a refill on my scotch, too."

The waiter smiled back, no longer alarmed and confident he knew how to soothe this ruffled guest. "Yes, sir. I'll have her come out right away."

Nick waited until the man was walking away before he opened the envelope. It held two items: a piece of stationery and an 8x10 photograph.

The note consisted of four words: *Payback is always personal.*

The picture was of a shirtless, platinum blonde woman

seated in front of his brother's Christmas tree. His niece's and nephew's Christmas stockings were behind her on the mantel, and a *Dallas Morning News* paper was propped in her lap.

He studied the woman in the photo. The hair color was right and her face shape, but Angela wasn't as slim. Nick was fairly certain his sister-in-law didn't have a tattoo on the inside of her right breast peeking out from her pushup bra, either, or she'd really taken a walk on the wild side. His ultraconservative brother had become more broad-minded, as well. He peered closer at the photo and felt the oxygen clog in his lungs.

Holy shit. Was that a unicorn?

He swallowed hard as recognition hit him upside the head like a two-by-four. He'd seen that delicate tattoo before. At one time he'd been intimately acquainted, so to speak.

Jennifer Grayson. *Jenny.*

How was this possible?

Nick studied the photo again and noted the date on the newspaper—this morning's headlines, last night's Mavs game, a standard "proof of life." Not bothering to glance at the ocean again, he rose from the lounge chair and stalked to the lobby, the sunbathers and scotch refill forgotten.

THE SHIP-TO-SHORE PHONES lived up to their notoriously bad service, and it took Nick forty-five minutes to reach his brother on the *Norwegian Dream* in the middle of the Mediterranean. By that time he was packed and ready to leave for the airport.

"Drew, is everyone okay?"

"Absolutely. We're terrific and having the time of our lives, just leaving port. When are you meeting us?"

"Not sure, something's come up. Tell me. Is anyone staying at your house while you're gone?" Nick looked out the sliding glass door toward the beach and the beautiful water. It was difficult to believe something so bad could be happening when the scenery was so stunning.

"No, we didn't do that this time. You told us not to. Is everything alright?" asked Drew.

"I don't know. You're sure about no one staying there? Ask Angela. There's no one who has a key who might have needed a place to crash?"

"Hang on a sec." There was silence, and Nick could hear his brother and sister-in-law talking. "Jenn what? Yesterday? Why didn't you—Oh?"

Nick's heart sank. He'd been hoping he was wrong on the visual ID, but he wasn't. It was Jennifer Grayson in the photo, Angela's best friend.

Drew came back on the line. "I take that back. There is someone at the house. Jennifer Grayson, you remember? Jenn? We all hung out that summer after Mom and Dad's accident . . ." Drew's voice drifted off. "She's Dr. Grayson now."

Oh yeah, Nick remembered all right.

The summer my life imploded.

Drew's voice pulled him back to the conversation at hand. "Jenn was coming by to get the mail, feed the cat and guinea pig, and generally look after things. She called Angela yesterday while we were shopping in port. The bottom of her water heater had fallen out, and her house flooded. She needed a place to stay until everything dried out and was repaired. Angela told her to stay at our house. It never occurred to her that might be a problem. Is Jenn alright?"

"I don't know yet." Nick explained the package he'd received on the beach. "I'm emailing a photo to your cell. You should be able to get it if you're just leaving shore. Tell me if you recognize the woman. And Drew, don't let Angela see it."

Nick put the picture through his portable scanner and waited. He could hear his brother's breathing over the phone. When he was agitated, Drew's asthma made him sound like he was climbing stairs, even if he was sitting still.

Nick could hear Stephanie and Jeff playing in the background, the sound of his niece's and nephew's high squeals as they laughed and giggled with their mom made his chest hurt. God, he wished he was there and away from this mess. He loved his family, but separating himself from them sometimes seemed the kindest thing he could do.

"It's coming through," said Drew. There was a beat of silence. "Shit. That's her. She did something to her hair. God." His breathing sounded worse.

"I need you to erase the email now."

"Alright. Done."

"Good. Take a deep breath," said Nick.

"Yeah. Thanks. Aw, Christ. Angela's going to go crazy when she hears this."

"Don't tell Angela 'cause we don't know anything yet. I need Jennifer's cell number."

"Sure. Just a minute. I have it in my contacts list." Drew rattled it off and Nick copied it down, though he didn't hold out much hope that Jennifer would be answering her phone.

"I'm catching the first flight to Dallas, and then I'll let you know what I find. Keep Angela and the kids close. And don't tell anyone about this."

"Be careful, Nick. Find Jenn."

"I will." He hung up and dialed Jennifer's number on the very off chance this was all some sick joke.

He got a recording. Jenny's voice was like he remembered. Soft, low. He asked her to call him as soon as she got the message.

Next he called Marissa, his boss and the co-owner of AEGIS, to explain the situation. Again, he wasn't holding out hope that he'd get the answer he was looking for. Two hours later he was on a redeye flight bound for Dallas.

His vacation was over and he was back to work, whether his doctor liked it or not.

Saturday morning
Dallas

FIFTEEN HOURS LATER Nick sifted through the rubble of Drew's living room in North Dallas. The Christmas tree was tumbled on its side, decorations and lights tangled. The stockings had been slashed with malicious abandon, the sofas overturned, knickknacks toppled to the floor.

Every surface in the house was swept clean or scattered with pieces of something that had been destroyed. The one surprising thing Nick found intact was a handbag sitting in a puddle of red wine at the back door. He assumed it was Jennifer's. He reached inside and found car keys, a makeup bag, and a wallet with an ID.

He wasn't positive it was Jennifer's bag till he opened the wallet and saw her driver's license. This was the Jenny he remembered: dark blonde hair, big green eyes, dewy skin, generous smile. Even in a DMV picture, she was beautiful. She'd obviously dropped her bag on the way into the house, along with the bag of groceries and bottle of cab. He set the bag aside to return to her, *when* he got her home.

Somehow the kids' guinea pig was still in its cage, even though the enclosure had been knocked to the floor. Nick righted the cage, cleaned it out, and gave the animal some water along with an extra-large portion of food before hunting down the family cat in the laundry room. He fed her as well, dumping what he estimated would be a week's worth of kibble in her dish.

The normalcy of those actions kept his fury at a slow boil, but when he was done with the simple chores, his anger roared to the surface again. Still, he knew fury was better than the naked fear that lay under that anger. He ignored the white-knuckle terror as he continued searching, hoping to find some scrap of evidence that would give him a clue to Jennifer's whereabouts. He already had a fair guess as to who'd taken her. Most likely it was Cesar's brother, Ernesto Vega.

Amid the debris he spied the ladder-back chair from the photograph he'd received. The chair was upright in front of the fireplace with a manila envelope on the seat, just like the one he'd received in Grand Cayman. His name was printed on the outside. Inside was a piece of stationery, and another photo.

He took a gulp of air before studying the picture. Jennifer was lying on a bed—asleep or dead, he couldn't be sure. He prayed she was merely sleeping. She wore a blouse and a trim tailored skirt, but her shirt was torn and simply knotted at her waist. She looked extraordinarily vulnerable: hands tied behind her back, eyes closed.

If you want to see your sister-in-law alive again, come to the Gaylord. Suite 345, Saturday at noon. She'll remain drugged until then. Remember, it's always personal.

Damn. Nick wasn't sure whether he was relieved or terrified at the confirmation. They thought Jennifer was Angela. How could they have made that mistake?

The two women didn't look at all alike. Then he remembered the platinum blonde hair in the photo, and it was easy to understand how the error had occurred.

God. It was what he'd always been most afraid of and what he'd worked so hard to prevent—his work putting the people he cared for at risk. Still, he was grateful that Ernesto didn't know as much about him and his past as he'd originally feared. Except by now, of course, they might have figured things out.

He reread the note. He had to focus. *Saturday at noon.* That was in two hours.

Drugged.

He recalled Jenny's affinity for health food and her aversion to even taking aspirin from that summer they'd spent so much time together. A future doctoral candidate, she'd already been a natural teacher. Late at night, lying side by side in his bed, she had made the history of dinosaurs come alive, a topic that hadn't interested him since he was a child.

She'd understood him in ways no one had, before or since. In the weeks after his parents' accident, as his father's reputation was destroyed posthumously in the press, Jenny had been the person he could count on when it felt like everyone else had turned their back.

Her support had enabled him to sort through the horrific media storm surrounding his father's alleged embezzlement and the subsequent dismantling of the Donovan law firm. That summer had led Nick to re-evaluate everything in his life, and he'd chosen to join the Navy instead of attending law school. He'd never told Jennifer how much she'd influenced that decision, or that she'd held him together when he'd felt like his world was falling apart.

They'd stayed in touch, for a few months at least. Even when she'd quit returning his calls and emails with no explanation, he'd kept up with her through Angela. Had he really thought Jenny'd wait for him?

Why had she quit returning his calls in the first place?

God, he was tired, as evidenced by the fact that he was revisiting past history and particularly that question.

The reason she'd quit calling didn't matter anymore.

He took another steadying breath to pull himself back from memories that would do him no good right now. Exhaling, he smoothed his clenched fist along his jean-clad thigh. He had to file those thoughts away.

Someplace where it wouldn't be personal. Someplace where he could stay cold and untouchable.

Chapter Three

"I AM ERNESTO Vega. I believe you knew my brother." Two bulky-looking guards stood across the room as a distinguished-looking Hispanic man seated himself across from Nick. His eyes were disturbingly familiar.

Nick's gut tensed at the introduction, but he didn't give any outward appearance that the knowledge disturbed him. That Ernesto would risk coming into the country was an indicator of how important this was.

"Yes, I knew Cesar." Nick gave a small nod as an exotic-looking woman handed him a bottle of mineral water from a refrigerator in the suite's wet bar.

"You're surprised I'm here in the U.S., are you not?"

Nick shrugged. "It would seem rather rash given that you're on the most wanted list for the DEA."

Ernesto smiled, but the expression didn't reach his eyes. The men stared at each other in silence.

Nick unscrewed the top on the water. "Are you here to kill me or give me back the woman?"

Ernesto shrugged. "I haven't decided. Perhaps both. For now, let's call it a mission of diplomacy."

Nick raised an eyebrow and looked pointedly at the bodyguards. "If you're planning to kill me, you're going to need a hell of a lot more men than you've got right now."

Ernesto sipped his drink. "Oh, I don't think so. Remember, I have your sister-in-law."

They still didn't realize their screw-up. Nick took a swallow of water to cover his relief. "For the time being. We're here because you kidnapped my brother's wife. That beats the hell out of any kind of diplomacy I've ever seen."

Ernesto swirled the liquid in his glass. "Tomas Rivera's wife, Carlita, was my sister. She's dead. So is my brother, Cesar. I don't give a shit about diplomacy."

"I had nothing to do with your sister's death," said Nick.

That was true. Ernesto's sister, Carlita Vega Rivera, had been killed in a violent explosion in November, the day before her brother, Cesar Vega, tried to kill Nick in a back-alley Mexican vet clinic.

But Carlita had been doomed long before the unexplained detonation that destroyed her husband's home. Having a very rare blood type, she'd been days away from death and in desperate need of a bilateral lung transplant that wasn't going to come in time.

In hopes of saving Carlita, Tomas Rivera had kidnapped a boy whose mother, Anna Mercado, had the same rare blood type. Leland Hollis, the newest member of AEGIS, had gone into Mexico to get the boy. Nick had been part of the extraction team.

Getting everyone out was where things had fallen apart.

Ernesto waved his hand impatiently. "You left Tomas Rivera's compound minutes before it was attacked. I refuse to believe you and your employer had nothing to do with its being destroyed."

"You're certainly entitled to your opinion, but I had nothing to do with the explosion. Neither did the people I work for." Nick was telling the truth, even if it could be interpreted to mean he was still working for the CIA as well as AEGIS. But he wasn't about to explain. Ernesto would never believe he'd quit the CIA anyway. No one believed him when he said he'd quit.

"So you say. But it seems suspicious to me that you were present at both blasts where my sister and brother died."

"Are you certain another cartel wasn't responsible? Your brother-in-law, Tomas Rivera, is not without enemies. Not to mention your own enterprises in the area."

Ernesto's smile was grim. "I would not order a hit on Tomas's compound with my sister inside."

The sister married to Ernesto's number one competitor, a man to whom he hasn't spoken in years, Nick thought. But he couldn't say that if he was trying to keep the peace. "You and I both know that there's been bad blood between the Vega and Rivera cartels for a while. Ever since your sister's marriage."

Ernesto leaned forward, his eyes glittering with anger. "You were seen on the security tapes inside Rivera's compound, setting up some kind of device moments before the explosion. Can you explain that?"

Nick wanted to ask how Ernesto knew that, but the answer was obvious. Tomas Rivera must have had security camera feeds running to an offsite location. "I never said I wasn't there at Rivera's, but I wasn't setting explosives. I was installing listening devices, trying to find out if Rivera knew anything about Elizabeth Yarborough's disappearance."

Ernesto raised an eyebrow. "The young woman doing charity work for your Peace Corps in Mexico? I thought authorities had proven that the boyfriend killed her?"

Nick stifled a sigh. Everyone thought that. Yarborough's boyfriend was currently in a Mexican prison accused of her murder, but AEGIS had been hired to find out what really happened.

"There is some speculation that she's not dead and was possibly sold into the sex trade," said Nick.

"And you thought Tomas Rivera might have information about this unfortunate American's kidnapping because . . .?" Ernesto studied Nick as he asked the question.

Nick didn't blink. Instead, he shot Vega a grim smile. "You know as well as I do that your brother-in-law has connections to human trafficking throughout Latin America. You and he both do. It seemed as good an opportunity as any to find out if that supposition was true while going in to retrieve our operative and the Mercados."

"And just what did you find?"

Nick shook his head. "Our bugs weren't in place long enough to yield any information before they were blown to hell along with the rest of Rivera's compound."

"But Rivera survived. Chasing after you at the time, I believe." Ernesto stood, seeming to debate what he wanted to say next. He walked to the sideboard to refresh his bourbon, but Nick felt no need to fill the silence.

"My sources have confirmed that a drone was used at Rivera's home and at the clinic. I want to know how that happened," said Ernesto.

"A private drone?"

Ernesto shrugged, but at the same time his eyes lit with a bitter fire. "I didn't say if it was government or private. That's what I'd like to know. Who would do such a thing? Neither myself nor Tomas Rivera has access to drones. But your government does. There is something bigger going on here than a feud between two families. I want you to find out what that 'something bigger' is. Someone at AEGIS knows."

"You have a great deal of faith in my abilities," said Nick.

"I know what you used to do for the U.S. government, Mr. Donovan. I understand that you were quite good at your job." Ernesto remained beside the bar and seemed content to let the question of whether Nick still worked for the CIA hang in the air.

"Since Cesar died in an explosion that almost killed you both, I'm assuming it wasn't your idea to blow the vet clinic. But I'd like to know what is going on, and I'm offering an exchange. I want you to find out who was behind the drone attacks on Tomas Rivera's home in Heroica Veracruz and on the vet clinic in Antón Lizardo. I believe that will explain who was responsible for the deaths of Carlita and Cesar both. When you tell me that, you may have the woman back."

Nick's mind raced. He had no clue who had blown up the Rivera compound or the vet clinic, and he had no intention of investigating those mysteries before locating and extracting Jennifer from wherever Ernesto Vega had taken her. He was certain that AEGIS had had nothing to do with either event, but all bets were off as to his former employers' involvement or that of any other government agency. Still, he had heard nothing about the incidents being drone attacks. He didn't believe Gavin Bartholomew, his boss at AEGIS, would have kept something like that from him.

"I've always assumed this was some kind of turf war, and I got caught in the cross fire. That was the official word in the debriefing I was privy to."

Ernesto arched an eyebrow. "How do I know if you're telling the truth?"

"Why would I lie?"

"Why indeed? Surely you know just as I do that people lie for all kinds of different reasons. It would hardly be prudent when I have your sister-in-law, now would it?"

Nick again felt his insides tighten in apprehension at the mention of the mix-up but kept his expression carefully schooled. Ernesto couldn't know he held the wrong woman as hostage.

"Or rather I had your sister-in-law," said Ernesto.

Now Nick's gut twisted painfully. "What do you mean you had her? Where is she?"

"I gave her to Rivera's people in Tlaxcala to hold for me."

Nick's breath clogged his lungs as he stared at the man.

"Tlaxcala?" The smallest state in Mexico was located in the east-central portion of the country and known for two things: the Sierre Madre Oriental Mountain Range and prostitution.

"Just for a while," said Ernesto.

The only people in Tlaxcala were sex traffickers. The area was notorious for it. Nick shook his head once as Ernesto continued talking.

"I want you to have sufficient motivation for finding out what really happened to my family. But you needn't worry about your sister-in-law. Rivera's people will sedate her to keep her cooperative. It won't be too traumatic that way. She'll go back to your brother, if not untouched, at least not traumatized. Rivera's people are very good at keeping the women comfortable when they arrive to get them through the initial 'adjustment phase' of their new lives."

Jesus.

"Do you mean they'll just drug her into oblivion so they can fuck her without any resistance?" Nick's voice remained steady and conversational as he felt the tiny thread on his control stretch and snap. He focused on unclenching his fists and breathing slowly through his nose. *Stay calm.* "What have you done?"

"I've given you incentive to find out what I want to know. After I get my information, I'll tell you exactly where your sister-in-law is, and you can get her out of harm's way as quickly as possible." Ernesto sipped his drink, seemingly unperturbed by Nick's harsh words. "But don't take too long. Tomas may find his people have need of her services."

"You son of a bitch. You mean he'll put her to work in one of the brothels in the area, don't you?" White-hot rage raced through Nick's veins, but his voice remained icy calm, even as the thought of what they were discussing made him slightly ill.

Prostitution rings and black market porn were just the tip of the iceberg. Still, he kept his tone stable and businesslike while he forced himself to keep his hands loosely gripping his bottle of water. "How do I know Rivera hasn't put her to work already?"

Ernesto shook his head but raised an eyebrow at the same time. "Tomas says he has not, but you never know. That's why you don't want to take too long to get me my answers. Don't worry, I'll check in on her from time to time." He shrugged noncommittally and finished his drink.

Nick tried to ignore the threat along with the acid eating at the lining of his stomach and the fear clutching his throat with iron claws. He'd seen the places Ernesto spoke of, and he'd witnessed the methods used. These were places totally devoid of hope, where animals came to spew their rage on women and children . . . on those thought to be expendable.

Tlaxcala was the state name as well as that of the capital city. Covered with brothels, the area's primary source of income was prostitution. Searching for Jennifer down there would be like looking for the proverbial needle in a haystack, and Tomas Rivera's people would know Nick was coming. They could move her around in a tortuous shell game for weeks. Nick's heart rate ticked upward because Ernesto's assurances of "checking in on her" didn't mean squat. "Why use me? How do you know I can be trusted?" he asked.

"Because I have the power to keep your sister-in-law out of harm's way. You want her out alive, Mr. Donovan, because your family is everything to you. I understand that."

Nick took another sip of the bottled water as Ernesto continued. "My family was everything to me as well. While I can't have Cesar or Carlita back, I will have justice. And I will have them avenged. I'll even use you to do it."

Ernesto moved away from the sideboard, his black gaze never wavering from Nick's. "Your old contacts and your expertise will come in handy. If you do this right, we can both be heroes. And your sister-in-law can come home safely. But if it all goes to hell, I'm fairly certain you'll die in the process. So, it's—how do you say it in the U.S.—a win-win for me."

"And . . . my brother's wife?"

Ernesto tilted his head and frowned slightly. "An unfortunate casualty."

Nick stared back with his neutral game face in play. In the end it wouldn't have mattered if Jennifer was family, an ex-lover, or a stranger he'd met on the street. He was going after her. Ernesto's not knowing her true identity might lend him some kind of upper hand later, if she hadn't already given herself away.

Nick finished his water before he spoke. "Alright. You've got your bargain. But if Angela is harmed in any way, the people in Tlaxcala are going down and I'm coming after you."

"Ah, but you'll have to find me first." Ernesto laughed and turned to leave.

"That won't be a problem." Nick's lips curved in a grim parody of the smile Ernesto had given him earlier. "As you've heard, I'm very good at what I do."

Ernesto paused in the doorway. "For your sister-in-law's sake, I hope so."

Chapter Four

Saturday afternoon

JENNIFER LAY ON the bed as the room came into gradual focus. *Where am I?* This was a different place from where she'd woken last.

Light filtered through half closed mini-blinds in the window beside her and threw long shadows across the mattress. She'd been drifting in and out for what seemed like days, but in truth she had no idea how long she'd been unconscious. She assumed she'd been drugged. Her skin felt gritty and sticky at the same time. Her eyes were so dry they burned.

Were they putting something in her food? She hadn't eaten much, and she'd been somewhat lucid yesterday—or had it been the day before? She'd taken a few sips of the soup they'd brought her then and hadn't known anything until now.

She had no clue where she was, but she was wearing the same clothes she'd been in when they took her from Angela and Drew's house. Was that just one day ago? Two days? Longer?

Her scalp itched, and she felt nasty. She smelled, too, as if she'd needed a shower for quite a while.

She wasn't tied up anymore and rose from the bed gingerly, concerned her head might spin. It did at first, so she took a deep breath against the slight headache and made her way to the tiny *en suite* bathroom.

The dimly lit washroom was ancient but functional. The sharp tang of bleach perfumed the air. The rusty sink, toilet, and shower stall had recently been scrubbed thoroughly, if the smell of cleansers was any indication. Clothes and a towel were folded neatly on the counter.

What is this place?

She washed her hands and explored the bedroom. The other door to what she assumed led outside was locked. She beat on the wooden panels and hollered for five minutes, but no one answered. She sat on the bed, debating what to do.

The only window in the room was tiny. In addition to the blinds, it had burglar bars across the glass. The view was facing a concrete wall. She could tell nothing by looking outside except that the sun was still up. But she had no idea whether it was morning or afternoon light. The room was empty save for the bed, a nightstand, and a lamp.

Clean clothes, soap, and water beckoned to her from the bathroom. She reached up to scratch her head, and that cinched it. She couldn't stand herself any longer. As long as she was stuck here, she was cleaning up.

Carefully locking the bathroom door, she stripped off her filthy clothes and climbed into the shower, surprised to find a very exclusive brand shampoo and conditioner in the enclosure as well as a disposable razor.

She stood under the surprisingly strong spray, scrubbing her hair and shaving her legs, despite the near darkness. Her thoughts were jumbled, as if she couldn't concentrate or hold an idea in her head. That had to be from the drugs.

Stepping out of the shower, she felt more human again. And despite the dark, steamy bathroom, she slipped into the clean clothes from the countertop. She was a bit unnerved by the exotic lingerie: a delicate gray bustier and lacey thong panties. Still, there was no way she was putting any of her dirty things back on. A simple, elegant knit wrap dress and high heels finished up the ensemble. Every item fit perfectly, down to the bustier and stilettos. That was unnerving.

Who had done this? How did they know her sizes?

She opened the medicine cabinet over the sink and found a small but exclusive collection of cosmetics and toiletries. Knowing she'd feel more in control and not as frightened if she was groomed, she dried her hair with the tiny blow dryer attached to the wall and applied the clear lip gloss and lotion she'd discovered.

When Jennifer unlocked the bathroom door and stepped into the bedroom, she barely contained a gasp. A beautiful older woman was seated on the edge of her bed.

She was exquisitely dressed and nodded approvingly. "You're awake and dressed, Miss Angela."

They still think I'm Drew's wife.

What would they do when they found out she wasn't? Why would they want Angela in the first place? Could this have anything to do with Nick and his work?

Angela had told her once that Nick did "work for the government" that he couldn't talk about. Jennifer had assumed that meant one of the intelligence services, but she'd never felt right about prying. It had been easier not to have any details. Now she wished she had at least asked a few questions, so she could know what she was up against.

Unaware of Jennifer's distress, the woman continued in heavily accented English, "That is good. I am Monique."

"You doped my food," accused Jennifer, still struggling to puzzle it all out.

"We had our orders. How do you feel?"

Jennifer frowned. *Confused. Scared. Pissed off.*

Monique smiled. "I meant physically."

"I'm hungry, and I feel hung over."

The woman nodded again. "That's to be expected. It's the drugs in your system. They make you feel that way when you're coming down."

Coming down? What had happened? Her stomach roiled when she thought of the man who'd groped her at Angela and Drew's house.

Caught up in her own private horror, Jennifer missed what Monique was saying: ". . . along. I'll feed you. You have to eat."

Monique rose to leave the room and indicated that Jennifer should follow. The older woman unlocked the door. Jennifer's mind was still fuzzy as she struggled to catch up. The horror at what might have been done to her while she was out cold crashed through her.

Monique was talking again, and Jennifer realized she was expected to say something. The older woman looked at her intently. The bedroom door stood open behind them.

"Are you just going to let me walk out of here without guards or anything?"

Monique smiled with a knowing gaze that Jennifer was beginning to dislike. "Of course. You'll understand soon."

Jennifer wasn't sure what that meant, but the woman's next words held a chill of foreboding. "There's nowhere for you to go."

She followed Monique slowly down the hall. As they neared the stairs, the rooms became more polished. It was clear that she'd been kept in a part of the house that was closed off. A place where no one could hear her beating on the door, perhaps?

Here there was fresh paint and carpeted hallways. Jennifer ventured to guess there were no rusted sinks or showers, either, in the guest rooms beyond the doors she now passed. The house was massive.

"What is this place?" she asked.

"It was actually considered a showplace at one time," Monique explained. "I've lived here for two years, and we are slowly refurbishing. The previous owners let it fall into a terrible state of disrepair."

They passed another door, and Jennifer heard the sound of weeping. She started to slow, but Monique kept walking. Clearly not everyone was happy in this paradise. There was a simple thumb latch on the door in the locked position, indicating that Jennifer wasn't the only one being held against her will.

Up ahead, light spilled from a cavernous glass dome that opened into a huge circular room stretching upward two stories. From the second floor, Jennifer and Monique stood on a balcony looking down into a massive foyer that had clearly been a recipient of the aforementioned refurbishing. The decorating was overdone with too many competing colors and fabrics—like a dessert that was too rich, too much, too everything.

They made their way downstairs and passed through the grand entryway, pausing before an opulent dining room. A long sumptuous table had been set, and several women in overtly sexy lingerie sat around it, eating in noticeable silence. They were all fairly young, although several wore so much makeup it was difficult to discern their ages. There were ten women total.

A burly man sat alone at a desk by the door to the room. He was reading a newspaper written in Spanish and had a computer in front of him. It looked almost like a check-in counter for the dining area.

"Would you care for something to eat?" asked Monique.

Jennifer's tummy rumbled, but she remembered what had happened the last time they'd given her food. She had to stay awake if she was going to find a way out of here. "No, I wouldn't."

"This food is not drugged," Monique said.

"Excuse me if I don't believe you." Hunger made Jennifer's tone sharper than usual.

"As you wish." Monique tilted her head and directed Jennifer to a large office next door. Bookshelves lined the walls from floor to ceiling, giving it a classic English library feel. A man sat at an immense desk in the center of the room with two chairs before him. He appeared to be in his mid-fifties: handsome with dark hair and slight graying at his temples. He was dressed in casual elegance with an open shirt and linen pants.

Pastries, eggs, bacon, and juice were all laid out on a tray before him, along with Georgian silver and Wedgwood china.

He looked up, and Jennifer couldn't stop herself from staring. His eyes were an ordinary brown but stunning in their intensity. He nodded to the chair and indicated she should sit.

"Tomas, are you sure you didn't hit the clinic? I find it hard to believe you don't have access to drones through your contacts within the military."

Jennifer was startled by the booming voice over the speakerphone. The caller had a sharp Bostonian accent and was obviously mad as hell.

The man Jennifer assumed was Tomas scoffed. "You forget yourself. The cost to me was quite dear in this case. I'm surprised you would think me that rash. I can't help but wonder if your associates are to blame."

"I assure you, my friend, I had nothing to do with the two incidents. My people didn't either." The voice was placating. "I am terribly sorry for your loss, but we still need to nip this issue in the bud before the delivery in Constantine."

"I agree nothing can interfere with that. All the arrangements have been made," said Tomas.

The voice on the line was quiet. Jennifer sat, trying not to look as if she was listening. Tomas took another sip of coffee from the fine china cup and poured himself a warm-up from the ornate silver pot on his desk. "I still think you need to look to your own people. Someone in your organization knows something."

He glanced up at Jennifer and dismissed her again as the clipped voice rumbled over the speakerphone. "I repeat. I had nothing to do with either of these horrific events. Nor did any of my people. But I'll be glad to help you find the son of a bitch who did."

"I may just take you up on that offer. We'll talk again soon." Tomas hit the OFF button and addressed the two women before him.

"Monique, thank you for bringing our guest down. Did she have breakfast?"

"No, sir. She said she didn't care for any."

"Ah, she's worried we'll taint her food." He turned to Jennifer. "I trust you rested well?" He raised an eyebrow.

The anger she'd felt before was nothing compared to the fury flooding her system now. Tired of being scared and feeling like a victim, Jennifer decided there wasn't much to lose by saying exactly what she thought. It was so much better than being frightened.

"For one who's been drugged into oblivion, I suppose you could say I slept like a baby," she snapped.

"It seemed best. Would you have preferred to have been awake on your journey down here, Mrs. Donovan? That would have been most unpleasant."

"I would prefer to go home."

"I'm sure you would. And the quicker your brother-in-law delivers the information we've requested, the sooner it will happen."

Her brother-in-law. They meant Nick. "I don't understand." She wasn't going to think about what would happen if they found out she wasn't Angela.

"I'm sure you don't, but no matter. Nick Donovan has quite the motivation to quickly provide a particular service for us so he can fetch you home. The big question is, what do we do with you in the meantime?"

Tomas gave her an assessing look, and she was instantly uncomfortable. "This is, after all, a business. And a white woman with your"—he looked her up and down as if he were undressing her—"*attributes* would be in demand. If you live here, no matter how short a time, you work here."

He stirred creamer into his coffee.

"What?" She could feel the confusion showing on her face.

"You still don't understand, do you? But why would you? This is all so far removed from your rather sheltered life."

She felt her anger spurt again. "There's no reason to be insulting, just because I don't understand what you're alluding to."

He smiled. "Ah, a woman with spirit. That is excellent.

You're already adding to your résumé. Don't worry, Monique will look after you and explain the job here."

"Job?" Jennifer echoed. *What is this place?*

"Naturally you'll have a job. You're in Tenancingo."

"In Mexico?"

Tomas smiled. "Of course."

What the significance was of Tenancingo, she had no idea. The confusion she felt had to be evident on her face.

"You *are* an innocent, aren't you?" laughed Tomas. "This is one of the *calcuilchil*. In English that means 'houses of ass.'"

She was starting to feel like a broken record. "I still don't understand." But she had the terrible feeling that she was beginning to. The overdone makeup, the young women, the lingerie—it all made a horrible, morbid kind of sense.

Tomas Rivera smiled proudly. "This is the finest brothel in Tlaxcala."

Chapter Five

Saturday afternoon
Dallas

NICK LISTENED TO Gavin's disembodied voice over his car's speakerphone as the speedometer crept up to ninety-five miles per hour. Gavin had gathered information about Tlaxcala and was sharing the not-so-fun facts while Nick drove back from the Gaylord.

"The real center of Tlaxcala's prostitution is the city of Tenancingo. It's called *cuna de los padrotes*. The crib of the pimps. Leland Hollis worked with the DEA down there before he came on board with us. I'm adding him to this call now. Hang on."

Darkness fell as Nick raced across LBJ. He needed to get to the AEGIS office, get his bag packed, and get to Mexico—an hour ago. He knew it was hopeless to think he could find Jennifer with the little bit of intelligence he currently had, but he was flying out tonight anyway.

Ernesto Vega and Tomas Rivera would not expect him in the area so soon, or at least he hoped they wouldn't. The element of surprise was all he had going for him in finding her.

Gavin seemed to read his mind. "I understand you're in a hurry, but I'm not letting you go off half-cocked and by yourself, so just chill. Here's Leland beeping in."

Nick pulled his mind back to his boss, grateful Gavin was thinking more clearly than he was. The man was a machine when it came to setting emotions aside from his work, as evidenced by his being back on the job less than a month after his wife's death. Nick figured Gavin was doing this simply to keep himself sane, but whatever worked.

A deep Southern-fried voice floated over the car's speakerphone. "Hey, Nick. It's Leland."

Nick felt a grim smile tug at the corner of his mouth. As if he couldn't tell who it was from the man's accent.

"Gavin says you're going to Mexico in a hurry. I don't want to cover ground you've already travelled. Tell me what you know about Tlaxcala."

Grateful Leland was cutting to the chase, Nick took a deep breath and focused. "The state is a mess. Lots of sex trafficking and drug running, sometimes together, with no enforcement by the local government or police."

"You got it in a nutshell. I worked the area for several years. Tlaxcala generates eighty percent of the sex trafficking in Mexico. It's a direct pipeline to New York. They ship women all over the U.S. and South America, and that little town turns a blind eye to it. They even host a carnival each year where pimps show off their cars and women.

Gavin cleared his throat. "We tried to get some traction there with the Yarborough case last spring but turned up nothing. That was before you got here, Leland. It was why we went looking at Rivera's compound for information."

"I understand why you didn't get far. That piece of the criminal element in Mexico is as closed as a nun's knees to outside intervention. Tlaxcala's sex trafficking is the most dysfunctional thing happening in Mexico from a generational standpoint. And Tomas Rivera is smack dab in the middle of it.

"Grandfathers, fathers, sons are all involved in the sex trade with the children aspiring to be just like their uncles, cousins, and older brothers. Ask a young boy who lives there what he wants to be when he grows up and he'll most likely say a *padrote*. A pimp."

Nick's abdomen tensed, and he pressed his foot down on the accelerator, passing several cars at once. "How has it become such an international center for exploitation?"

"It's insidious," said Leland. "They send their most handsome young men all over Mexico to romance young women and lure them back to the area, promising a better life, marriage, an opportunity to meet their boyfriend's family. After they get there and are cut off from their own families, the women are forced into prostitution in the local brothels or shipped out all over. They call it 'love coercion.'"

"Christ. What a mess," said Gavin.

Nick couldn't think about that right now. It was too damn sad. The thought of Jennifer in that situation for a moment longer than she needed to be had him tightening his fingers on the steering wheel until his knuckles ached.

He wasn't ignoring Ernesto Vega's order to find out what had happened to Carlita and Cesar Vega, but he wasn't going to do that first. If he could find out where Jenny was, he could get her out before anyone even knew he'd been in Mexico.

Leland was still talking. "I chatted with my old boss, Ford Johnson, before I called. He said you might not remember him, but you two met when you first came on board at the CIA."

Nick tried to focus, bringing up a hazy image of a fit, sixtyish-year-old man.

"Ford's going to get back to me if he can find out anything from his end. I've got a confidential informant here who used to work for the Vegas down there. I'll reach out to him, see if he knows anything."

"Got it. Thanks." Nick turned off LBJ onto the North Dallas Tollway. The traffic was heavier than he'd expected. Holiday shoppers probably had something to do with it.

"Tell me a little more about Jennifer Grayson," said Leland.

Nick's mind flashed on the lush figure in the sexy bra

he'd seen in the picture. "I sent the proof of life picture to Gavin."

"Right. Bombshell blonde. Unicorn tattoo."

Something hard and unpleasant unfurled in Nick's belly. That Leland had noticed, even though the man was happily settled with someone else, bothered him.

What was that?

"Yeah. She's Dr. Jennifer Grayson now. PhD, not MD. Something to do with paleontology. Not sure of the specific area. She was studying dinosaurs when I knew her years ago. She's about five-eight. It's been a while since I saw her. The hair's new. I almost didn't recognize her." *Until I saw the damn tattoo.* He heard the surliness in his own tone.

"'Kay. Let me clarify the question. What is she to you?" Leland's voice was patient.

What was she to him? God, Nick had no idea. Not anymore. He didn't even want to acknowledge the thought. At one time he'd almost changed the course of his life for her, but that seemed crazy since he hadn't spoken to her in over ten years.

Honesty was the best way to handle this. He knew that in his gut. But if he couldn't be honest with himself, telling the men he worked with about his feelings for Jennifer was out of the question.

"A family friend from long ago."

"You're sticking with that story?" Leland's disbelief was evident in his tone.

Gavin broke in before Nick answered. "I don't want you going in by yourself. Marissa's out of the country right now, but Bryan's around. He should be at the office when you get there or shortly after."

"Excellent. I'm leaving tonight. I can't wait on anyone. It's my fault she's there. They took her thinking she was part of my family."

"You realize that's insane? You don't even know where you're going," argued Gavin. "And this is not your fault."

"But you two are going to find out where I need to go, right?" Nick ignored the discussion of whose fault it was and forced a levity into his tone to keep Gavin and Leland onboard with helping him. "Gavin, I was doing this for years before you hired me. Between your information and Leland's CI, I can figure it out."

Nick took the exit from the Tollway too fast, slowing down only when he approached the residential area where the AEGIS office was located. Cheery Christmas lights lit the night all around him in the upscale neighborhood.

"Give me a little time, man." Leland's voice sounded like a radio announcer's over the car's speakerphone. "An hour? Two max? I can get you more information. Let me talk to my contact."

Nick took a deep breath. Both men were right. He knew they were. Then he thought of Jenny, drugged in a bordello somewhere in Tlaxcala. His stomach twisted.

The line was quiet as he went through security at the gated community that housed AEGIS's unorthodox office space. Walnut Creek Residential Airpark had been his home since he'd left the CIA and had come to work for Gavin. The subdivision looked like any other North

Dallas gated community, except alongside the garages and driveways there were also hangars and taxiways.

Bryan's car was already there. *Good.* He grabbed Jennifer's purse that he'd brought with him from Drew's house. They were leaving for Mexico as soon as he could pack a bag.

"Look guys, I'm at the office. Bryan's here, too. I understand your concerns, but I gotta go. Leland, I'd appreciate whatever intel you can send, but I won't wait. Text or email me everything you got. I'm leaving as soon as I get packed. I'll take any other information you gather once we land."

It was obvious they weren't going to talk him out of this. Gavin's sigh was audible over the phone. "Dammit. You be careful. I don't want to come pull your butt out of another Mexican hospital this month. You understand?"

"You know me, Gavin. I'm always careful." Nick ended the call and headed inside to find Bryan Fisher—aka Hollywood, for a reason Nick wasn't entirely clear on—waiting in the conference room. Bryan was already bringing up maps and pictures of Ernesto Vega along with information about the Vega cartel on the large computer screen in the AEGIS conference room.

Hollywood didn't spend time asking questions like everyone else had. Instead, he simply went to work. It occurred to Nick that Bryan might know more about sex trafficking south of the border—and in Tlaxcala, specifically—than anyone else at AEGIS. He'd been working the Yarborough case in that area last month when he stopped to help get Leland and the Mercados out of Tomas Rivera's compound.

Since Nick had been in the hospital recuperating after that misadventure, he'd never heard the debriefing on everything Bryan had found. Given that there'd been no more news of Elizabeth Yarborough, Nick just assumed it hadn't been good news.

Still, he got the feeling Bryan had been looking for her on his own time for several months. Amid all the ensuing chaos with Rivera and his own detour last month, Nick had never gotten the full scoop on the connection—if there was one—between the kidnapped woman and Bryan.

Together, the men pulled supplies from one of the house's bedrooms that had been turned into a storeroom. Those supplies included ammunition, multiple weapons, K-rations, a water filter, a first-aid kit, and a change of clothing for Jennifer.

He wasn't sure what kind of shape she'd be in when they found her. Drugged, beaten, naked? Sadly, all three were commonplace with what they'd found on past jobs and a distinct possibility here.

Neither man spoke as they packed. Nick changed clothes, pulling on camouflage pants and a dark T-shirt with hiking boots. He took a couple more changes of clothes, having no idea what kind of cover he might have to use once they arrived.

He refused to let himself think about the odds of finding Jennifer without more information. Was he making a huge mistake, taking off with no specific knowledge of her location? They had three different landing sites picked out in Tlaxcala, depending on what information Leland could get them in the next hour. Otherwise, they'd hope for more intelligence once they landed and drive to wherever they needed to go.

Bryan closed the last duffel bag. Nick stuffed extra energy bars into his backpack. His phone buzzed as they walked downstairs to the hangar, carrying the supplies. It was Leland.

"Tell me something good," Nick said with a tone significantly more optimistic than he felt.

Bryan opened the plane's cargo door and loaded bags. He would be the pilot tonight.

"I heard from my CI," said Leland. "Jennifer Grayson is in Tenancingo. Right now they still think her name is Angela Donovan. My informant is there, too. His name is Hosea Alvarez and he's agreed to work with you. He knows where she is being held."

"Isn't it a bit of a coincidence that your guy just happens to be there?" asked Nick. Bryan started the preflight check as Nick strapped himself in.

"Don't worry about my guy. Alvarez used to work for the Vegas before he got popped for possession with intent to sell and went up to Huntsville for a while. Hosea Alvarez and Ernesto Vega are still tight, but Alvarez refuses to run drugs for Vega anymore. Vega trusts him because Alvarez did the full sentence in Huntsville without rolling on him."

"But why do *you* trust him?" asked Nick.

"Alvarez has been my CI for five years. Even though he's in deep with Vega, he still works for me. Probably more for self-preservation than anything, but he always has good intel. He's stuck his neck out for me when he didn't have to. I trust him."

"A CI that helps with sex trafficking?" asked Nick. The moral ambiguity did not fill him with confidence.

"Yeah, I understand why you'd question this. My guy isn't a choirboy. I thought he had completely washed his hands of Ernesto Vega, but apparently he's not above working for the cartel occasionally. And he's not squeamish when it comes to prostitution or sex trafficking."

Nick shook his head. The man wouldn't run drugs, but he'd sell women into slavery. And Nick was supposed to trust him?

The irony of the situation struck him immediately. Nick was condemning Alvarez when he himself had committed murder on more than one occasion for the U.S. government. Yet clients now trusted Nick to keep them safe. It was kind of the same thing. If he thought about that for too long, his head would explode. So, no more judging Hosea Alvarez, whoever the hell he was.

"What did Alvarez tell you?" Nick asked.

"Your girl is in one of the 'training houses' in Tenancingo," said Leland. "Ernesto hired Alvarez and a crew here to pick the woman up in Dallas and take her to Mexico. Tomas Rivera's men run the place. They've been keeping her drugged, but she's up and around."

"What?!" Nick flashed on the picture he'd received of Jennifer: the fear in her eyes, the tears on her cheek, the blood on her lip. CI or not, similar situation or not, Nick would like to wrap his hands around Alvarez's neck and not let go till the man was dead. "Your guy was one of the people who took her?"

"That's how Alvarez got involved. He was in Dallas and normally doesn't leave the area. He didn't know it was a kidnapping until Ernesto offered him more money than he could refuse and not look suspicious."

Jesus. It shouldn't surprise Nick but it did. What people could do to each other for money.

Shit. He closed his eyes and pinched the bridge of his nose for a moment. "Can Alvarez get word to her that we're coming?" he asked.

Leland cleared his throat. "He'll try, but I won't guarantee it. I don't want Alvarez to blow his cover. The Vegas would take him apart if they knew he was giving me information."

That was a certainty. Whoever this Alvarez was, he was walking a very thin line.

"The house is on *Calle Pino*. Pine Street. Alvarez says it's impossible to miss. It looks like a Japanese temple with huge bushes out front shaped like dolphins, a tacky version of Disney World. He's going to get you inside by having you pose as a customer."

"They run the brothel out of the house where they are holding her?" Nick asked.

"Training brothel, remember? They bring young women there initially to convince them that prostitution is the way to make dreams of a better life come true. Some of the girls aren't even teenagers yet. If the women refuse to cooperate, they're gang raped or beaten, their families threatened. Later they take the girls to Mexico City or to U.S. cities to be sex workers."

"Doesn't the town know what's going on?"

"There's a lot of denial," said Leland. "Tenancingo has a population of about ten thousand, but probably three thousand of those residents are involved in the business. There's not much chance for escape. Who would help them?"

Damn. The thought of women being treated like that nauseated him. Some people got sick over gore, for Nick it was witnessing the abuse and pain of those weaker than he was. That was how he'd known for certain that he had to leave the CIA. Being able to stay cool and unemotional in a crisis was one thing, but when he didn't feel anything watching his niece fall out of that tree, he'd known it was time to find something else to do or risk losing a part of himself he'd never get back.

Was it possible to recover what he'd already lost?

"How is Alvarez going to get me in as a customer?" asked Nick.

"He has a plan he's working on. You'll be there for one of their 'training' sessions. He'll have all the details by the time you land."

Nick swallowed hard as Leland kept talking. "I'm sending Alvarez's contact information now."

Nick's phone beeped with Leland's incoming text. He ended the call and told Bryan the news. They had their location.

Hollywood stopped in the middle of the pre-flight check and pulled out the map again. "I can get us a truck. I know a guy in that area." He reached for his phone.

"Of course you do," muttered Nick. "Is he a pimp?"

"Nope. He's a priest."

Nick shook his head. Hollywood wasn't joking. Moral ambiguity, indeed.

Bryan fired off a text and finished readying the plane for takeoff. Five minutes later he had a reply. "Truck will be there," Bryan said.

"Excellent," said Nick. "I just hope Jennifer is."

Chapter Six

Saturday evening
Tlaxcala, Mexico

IT WAS ALMOST ten PM when they circled the deserted airstrip near Tenancingo. The night sky was clear and illuminated the retro-reflective lighting system perfectly. In the moonlight Nick could see a Jeep parked at the edge of the field as promised. The outbuildings were long gone, but according to Bryan's priest, a water well dug years ago when the airport was used for legitimate business still worked.

Bryan rolled the plane to a stop beside the Jeep. "My guy says there are no drug deliveries slated for the next twenty-four hours, so we're probably okay with leaving the plane here. I can cover it with camouflage netting if you'd rather."

"How can your priest be so sure that there are no scheduled deliveries?" asked Nick.

"The guy's brother works for the Riveras."

Of course, thought Nick, nodding his head. *Moral ambiguities. Nothing else would make sense, would it?* "Go ahead and cover the plane, just in case."

Nick called Gavin's cell to tell him they'd landed, but when his boss didn't pick up, Nick followed AEGIS protocol and rolled his message to the main office voice mail system. Next he phoned Hosea Alvarez on the road to Tenancingo. Leland's CI answered on the third ring, and Nick stated the pre-arranged code.

"I received your number from 'a friend in Texas.'"

Alvarez hacked a smoker's cough before speaking. "I don't have much time. You have the address?"

"Yes," said Nick.

"You'll be a walk-in. It's a 'Saturday Night Special.'"

Nick's throat narrowed. He had no idea what to say other than, "How market savvy."

Alvarez's laugh was hoarse and gravelly at the same time. "They are out to make money. I've put you in the appointment book." Nick pictured a large book like doctors used before computers and electronic planners. Alvarez kept talking: "You'll meet with Monique or Tomas first. I've told them you're a dealer out of Chicago who was arrested in Texas. We met in Huntsville. You're recently released and looking to expand your reach in the Midwest. They'll roll out the red carpet because you're planning to move a lot of product. Your name is Nathan Fisk. They'll make sure you get everything you ask for."

"How deep does the cover go?" asked Nick.

"Deep enough. Nathan was a cellmate at Huntsville.

He got out a couple of weeks ago and is setting up shop again."

"And you know this how?" asked Nick.

"He called and asked me for an introduction. I put him off. The story should hold up long enough for this to work."

Nick swallowed and hoped to hell the real Nathan Fisk didn't have any other friends in Tenancingo.

Alvarez continued. "I've told them your preference is for a white woman who's not 'broken in' to this yet. You'll probably be allowed to choose your own. If it goes as expected, you should end up with your sister-in-law."

Nick cringed at that mental picture. "Can you let her know what's happening?"

"I'll try, but I can't guarantee it. I don't know that I'll be able to see her before you arrive."

"How early can we be there?" asked Nick.

"Any time. They're open round the clock."

"I'll text you when we are on the way. It should be within the hour."

"Excellent. As long as you remember your cover, everything will be fine," said Alvarez.

Nick wasn't so sure about that last statement, but at least they had a plan. After they found Jennifer, Hollywood would create a distraction and they'd get out. There were some holes in their plot, but it was a start.

Nick and Bryan arrived in Tenancingo in record time. Both men were dusty and dirty after the drive from the airstrip in the open-air vehicle. True to Leland's description, the place looked exactly as the former DEA agent had said it would: a typical Mexican town until you got to the side streets with the outrageous architecture and outlandish landscaping.

They found a hotel and checked in. Nick took a quick shower to wash off the road dust and dressed in the jeans and the button-down shirt he'd packed. He needed to look like a businessman, not a soldier, when he arrived at the brothel.

Bryan was coming with him. With his cover story, it would make sense for Nick to bring security. They didn't check out of the hotel but brought their luggage back downstairs with them. The lobby was deserted, even though it was Saturday night. Nick texted Alvarez as they drove through the darkened streets of Tenancingo to *Calle Pino*.

It was close to midnight, but the house was lit with a jaw-dropping number of white Christmas lights. A surreal scene, the architecture was equally outrageous with an outlandish mix of Asian pagodas, gingerbread trim, and a hedge that looked like dolphins rising up out of the water. The dolphins blinked off and on in time to the Christmas carols blaring from a hidden speaker in the front yard.

Bryan parked in front on the street. Together they went to the door, rang the bell, introduced themselves, and were admitted by a heavily armed man. An attractive older woman introduced herself as Monique and showed them into an opulent sitting room before offering them both drinks.

Monique apologized for Tomas Rivera's no longer

being in residence as an urgent business matter had called him away. "Tomas should be back by tomorrow morning and asks if you can talk then? In the meantime, he'd like you to avail yourself of the pleasures we offer here."

Nick shrugged and smiled. "I could do that."

Monique nodded. "Excellent. We'll be showing you the women you can choose from through a closed-circuit system."

She served them their beers and handed Nick a tablet that had a camera feed to another part of the house. Several women were seated at a large table and eating what appeared to be a late supper. They were dressed in exotic underwear that left very little to the imagination. Nick searched for Jennifer, but didn't see her at first. Finally, there in the corner, he spied her talking with a young girl.

The relief welled up inside him. Still, he forced himself to show no more than a passing interest. Jennifer was the only woman in street clothes. Even the child she was talking with looked like an underage model for a sleazy lingerie magazine.

Besides the scanty attire, something else was "off," but he couldn't put his finger on it. Then he realized the women weren't talking at all. They were simply staring straight ahead as they ate with no one making eye contact.

He studied the room and its occupants a few moments longer before focusing in on Jenny. He allowed himself to get lost in her, assuming that was the point of this particular exercise with Monique.

Except for the platinum blonde hair, she looked almost the same as he remembered. He studied her image on the tablet closely. Her peaches-and-cream complexion looked just as silky smooth as it had ten years ago. Her face was a little fuller, her figure a bit more lush. She had a woman's body these days, not a girl's. But she was still his Jenny.

His Jenny?

He pulled himself back from that startling thought and pointed to her image on the screen. "I want that one," he said. Thinking of Jennifer as "his" right now could get them both killed.

The woman appeared a bit nonplussed. "Are you sure? She's very new. Not as biddable as the other girls. Perhaps the other woman next to her appeals as well? I only want you to have the very best of experiences."

Nick forced himself not to laugh. The Jennifer he knew and the word *biddable* didn't belong in the same sentence. And the other "woman" Monique referred to looked as if she was barely fifteen. He clenched his jaw against the burn in his gut.

"I like a woman with fire," he insisted, handing the tablet back to her.

"Very well." Monique spoke into a small intercom and handed the tablet over to Bryan Fisher, obviously expecting him to go through the same exercise.

Hollywood looked to Nick, for all practical purposes appearing as if he were asking permission from his employer to partake of such a treat. Nick nodded, and Bryan studied the tablet. Hollywood's hand gripped the seat of his chair as he stared at the screen, but his eyes gave nothing away.

Bryan took only a moment to make his choice and pointed to the youngest looking girl in the room. "I'd like her."

The older woman nodded. "She has been here several months. She will do whatever you wish."

Nick's stomach roiled as the woman spoke.

"Excellent," said Bryan. "I prefer my fucks biddable and young."

Nick was glad he wasn't sipping his beer. He would have snorted it through his nose. Bryan never cursed in front of women and had this thing about manners that was a cross between Rhett Butler and an Eagle Scout. To use that kind of language was completely out of character.

Still, Nick would have believed his friend was looking forward to sex with a minor, if he hadn't glimpsed the man's knuckles turning white as he clenched the chair cushion. Hollywood was living up to his nickname. When he leaned back in his seat, Bryan folded his hands in his lap, no sign of the tension Nick had seen seconds before.

The woman spoke into her intercom again before turning to the men. "The women will be ready shortly. Perhaps you'd like another beer while you wait. Tomas said you were to have anything you wanted."

"Excellent," said Nick, grateful that Alvarez had been so thorough. "I'd like another beer." That would be expected of a man in his position.

Bryan asked for another beer as well. "I don't usually drink when I'm working, but I'll make an exception for screwing."

Nick gave up on trying to sip his drink if Bryan was speaking and instead, settled in to wait.

JENNIFER STUDIED THE girls in the dining room. None of the women looked over twenty-five, and there was one who couldn't have been twelve years old. Two had bruised faces, and one had a black eye.

No one spoke or made eye contact. It was extraordinarily odd to see a roomful of young women not talking to or even looking at each other. No one appeared happy to be here, and they were all dressed in lingerie that was straight out of a Hookers-R-Us catalogue.

Monique again encouraged Jennifer to get some food. She'd been locked in her room since the meeting with Tomas and was starving. Looking at all the other women eating, Jennifer assumed they weren't drugging the buffet. If she was going to figure a way out of here, she had to be able to think straight, and right now she was so hungry she was light-headed. There was a platter of *migas*, a plate of fruit with cut watermelon, and a box of pastries. She helped herself and tried to figure out exactly what was going on with the other women as Monique left the dining room.

Jennifer sat beside a young woman dressed in a provocative bustier and thong set under a filmy robe and another even younger girl who looked to be in her early teens, if that. Both kept their eyes downcast, focused on their food.

"¡Hola! ¿Cómo te llamas?" Jennifer asked their names, remembering at the last minute that everyone thought she was someone else. "Mi nombre es Angela." My name is Angela.

Neither girl answered. Out in the hallway a doorbell rang.

Jennifer tried again, but her Spanish was so rusty she switched to English, hoping someone could answer. "How long have you been here?"

The younger girl gave her a furtive look and shook her head. The older teen spoke under her breath in accented but unbroken English. "Por favor. They don't like us to talk."

"Why not?" asked Jennifer. "What can we say that would harm them?"

The older of the two replied: "They get angry when we talk. You don't want them angry."

For an incongruous moment, Jennifer was reminded of the dialogue from The Incredible Hulk: "You won't like me when I'm angry." She felt the unwelcome urge to giggle, but the women's bruises and black eyes weren't remotely amusing and took on a whole new meaning in light of what the girls were telling her.

"Just your names then," she whispered.

The younger girl moved the food around on her plate and cleared her throat. Jennifer glanced down. Seeds from the girl's watermelon were arranged on the white dish to form letters.

M-I-A

Jennifer nodded and smiled. "Nice to meet you, Mia."

The young girl's eyes watered for a moment, and she gave the barest hint of a smile.

"How old are you?" Jennifer asked.

The girl formed the number *ten* with her watermelon seeds. No one was paying any attention.

"How long have you been here?" Jennifer asked.

The girl formed another number with the seeds. *Six.*

"Months?"

Mia nodded. Jennifer felt her own eyes water. *Good God.* How had a ten-year-old ended up in this place?

The guard at the desk looked up. *"No hablar,"* he muttered. No talking.

Mia startled and reached for Jennifer's hand under the table as her eyes filled. "I want to go home," she mouthed.

Jennifer gave the child's fingers a reassuring squeeze. "It's going to be okay."

The guard stood and moved to walk toward them. *"¡No hablar!"* he shouted this time, leaning down into Mia's face.

"¿Por qué?" Why? asked Jennifer, in an effort to get his focus off of Mia. "What's wrong with talking?" She raised her voice to her best "teacher tone," which translated from English to Spanish perfectly.

The angry guard glared, looking her over as if he was stripping her with his eyes. She hid the shudder of revulsion and stared him down like she would one of her grad students.

Mia focused on her plate and brushed the seeds away so they no longer resembled letters or numbers. The guard continued his death stare until the cell phone lying on his desk buzzed. With a final malevolent glare at both Jennifer and Mia, he stalked to the table.

Mia squeezed her hand again, and Jennifer squeezed back. "It's going to be okay," Jennifer repeated. "I promise." She had no idea how this situation was going to turn out okay, but she was determined to give Mia hope.

The guard was talking on the phone in Spanish so fast that Jennifer couldn't follow. But "pissed off" translated perfectly from Spanish to English.

"Where are you from?" Jennifer asked, ignoring him for the time being.

Mia stiffened beside Jennifer as the guard left the room, still complaining on the phone. She obviously understood every word he was speaking. "You're like the other," Mia said.

"The other?"

Mia nodded. "The other *guera*. She's not here anymore." Jennifer wanted to know what Mia meant by that, but there wasn't time to ask before the irritated guard was hurrying back into the room. He shot another withering glare toward Jennifer.

Mia squeezed her hand and slipped something into her palm out of sight under the table. "You've been kind to me," she whispered.

Jennifer closed her fingers around the item and realized it was a ring as the guard traipsed over to glower down on her. He indicated that Jennifer should follow him. She didn't want him to see that Mia had given her anything, sensing he might take it out on the child. Under the tabletop, she slipped the ring onto her middle finger and rose from the bench seat, belatedly realizing she hadn't eaten a bite.

The surly guard wanted to hustle Jennifer out of the dining room, but she took her time, nodding to Mia as she left. The guard was hurrying her up the staircase when the man she knew as Hosea approached. He said something to the guard Jennifer couldn't understand, apparently some kind of order. The guard shrugged and turned to head back down the stairs.

Smelling of cigar smoke, Hosea led her onward. "We don't have much time," he said, directing her up the stairs but not turning to her as he spoke. "Help is coming. Go along with whatever comes next, and remember, there are eyes everywhere."

"What?" She stopped climbing mid-step.

"Cameras. They are watching all the time."

She shuddered. The revulsion of someone watching her unawares made her slightly queasy. She wasn't sure she could do what was necessary to get out of here, but the thought of the alternative chilled her blood.

"Are there microphones, too?" Her mind whirled at the implications, but Hosea didn't answer her question.

"Keep walking," he hissed. "We must hurry."

They reached the top of the staircase and moved a short distance down the hall to one of the bedrooms.

"Who are you?" she asked, as he rapped sharply on the door.

"A friend," he mumbled, moving away before the door swung open.

The room before her was beautiful, with tapestried furniture and a four-poster canopied bed, like something out of a magazine article on how to seduce your lover. Another woman stood beside a desk, dressed with the same care that Monique had been, but there the similarity ended. This well-dressed woman looked much older and harsher as she held out a flimsy robe.

"Strip," the woman ordered, with none of the odd politeness Jennifer had encountered since she'd been here.

"What?"

"Do it, or I'll break your arm and Mia's as well." The woman said the words as casually as if she'd offered Jennifer creamer for her coffee. The old witch obviously wasn't going to take no for an answer. Her accent was heavy, but it wasn't Hispanic. It sounded more European. Whoever she was, she spoke flawless English.

Jennifer slipped off the dress without arguing. Her hands trembled when she understood that the transparent robe was all she would be given to wear. She was now very grateful for the exotic bustier and panties she'd put on earlier and slid the transparent wrap over her lingerie. She hoped that would be okay with this drill sergeant.

"An important client is seeing you tonight. It's imperative that you please him. He knows you're new, so don't worry about that. But don't fight him. It won't go well for you if he doesn't enjoy his time here." The woman's voice was cajoling and threatening at the same time.

Jennifer felt a cold finger of dread walk down her spine as she listened to the surreal demands. Hosea had said someone was coming. She just hoped they got here before she had to deal with the "important client."

"Cameras. They are watching all the time."

God, was this really about to happen?

How had she gone from being a freshly divorced college professor worrying about her Christmas break to turning her first trick in a Mexican bordello?

Chapter Seven

Saturday, late evening
Tenancingo

FIFTEEN MINUTES AFTER they had made their "selections," Monique led Nick and Bryan upstairs. They arrived at Bryan's destination first.

"For all the ruckus out front with that music, it's very quiet up here," said Bryan. "No distractions."

Monique smiled, her hand on the bedroom doorknob. "Yes, we find our clients prefer a peaceful atmosphere."

Nick nodded. Message received. Bryan would be causing a "distraction" soon. He was thinking about which side of the house they'd need to leave from to get Jennifer out when a heavy oak door swung open. He caught only a glimpse of a king-size bed before Bryan walked inside and shut the door behind him.

Nick hoped Hollywood could slip the child out of the house without frightening her. There might even be a back exit. He forced himself to focus on the details of the rescue in order to avoid thinking about seeing Jenny for the first time in a decade. He was honest enough with himself to know that dwelling on that particular fact would decimate his concentration. Jennifer was the mission right now. That was the only way he could think of her and make it through this.

A few steps away, Monique knocked at another intricately designed door before swinging it open. The room was so different from what he'd expected that he paused in the doorway. Oversized furniture and a massive canopied bed with tapestried coverings filled the room. The glow of candles cast a dim light, illuminating a table covered with food and wine chilling in an ice bucket. A woman was seated at a vanity. Her back was to the door; her face reflected in the mirror.

"The phone is there beside the bed. Please dial zero if there's anything further you require." Monique sounded like a bellhop as Nick moved into the room. The door closed behind him with a snap.

The woman at the vanity turned, and his breath caught in his throat. Nick had known it would be Jenny, and despite what he'd thought about downstairs when he'd seen her on the tablet screen, he hadn't prepared himself for seeing her like this. Seated at the table with candles all around, she was wearing a sheer robe over a gray thong and a bustier kind of thing, or that's what he thought the full-length bra was called.

He spotted the small unicorn tat peeping out from the edge of whatever the lingerie piece was and his brain quit processing details as all the blood in his head rushed south. He'd been primed to come in and tell Jenny exactly how they were getting out of the house and away from these people and now . . . this. His mouth went dry at the sight of her. She looked like every fantasy he'd ever had about her rolled into one.

He continued to stare as recognition flared in her eyes. "Oh my God," she said. "It's . . ."

She clapped her mouth closed, and her eyes widened. That struck him as odd. The relief on her face was obvious, but instead of looking at him, she took an audible breath and studied the walls of the room. When she finally did glance at him again, her eyes had changed.

"So you're who they've sent me for my first time?" Her voice sounded bored, not the tone he remembered. "What do you want me to do?"

What a question. He raised an eyebrow, but she shook her head. In warning?

Nothing here was as he'd anticipated. He continued staring at her, hoping the lust would quit fogging his brain long enough for him to figure out what was going on.

"I've been told to show you a good time." Her voice was cold, downright chilly. Without another word she stood and crossed the floor, slipping into his arms with her breasts pressing into his chest. "It's you." She murmured the words in the barest of whispers.

Nick's mind froze, but his body didn't. On autopilot his hands automatically went to her waist as she kissed his neck, working her way up to his ear. This was not at all what he'd planned.

"I can't believe you're here." She breathed the words into his ear.

Me either, he thought, but kept the news to himself as he pulled her closer. His senses flooded with all that smooth skin pressing against him. His body tightened, and his right hand moved to cup her ass. Her cheek's bare skin was silky soft, like he remembered. God, he'd missed her. She melted into him as his body switched into overdrive.

"What do you want?" She spoke louder. The artic tone was back. He was confused and knew he was just too stupid with wanting her to figure out what the hell was going on. There was no way the woman could mistake the effect she was having.

She moved her lips closer to his ear and nipped his earlobe before she spoke in a hushed tone. "Cameras are everywhere. I'm not sure about microphones."

And just like that, cold reality slapped him in the face. He should have been expecting it, but he'd been so focused on getting her out and making sure she was all right. She might be glad to see him because he was there to save her, but throwing her body at him was an act.

Jesus. He had to get them both out of here without tipping his hand to the cameras and those watching what he was doing. He was crazy not to have considered it once he saw those tablets downstairs, but it had never occurred to him that he would have to play this encounter through as if he was really a client.

He slipped her arms from around his neck and moved to the table to pour himself some wine, willing his hands not to shake. "I want you," he said, clearly and loudly enough for any microphone in the room to pick up.

She smiled, but her expression wasn't warm. "Do you now?" Her frigid tone was so at odds with the woman he'd known years ago.

He knew what he had to do. Monique and company were expecting them to have wild sex. If they'd been truly alone, it wouldn't have been a hardship. And regardless of the circumstances, that's exactly what he was going to have to pretend to do. He had to make love to Jenny knowing others were watching, at least until that distraction of Bryan's came through.

There wouldn't be any sneaking out of the room or the house before then. Guards were most likely gathered around security monitors at this very moment, drinking beer and taking bets as to how long Nick would last before he came. They were expecting to see some action.

"What do you think I want?" His voice was pitched low but loud enough for the mics as he took a sip of the wine. "I'm here to fuck you. Isn't that what they told you to expect?"

Her eyes widened in shock as he silently pled with her to understand that this, too, was a charade. He put the wine down and stepped toward her, kissing her with an intensity that wasn't at all make-believe for him and breathing words into her mouth before he pulled away.

"We're going to have to pretend to do this," murmured Nick. "I'm sorry. You don't have to be enthusiastic. They expect me to be practically raping you."

She froze and leaned back to stare at him for a long moment. Her eyes filled with revulsion, sadness, and then acceptance. Nodding her head, she moved to his other earlobe. Her breath was hot on his cheek, and that alone would have turned him on if they'd been by themselves.

But her whispered words were like a cold shower. "They've threatened to hurt one of the other girls if you don't enjoy yourself."

He forgot about the cameras for a moment and stopped to stare at her. "Is this really—"

She kissed him before he could say anything else. Her lips fused with his, and her tongue plunged into his mouth. She pulled back slightly, only after his growing erection pressed into her belly.

She smiled and sighed, "I'll be fine." Taking his left hand from her waist, she placed it on top of her breast and began unbuttoning his shirt.

"Come on, we've both done this before." Her voice was louder, and he realized that was for the onlookers, even though it had a totally different meaning for the two of them. She slid a hand inside his shirt and brushed fingertips over his chest.

He couldn't answer. Of all the wild, fantastic ways he'd dreamed of being with Jenny again, this had never been a scenario. Gripping his shirt, she tugged him toward the bed, and he followed.

Slipping her fingers into his hair, she kissed him, and for a moment he might have thought she really meant it. Her enthusiasm was tangible as she pushed him down to sit on the mattress, and he pulled her between his knees.

If he thought about cameras, he wasn't going to be able to do this.

He pushed the barely-there robe aside and trailed kisses across her stomach. His palms brushed upward from her waist. Her generous breasts filled his hands. She moaned when he slipped a finger inside her bustier, and his lips trailed lower on her abdomen.

He wasn't sure if this was pretense or not, but he wasn't going to think about that now. She bumped him backward onto the mattress and climbed on top of him, straddling his hips and seating herself on top of him. They were almost to a point of no return. Where the hell was Nick and that "distraction"?

He moved a palm from her breast to the front of her thong, and she leaned into his fingers, pressing him closer. He imagined he could feel her temperature rising.

She reached into his waistband, and before he knew how she'd done it—he was unzipped, and she was holding him firmly in her hands. She bent all the way forward and kissed him again, slipping her tongue past his lips as she stroked him.

The two sensations combined to make him feel as if the top of his head were going to fly off. He groaned and pulled her closer, sliding his fingers past the silky lace thong and into her. Nick could feel his breath coming faster. They were really going to do this—have sex with God knew who watching. And right now Jenny had him so turned on, he didn't care.

How much of this was acting, and how much was real? He had no idea, but he had the vague notion that he probably should be concerned. Still, she was here, doing things to him in the flesh that he'd only dreamed about for so damn long.

He was pushing the scrap of lace that passed for panties aside when there was a furious pounding on the door. Screams and running feet sounded in the hallway.

"¡Fuego! ¡Fuego!" a woman's voice screamed. "¡La casa está en llamas!"

The house was on fire.

Thank God.

JENNIFER FELT HER eyes widen as Nick broke the sizzling kiss, stared into her face, and untangled himself from her body. She couldn't even think about the fact that they'd been about to have sex. He'd put his hands on her, and she'd forgotten where they were—just like that summer so long ago. And hadn't that led to enough heartache to last a lifetime?

Her vision snapped back into focus when he slid his hands from her and zipped his jeans. Handing her his button-down shirt, he headed for the door and left her on the bed to pull herself together.

She heard more screams of "¡Fuego!" and what had to be gunshots. Before she could sort out what was happening or do anything with the shirt, Nick was back. "We've got to go. Do you have any more clothes in here?"

She shook her head. Of course she didn't. The old battle-axe who'd forced her to strip had taken the dress, leaving Jennifer in only the beautiful lingerie. She pointed to the stiletto heels and gave him a grim smile.

"Can you run in those?" he asked.

"We'll see."

He nodded as she slid into his button-down. "The shirt'll do for now. Let's go."

She pulled the shirt on but didn't bother with the buttons. Grabbing her shoes, she followed him to the door and slipped the high heels on. He grabbed her hand in preparation to pull her along. She forced herself not to clutch at his fingers.

"Do what I tell you. No questions, and you'll be fine. We're getting out of here and going straight for my Jeep. No one will think running out of here is odd when the building is on fire. It's just that we're not stopping once we're out. Got it?" he asked.

"Yes." She didn't trust herself to say anything else.

So many times she'd planned what she would say if she ever saw him again: carefully prepared words and explanations. In the current situation, it wasn't surprising that none of those planned speeches came to mind. This was surreal.

He was the same, down to the dimple in his chin and the electric blue eyes that had haunted her dreams for ten years. His hair had a couple of gray streaks shot through at the sideburns, but it didn't seem possible that he hadn't changed when she felt so completely different.

Nick gave her one more searching glance before he opened the door, looked both ways, and crept forward. She followed him, feeling slightly ridiculous in stilettos and a white button-down. But it was better than being naked and barefoot.

Nick didn't seem too worried about the house fire or in any great rush to get out. Still, he kept a tight grip on her hand as they hurried down the long staircase. Smoke rose from the bottom floor and appeared to be coming from the back of the house. The foyer was empty, but shouts drifted up the stairs from outside, punctuated by the popping sound of gunfire.

From out of nowhere, Mia dashed toward the front door as Jennifer hit the bottom step. The girl was wearing a man's collared golf shirt that came past her knees.

"Mia!" Jennifer called. "Wait. Come with us."

The girl stopped and looked back at them over her shoulder. Her eyes filled with fear when she saw Nick. She shook her head, making for the front door again.

"It's okay. He'll get us out of here," Jennifer called.

"He's one of the bad men," she argued.

"No, Mia, he's not. He'll help us."

The girl hesitated a moment longer in the doorway.

Another shot rang out, sounding like a lone firecracker in the cacophony around them. Mia crumpled to the floor. Jennifer stood in shock for a beat before she dropped Nick's hand to run toward the girl.

Nick called out, but she ignored him. Mia was so still. Her eyes stared, unseeing, with only a small red mark on her forehead to indicate what had happened.

Was she alive? Jennifer didn't want to admit the obvious to herself. *Mia had never had a chance.*

She dropped to her knees beside the body and immediately felt the sticky warmth on the tops of her feet and shins. Blood was pooling around the base of Mia's head at an alarming rate. Jennifer stared in horror. The back of the child's skull was gone.

A bitter taste rose in her throat. Despite the terror coursing through her body, Jennifer stayed and gripped Mia's hand. No one should die alone. More smoke drifted in from the back of the house. Christmas music from the decorations outside blared through the entrance like something from a nightmare.

"Mia. Mia, I'm so sorry," she whispered.

Nick was there, bending down at Mia's shoulder and pulling Jennifer out of the doorway as another shot whizzed through the entrance and hit the wall above her head.

"Move! You can't help her." His voice was sharp, and he tugged at Jennifer's wrist with a vice grip.

She stood, looking down at her hands. The blood on her palms was warm and black in the strange light of the fire, just like on her legs. The coppery scent wafted through the air along with smoke. A combination of nausea and terror still paralyzed her.

"She's dead, Jenny. We've got to go. Now." The words were harsh, but his voice sounded so different. Finally, she looked up. His eyes were dark and haunted as he drew her away from the doorway toward the back of the house and into the haze.

She focused on his voice and on the inconsequential fact that he'd called her Jenny. Nick was the only person who called her that.

She let him haul her away, unable to fully comprehend the horror of what had just happened. Yet the blood covering her hands, legs, and the bottom of Nick's shirt testi-

fied to it. She glanced back toward the entry hall and saw
Monique's body on the front porch and another sprawled
on the steps leading to the lawn. The white holiday lights
blinked on and off as if highlighting the bodies. She
stumbled and would have gone down if Nick hadn't been
holding on to her. Another bullet flew past her head.

"Damn. It's the shoes," Nick muttered, bending to
pick her up.

Both stilettos fell off as he slung her over his shoulder in a fireman's hold, but he didn't stoop to grab them.
Instead, he moved through the entrance toward the
dining room where Jennifer and Mia had met earlier. The
dreamlike quality of the scene increased exponentially
from her upside down vantage point with the curtains
fully engulfed in flames, smoke pouring from the room,
and Nick's bare skin beneath her.

Unbelievably, they ran toward the back of the house
where the smoke thickened by the second.

Chapter Eight

NICK SPED THROUGH the back hallway, searching for another way out while more gunshots echoed from the front of the house.

What the fuck? Who was shooting? Where was Bryan?

He'd assumed Hollywood had set the fire as a distraction, but now he wasn't so sure.

His lungs burned from the acrid haze that had thickened to the point where he was running with one palm along the wall, feeling his way down the hall. He hadn't been taken this far back into the house when he and Bryan were shown to Monique's sitting room earlier.

His hand brushed along the stucco surface, across what he assumed were large pictures. He heard a loud thud when something fell to the floor in his wake. His eyes watered, and he coughed like a three-pack-a-day smoker. Jenny wasn't heavy, but he wasn't operating at full capacity after his injuries last month. He could hear his own labored breathing as he raced down the corridor.

Finally, there was a break in the seemingly end-less hallway with what felt like a doorframe. He had to make a split-second decision: keep going into the smoke toward the back of the house or turn here and search for a quicker way out.

He turned and pushed the door open. Smoke cleared marginally. Closing the door behind him, he saw the vague outline of furniture as he moved into what ap-peared to be a small office. He ran his hand along the wall, making a circuit of the room, and prayed for a window, a door, anything that led out of what he feared had become a death trap.

At last, his fingers touched smooth glass. He took a quick measure of the opening and searched for some-thing to throw through it. A chair sat just to the side of the window. He settled Jennifer on her feet. He couldn't see her face clearly in the haze but made sure she was steady before he picked up the sturdy wooden chair and hammered at the floor-length window.

It took three whacks and a surge of adrenaline to break the double panes. Smoke streamed through the opening as he pulled Jenny along with him. He carried her several feet from the window to avoid broken glass. Coughing and hacking, neither spoke for a moment.

They'd exited along the side of the house into darkness beyond the holiday decorations and now stood in a flow-erbed. Fire devoured the roof along the front of the build-ing, but here there was only smoke. Nick grasped Jenny's hand and pulled her with him as he peered up the side yard. There was probably no way to spy the sniper in the dark, but he didn't want to walk straight into the line of fire either.

No curious neighbors gathered to watch the house burn. That was unusual in an area where the houses were fairly close together and the neighbors most likely knew one another, even if they didn't know the occupants of the bordello. Unusual, until one thought about a sniper running loose.

Nick studied the street and surrounding area for any further sign of the gunman. He focused on the front yard and froze. At least five bodies lay at odd angles across the lawn.

Even without being told, he knew none of those people had been dragged from the house. There was no one there to do it.

He tried to shield Jenny's line of vision as his mind reeled. She'd already seen enough tonight. He had, too, for that matter.

His stomach tightened. Those poor souls had been shot as they exited the burning building.

God, why?

He moved farther into the shelter of darkness and gripped Jenny's hand. A shadow stood up before them. Nick braced, pushing Jenny behind him.

God, WERE THOSE *bodies in the front yard?*

Jennifer woke from the fog when Nick placed the hand she'd been gripping on her hip and shoved her firmly behind his back. She felt every muscle in his body go on alert. A man rose out of the shadows.

If possible, Nick tensed even more.

"It's Hollywood," said a deep voice. "You okay?"

Just as quickly, Jennifer felt Nick relax.

"I couldn't find you," continued the shadow man.

Nick nodded. "We had to go out the back. What happened? Did you start the fire?"

"No. I've no idea what happened. Everyone who ran out the front door of that building was shot." The shadow man, aka Hollywood, stood in front of them. He was dressed the same as Nick, in jeans with no shirt. A big man, he was built like a tank but taller than Nick, at least six foot five, with short hair almost military in its severity. He had the bulky build of a bodyguard, but even in the shadows Jennifer could see that he wasn't fat, just large and extremely ripped. She couldn't see his face, but his voice was deep and soothing with no noticeable accent.

"What happened to the little girl? I sent her out the back when the screaming started. Did you see her?" asked Hollywood.

Jennifer stopped short. The collared shirt Mia had been wearing was this man's. The shock of everything made her feel blessedly numb as she digested all that was happening—the bodies, the fire, the blood.

"Yeah, we saw her." Nick put his hand on Jennifer's elbow. "She ended up trying to go out the front door."

Jennifer watched the newcomer's shoulders droop and thought she heard him curse under his breath. "She was so scared. I thought she was behind me and . . ." He trailed off. "It was a massacre."

Nick nodded again. "That's exactly what it looks like. Let's get out of here before anything else happens. Where's the Jeep?"

"Around back. I moved it before the shooting started."

They turned and Nick slid his hand from her elbow to her palm, grasping her fingers as they hurried toward the rear of the house and the alley. In the darkness, she stepped on something sharp with her bare foot and winced. Nick stopped and, without a word, scooped her into his arms.

People were shooting at them, and others were dying all around her. But being held like this, she felt surprisingly sheltered. She was just coherent enough to realize it was most likely an illusion, but she was going with it for now.

Nick and Hollywood crept farther into the gloom. Smoke rose from the roof in the back. An open-air Jeep with its engine running was parked twenty yards down the alley.

Jennifer's mind raced as she clasped her arms around Nick's neck. The shock was starting to wear off, or more likely she was beginning to think through it.

What is going on? Who is that other shirtless guy? What is Nick doing here?

Nick squeezed her shoulder as they reached the vehicle. "I know you have questions. We're getting out of here to a safer place, and I'll answer what I can." He opened the back door and put her gently on the seat before climbing in beside her.

Hollywood drove. "Back to the hotel or straight to the airstrip?" he asked.

Nick stared at her a moment, and the safety she'd felt moments before in his arms melted away. There was a calculating look in his eyes she didn't recognize. Despite the heat of the night, she was freezing—covered in blood, wearing a man's dress shirt and little else. Her exotic underwear hardly counted as clothing.

Nick turned to face the front of the Jeep and answered Hollywood's question. "Airstrip. This place is going to be crawling with local law enforcement, such as it is, in the next hour. The sooner we get off the ground, the better."

He turned back to her, his gaze softer. "I'm sorry. You'll have to get cleaned up at the airstrip outside of town. I have some other clothes for you in my bag."

She nodded. More than anything she just wanted to go home, wrap up in her grandmother's afghan, and sit in the overstuffed chair in her living room. She'd welcome the ordinariness of her busted water heater with open arms. The shock and horror of the past half hour and of the past few days—she still wasn't clear on how long it had been—won out over any questions. As tired as she was, explanations of anything were completely beyond her.

She felt Nick's stare as lights from the few buildings they passed flashed sporadically across her face. She wasn't sure what he was searching for, but once they'd left the town and the lights behind, he pulled her closer in the darkness, tucking his arm around her.

At that moment it didn't matter how long it had been since they'd seen each other. She didn't ask herself why he was holding her or what it meant. She didn't care that she'd sworn never to do this again. She just moved into his body, relishing the comfort there and the feel of his chest under her cheek, the tangy scent of sweat, and the man she remembered from her past. They'd talk later.

Maybe this was all a nightmare, and she'd wake up any moment in her own bed with her flooded living room carpet. She closed her eyes in an attempt to block out everything.

"Any idea why they were shooting those people?" asked Hollywood.

"None," answered Nick. His deep voice under her ear echoed inside her chest, even as she recoiled from what he was saying.

"Think it had anything to do with our visit?"

She could feel the motion of Nick shaking his head. "No one knew we were coming besides AEGIS and Leland's contact. I can't imagine anyone would have gone to all that trouble just to get to you or me, but the house was deliberately targeted."

He seemed so matter-of-fact about it. Mia was dead, lying back in that house's entry hall in a puddle of blood. Jennifer twisted the ring around her finger that the child had given her. Other women she'd seen only in passing were dead, too. She shivered, and Nick pulled her closer.

"Why would you kill everyone in a private brothel if you were after just one or two people?" asked Nick.

"I suppose it would depend on the one or two you were after," said Hollywood.

Nick shook his head. "It looks to me like someone was after Tomas Rivera. Or trying to start a war."

NICK HELD ON to Jennifer as Bryan drove through the dark countryside. His insides churned at the thought of that child shot dead in front of them. He couldn't get Jenny back to Dallas soon enough, away from him and the mess that was his life.

Holding her in his arms was not good for the emotional distance he was desperate to establish. Their forced "intimacy" was playing hell with his libido and his head. Within minutes of leaving town, they had turned onto a potholed road that threated to rattle the engine out of the vehicle and her butt directly into his lap.

After ten minutes of fighting the inevitable, he gave up on trying not to think about how good it felt to hold her again. He worried she was too still and too silent, but his body had no discernment with this woman. His dick didn't know the difference between holding as comfort and holding as a prelude to sex.

They wove through dense jungle before the Jeep emerged near the airstrip, and Bryan parked by the plane. Jenny sat unmoving, even when Hollywood got out and began uncovering the Cessna.

"It'll take about ten minutes for Bryan to ready the plane," Nick explained, trying to keep everything quiet and even-keeled. Still, she didn't move or speak.

He touched her face. "Jenny, let's get you cleaned up. There's an old well here. We'll get some water, and at least get the blood off your legs." He reached into the duffel bag by their feet and pulled out the dark T-shirt he'd worn on the trip down.

"Who's Bryan?" she asked.

He stopped, realizing that he'd never identified Bryan by anything other than his nickname. "Hollywood," he said.

"Oh." She nodded woodenly and took Nick's hand as he helped her out of the vehicle.

Together they walked to the old-fashioned pump that held a bucket beneath the spout. He rinsed the T-shirt so she could have something to wash with, filled the bucket, and helped her out of his bloodied button-down. Initially, she wasn't moving or helping. When the cool well water hit her legs, she seemed to wake up and took the T-shirt from his hands.

"Thanks, I'll be okay," she said.

He turned to give her privacy, and remembering he'd brought clothes for her, he went to retrieve them from the Jeep and to put on a shirt himself. He returned moments later to find her scrubbing her arms and legs in a frenzy.

She was still wearing the thong and bustier he'd first seen her in, but they were soaked through—lace and satin clinging to her skin. He watched a moment, not knowing how to help her, stepping in only when she took an entire bucket of water and splashed it over her torso.

She was crying now, and he could hear her gasping in great gulps of air. She was on the verge of completely melting down. He wanted to pull her into his arms, but instead, he pulled the camping towel he'd had the forethought to pack and wrapped it around her before setting her away from him. Emotionally drowning, he was desperate to save himself. If he held her while she was like this, it would be over.

Still sobbing, she tried to dry her body, but she couldn't coordinate her movements and eventually stopped to just stare at him. The clouds from earlier had cleared. Moonlight glistened in the droplets of water on her shoulders and chest.

The wet lace was transparent, and she might as well have been nude for all the modesty the clinging satin provided. Tears covered her face, and the devastation in her expression pulled at him, driving all thoughts of self-preservation aside.

He couldn't *not* reach for her, and finally pulled her toward him. Her skin was icy to the touch as she clung to him—soggy, shivering, and weeping. He held her as the moisture soaked through his clothes, but he didn't care. Having her in his arms felt so damn good. He'd hold her as long as she'd allow it. Gradually, she quieted and took a deep breath.

"I'm okay now. I'm sorry, I never cry. It's just—" She hiccupped.

"Don't apologize." He stepped back, his tone sharper than he'd intended. "Just get changed. We've gotta get out of here." God, he had to get her dressed, get her home and away from him. He was coming apart, losing all perspective, and he'd been with her for only a little over an hour.

She nodded. If she noticed the brusqueness of his words, she didn't show it. She simply followed his instructions, stripping down to nothing with zero modesty and no warning before taking the clothing Nick handed her.

He had grabbed stuff from Marissa's locker at the office, assuming Jenny would rather borrow clean underwear than go without. There were camo pants and a woman's dark T-shirt, too.

He tried to avert his eyes and succeeded for the most part. But given the transparency of her lingerie, there wasn't much that he hadn't already seen. His memories filled in the rest of the detail. Still, he turned his back as she pulled on the borrowed clothes. He was desperate to get his mind off his cock and back on the task at hand. She wouldn't be safe until they were off the ground.

Moments later, they were on the plane. Five minutes after that, they were in the air.

Getting Jenny to the safety of the U.S. border was predominant in his head. How he would keep her safe once they were there, he had no idea. But the first order would be getting himself as emotionally distanced as possible. For now, he was focused on getting her back to Dallas and secured. He'd never have to see her again after tonight, if that's what he wanted. AEGIS could help him set up security for her. With his head this messed up, there was no way to keep her safe and keep his sanity, too.

She was too distracting. Too tempting. Too dangerous.

It was almost six AM when they landed in West Plano at the residential airpark. Exhausted from her ordeal, Jennifer had fallen asleep as they flew. She hadn't spoken once during the flight. Nick knew because he'd watched her sleep and spread a blanket over her when she'd shivered.

When he wasn't studying her as she slept, he'd turned the dilemma over in his mind of how to keep her out of harm's way while also keeping his distance. He knew it was possible, he just wasn't sure how he would manage it.

She woke when the wheels touched the ground. The neighborhood was peaceful when Bryan taxied the plane to the garage under the house. Nick helped Jenny out of the plane while Hollywood did the post-flight procedures.

"I'll lock up. I've got to talk to one of my contacts," said Bryan.

Nick nodded and led her upstairs. She was still too quiet and asked no questions; she simply followed where he led her. He paused in the den to pour her a generous scotch, the same brand she'd introduced him to the summer they spent together. After that, he'd adopted the drink as his own, but he had never acknowledged the significance of his choice.

Wrapping her fingers around the glass, and without stopping to consider the implications, he took her to his room: the master bedroom suite. She was shivering again by the time they got there, and he turned the hot water in the oversized shower to full blast. She sipped the drink as he set clean towels out on the countertop along with his own robe.

He could feel her watching him and fought the urge to touch her. The bathroom had never felt small before, but tonight—with the steam, the pounding water, and the faint scent of her scotch—he could feel the walls closing in on them both.

His body was drawn to hers as if they were magnetized. He wanted to blame the feelings of intimacy on the setting, but knew it was more than that. He had to get out of here, or he was going to screw up.

"Will you be okay?" he asked. "I've got your purse from Angela and Drew's house in my office. I'll leave it in the bedroom while you shower."

She didn't speak. She just stared at him with eyes that seemed bigger and more luminous in the foggy bathroom.

"Call me if you need anything."

She didn't answer, even as her face filled with a sorrow and devastation he understood but couldn't fix. There was nothing for him to do but leave. If he didn't he was going to reach for her, and it would be all over.

He walked out and was almost to the bedroom door when he heard the shattering glass. Racing back, he found Jenny on the floor. The scotch glass was broken in the sink and whiskey was splattered across the counter. The peat and vanilla wood smoke smell of the single malt scotch liquor filled the air. He expected to see Jennifer shattered as well. But when he looked into her face, absolute fury blazed from her eyes.

"I can't believe they killed that child. Why? Why did they do that? She was just a baby. Why kill any of those women?" Tears of anger and frustration trickled down her cheeks. "It's all so senseless."

She shook her head. At a loss for what to do, he pulled her into his arms, even as he wondered if this was what she really wanted. It was what he'd been wanting since he'd let go of her beside the well a few hours before. What he'd wanted since he first saw her in that bedroom in Tenancingo. It was exactly what he knew he shouldn't be doing. She was weeping again, but this had more to do with anger than the sorrow and shock he'd seen at the abandoned airstrip.

Anger, he understood. The senselessness and waste of everything that had happened in Mexico made him mad as hell, too. Steam filled the bathroom as he held her. She trembled in his arms with the tumult of emotions. He kissed the top of her head and murmured soothing words in an effort to calm her, grateful he could hold her—and want her—without feeling like a jerk. Still, something changed as he embraced her, taking his touch from platonic comfort to sexual heat. When she turned her head up to look into his face, he was lost.

He shouldn't do this. It would be so much harder to leave her after touching her this way, but he dove in anyway, kissing her before his brain had a chance to evaluate the wisdom of his actions. Her lips opened beneath his, and she brought him closer, fumbling with his clothes as he tugged at hers.

He was about to have her naked in his arms, like they'd been earlier tonight in the brothel, but this time there was no audience. With unexpected clarity, Nick realized he was right where he wanted to be when she stopped and went completely still.

Pulling away from him, she took a jerky step back, breathing hard. "I'm sorry. I can't do this. I want to, but I just can't."

He gazed at her, trying to read the expression in her dazed eyes and clear the lust from his own. Whenever they were alone it was like this. Spontaneous combustion.

"This is a bad idea," she mumbled, and he knew she was right.

He dropped his hands and stepped back as well, opening a gulf between them that was more than a physical distance. Her lips were swollen from his kiss. Her clothes were askew. She looked like an advertisement for sex, and he had to get out of there—immediately.

He wasn't going to do this to himself or to her.

He cleared his throat before speaking. "Sleep in here. I'll grab some clothes and be in the other bedroom next door."

Her eyes were unreadable. Her only response was a nod. He left without another word and swore he wouldn't imagine the water beating on her naked body or the way it had felt to hold her in his arms like he remembered from so long ago.

He had to let that go. She wasn't his, she never had been, and she certainly wasn't now. The best thing he could do for her was get her out of town and to a safe house until this was figured out, and then stay the hell away from her. The best way to protect her was to make sure no one knew what she meant to him.

He yanked clean clothes from his closet before going to the guest room, determined to shower, sleep, and imagine sex with Jennifer no more. He got the cold shower right but lay awake for hours tossing and turning, thinking about her in his bed next door.

Eventually, he slept, only to dream of her body pressed to his as the water poured over them in the shower. He was inside her, pushing her into the tile wall and pulling her legs around his hips when he woke up, hard and frustrated.

Knowing that to dream like that was the road to madness, he got up and stalked downstairs to the AEGIS training gym. He punched at the heavy bag, angry with himself for his lack of self-discipline and desperately hoping he could exhaust his body enough to sleep with no more dreams.

Chapter Nine

Sunday morning
Dallas

NICK WOKE AROUND eleven AM and looked down the hall to see that the door to the master bedroom was open. He hadn't thought Jenny would be up yet. He pulled on a pair of gym shorts and a T-shirt before going in search of her. He'd expected to find her in the kitchen or on the deck, lounging in the sunshine and the morning breeze.

Where he didn't expect to find her was in his office—sitting at his cherry wood captain's desk, kicked back in a chair with her feet propped up, riffling through her wine-soaked purse while talking on the landline. Her back was to the doorway, but the robe he'd loaned her was open to her thighs.

The punch of lust hit him so hard, he didn't hear a word she was saying. He just stood in the doorframe and stared. He wanted to step back to get a grip on himself but couldn't tear his gaze away. Then her words started to sink in.

"So how would this work, Teddy? I understand the woman can't travel to Africa, but who'll teach my courses next semester if I go in her place?" Jenny's excitement was palatable: in her tone, in the set of her shoulders, in the tilt of her head.

Africa?

"They'd do that?" she asked.

Another pause. Nick's lust vanished in 2.4 seconds, changing to something infinitely more combustible.

"I know I organized the Paleo-Niger project, but that was volunteer work. I'd planned to go with you and pay my own way until my financial circumstances made that impossible. Now you're saying the Russ Foundation wants to hire me to go to Africa? This week?"

Part of him wished he hadn't heard anything. Jenny wanted to go to Africa? Getting her out of town was a good plan, but talk about jumping from the frying pan into the fire.

If Nick had stayed with the NCS, his next assignment would have been in Africa. Before he quit he'd done preliminary background work for the assignment. A year ago the Republic of Niger had been an extraordinarily dangerous place, particularly for foreigners.

Nothing had happened in the past twelve months to change that. If anything, the situation was even more out of control. He couldn't think about what it would be like for an American woman travelling alone there. His frustration level ratcheted up as he listened to Jenny's side of the conversation.

"Of course I want to go. I've just—it's, um . . . complicated. But yes, I can do it. You've already got my passport information, and I had the visa all arranged before I cancelled, so go ahead and make my reservations."

She was so caught up in what was happening, she didn't realize Nick was standing in the doorway hearing every word.

"I need only a few hours to get things together here. My dig pack is in my storage unit along with my passport and visa. I took everything over there when I thought I was cancelling last week. I never put the passport back in my safety deposit box, so I don't even have to wait on the bank to open tomorrow before I leave. I can fly into JFK tonight and catch that early morning flight to Niamey tomorrow."

She swung around in the chair and looked up at that moment to make eye contact. Her face was lit with an excitement Nick hadn't seen since the summer they'd first met. Despite finding him there in the doorway, her gaze didn't waver as she spoke into the phone. But something in her expression changed.

"On second thought, don't make the reservation for New York till tomorrow." She turned her back to him in the next pause. "You're right. I'm so excited, I didn't think about the holiday. It'll be crazy to travel. Okay, I'll just put my roller skates on and get it done. Tomorrow evening will be fine."

She listened for a moment. "Of course, just let me know. Sure, you too, and thank you. I'll see you soon."

She set the landline back down in the cradle on the desktop and took an audible breath before she turned to look up at him.

"Hi." She smiled. "I hope you don't mind. I needed to call my boss."

Nick studied her and considered counting to ten before speaking, but he knew that even if he counted to a thousand it wouldn't help. "No, I don't mind. But I would like to know what in God's name you think you're doing planning a trip to Africa less than eight hours back from that ordeal in Mexico?"

She tilted her head, and he could tell from the look in her eye that he was about to be handled. His pulse rate ratcheted up before she said a word.

"That's just it, Nick. I know I need to get away, to get out of town while you sort all this out. Isn't Africa far enough away?"

How could he argue with that? Of course, distance was the very problem. Africa was too damn far away. He didn't like the thought of Jennifer being where he couldn't see her, couldn't touch her.

Jesus. What had happened to getting the hell away from her once he got her back to Dallas? When had he become so incredibly possessive? When the woman he'd dreamed about for the past ten years had been kidnapped and he'd risked his life to rescue her from a brothel in Mexico, that's when. If that didn't inspire a slight feeling of possessiveness, he wasn't sure what would.

He leaned forward, meeting her gaze. "Africa is absolutely lousy with cartels, terrorists, and criminals who would just as soon shoot you as look at you. The Republic of Niger's government has become increasingly chaotic and unstable over the past year, and that's a generous assessment of the situation. At this point, it's possible you might be safer in Mexico."

"I don't want to argue with you—"

"Of course you do," he interrupted. "But you've got to listen." He took a deep breath, preparing to explain exactly what he meant.

"Where is Bryan?" she asked.

He blinked at the abrupt change in subject. "He's gone home to sleep, I'd imagine." Before he could say anything else, she stood and walked toward him.

"Good." With no warning, she slipped his robe from her shoulders.

He stood staring in shocked silence as he tried to process the conversation's appealing change of direction. She was naked underneath the robe. He'd known she would be, but he hadn't expected to see her standing so gloriously naked in his office.

"I don't want to talk right now. Can't we do that later?" She slid her arms around his neck and pulled herself to him as his brain shorted out.

Still, he recognized those words as his line. He was supposed to be the one not wanting to talk about things, not dealing with problems when he would be leaving. It took him a moment to piece that together as he was working with less blood supply to his brain than usual, but she was doing exactly what he'd done to her ten years ago when he'd left. She was planning to leave and not discuss things at all, and he was supposed to be okay with that.

He was more than a little surprised at how "un-okay" he was.

He tried putting his hands on her arms but couldn't quite bring himself to push her away.

"Jenny, we need to talk."

She kissed his collarbone and pressed all that lovely bare flesh closer to him, and his arms automatically went around her. She kissed the line of his jaw.

"Aren't there things you'd rather do than talk?" she asked.

"Is that a trick question?" He nuzzled the side of her neck.

No, he didn't want to talk. He wanted to take her down the hall to his bedroom and pick up where they'd left off a few hours ago. She was giving a fair impression that she wanted the same thing. But what had happened to the weeping woman at the airstrip and in his bathroom last night? Was she really recovered from the horror of the past two-and-a-half days and able to move on so quickly, or was this some huge act to distract him from her leaving town?

Why couldn't he turn his brain off and focus on this? On now? On her bare ass in his hands?

His slid his fingertips up her waist and pulled her closer. "Jenny, I—"

"Shhh." She kissed him again, this time sucking at his lower lip as she ran her hands around his waist and over his butt.

He gave up and quit arguing. Hell, if she didn't want to talk, why should he? He slipped one hand between her legs and felt the heat under her soft curls.

She moaned deep in her throat as he finally stopped thinking and melted into the moment. Her hands were back around at his waistband and she had him out of his gym shorts in record time. Her hand was stroking him as he backed her up to his desk.

With one swipe he cleared the neatly arranged pens and papers to lift her up and over the raised edge of the uniquely designed desktop. He'd always prided himself on keeping a ruthlessly spartan office. That came in handy now.

He was about to be inside her again. It was just as it had always been. One look at her and he was turned on. Her lips were moving against the side of his neck, and she was nibbling at his earlobe when the phone beside her hip rang with a startling vibration.

She jumped, and he would have smiled if he hadn't caught her guilty expression. Her eyes widened as she looked away from his face, but it was too late. He'd been seconds from being "played," his mind taken away from the real issue at hand.

Africa? Seriously?

After the trauma of what she'd experienced in Mexico, he wasn't sure if travelling to Niger was the height of idiocy, recklessness, or both. How could she possibly be considering going there?

The phone rang a second time, and he reluctantly checked the caller ID. It was Gavin. He couldn't ignore his boss, no matter how inconvenient the timing.

Jenny started to pull away, but he held her to him with one hand as he picked up the phone. They were going to discuss Africa, with their clothes on, as soon as he finished this call.

"Hope I'm not catching you at a bad time," said Gavin.

Nick snorted a grim laugh and wondered, not for the first time, if there weren't cameras in the office, even though he knew for a fact there were not. The man just had excellent "spidey" senses, more so than anyone Nick had ever worked with.

"No, boss. Everything's fine here. What can I do for you?" Jennifer again moved to pull away, and he held her firmly in place, not in the least bothered that he was standing there with his pants around his thighs.

"I talked to Bryan earlier, and he suggested I let you sleep in, so I did. But I wanted to talk about what you ran into in Tenancingo. It sounds like something more was going on there than just a simple turf dispute."

Nick cleared his throat. "I agree. It was a deliberate massacre. There was no reason to kill those people once the building burned."

Jenny stiffened in his arms. Nick ran his palm up and down her spine as he continued. "It's like someone was trying to start a war."

The connection was lousy, and Nick had to press the phone closer to his ear to hear. Still, Gavin's voice was staticky and dropped out every couple of seconds. "Tenancingo has been operating as a center for sex trafficking for a couple of generations now with little to no interference from local law enforcement. That level of violence doesn't make sense."

"The hits on Rivera's compound last month and the vet clinic take on a whole new meaning with this. No one is strong enough to take over both cartels, but someone could be trying to get them to fight among themselves. If they start destroying each other, the agitator wouldn't have to work as hard to stir things up," said Nick.

"Do you think Leland's contact, Alvarez, might know something?" asked Gavin.

Jenny quit struggling, making no secret of the fact that she was listening to both sides of the conversation. Nick figured there was nothing she shouldn't hear. If anything, it might make the argument to keep her out of Africa more forceful.

He tilted the phone so she could hear more easily. "He might, if he's in the loop with Vega. Should I talk to Alvarez or have Leland do it? Most of our communication was through text."

"You go ahead," said Gavin. "I've got Leland busy with a couple of other things now. But I'll have him check with his old contacts in the DEA."

"This didn't look like a cartel feud in the classic sense. And I don't see how it could have been about me or Bryan unless Leland's contact was dirty."

"Do you think this was some sort of hit on Tomas Rivera?" asked Gavin.

Nick straightened and pulled Jenny closer toward him, enjoying the feel of her bare skin against him but still smarting over the idea that she'd been trying to distract him with sex earlier.

"With the attacks last month on Rivera's compound and on Cesar Vega, it's not that farfetched. Someone was emboldened in a big way to think they could strike at the heart of the Rivera cartel one day and take out the enforcer for the Vegas the next."

"That kind of violence is all too common down there. It would almost prove the opposite of what we're saying here, that this is a turf war," said Gavin.

Nick exhaled. "Could be . . ." Even he heard the lack of conviction in his tone.

Jenny pushed at his chest again, and he was so surprised he almost took a step back. Anger flashed in her eyes. Apparently, she didn't like being held still while he talked. He let her go and watched reluctantly as she slid off his desk and bent to pick up her robe. She pulled it on before she left the room, covering the ass he'd been holding just moments ago. Obviously pissed with him, she snapped the door closed.

He pulled up his own pants with a sigh. "Gavin, what do you know about West Africa, specifically the Republic of Niger?"

"Geographically? Politically? What are you looking for?"

"All of it. Jenny is talking about going to Niamey on a paleontology dig."

"That's a very bad idea. It's a hellhole over there right now. The drought in the area has produced a political crisis, and they've got a new government in charge every other week with tribes fighting among themselves based on religious affiliations and allegiance to whichever group is in charge at the moment. Al-Qaeda connections run deep all over the area."

Nick had suspected as much but had hoped instead for something that would reassure him about Jenny's choice. Unfortunately, he'd have to settle for ammunition in their pending conversation about her travel plans. Gavin wasn't sharing anything encouraging.

"Drug cartels have moved from Latin America to the coast of West Africa. Niger is in the center of a prime shipping route across the continent for moving their product into Europe: mostly Spain, the U.K., and France. There's very little law enforcement, and the drugs travel with virtually no resistance."

"I thought the DEA had an office in Niamey," said Nick.

Gavin snorted. "Oh, they do. It's one of four DEA offices covering a continent spanning 11.7 million square miles and inhabited by one billion people. I think you can safely say that doesn't even qualify as spitting in the ocean."

Nick nodded, his worst fears confirmed about where Jenny was headed.

Chapter Ten

_____

JENNIFER MADE HER way back to the bedroom, struggling with her equilibrium. She'd acted on impulse. Thank God the phone had interrupted, or she would have made a serious error.

That Nick still held such a sexual thrall over her after all this time was disturbing on multiple levels. She'd stepped into his arms to stop an argument and had almost ended up having sex with him on a desktop. Who was she kidding? Certainly not herself. She was becoming addicted to him all over again and reminded herself of how well that had ended before.

Nick was definitely not excited about her field study in Niger, but that was too damn bad. She'd worked hard for this trip, and the idea that she could actually go was so thrilling she could barely contain herself. She'd been horribly disappointed when she'd had to cancel, particularly after the countless hours she'd spent painstakingly organizing the dig, dealing with the constantly changing government officials, and navigating the regulations to get the proper approvals and permits for the project.

And now she was going, all because one of the other professors couldn't attend due to health issues. Jennifer was sorry for the woman but incredibly grateful at the same time. She hoped that didn't make her a bad person.

The unexpected opportunity was enough to make her forget, at least for a little while, about the wretched circumstances of her time in Tenancingo and why she couldn't stay here any longer than absolutely necessary. As for Nick, he would just have to get over his concerns about her travel to Africa. She'd been perfectly safe the last time she was there with the Russ Foundation.

She'd known he was about to argue when she took her robe off. She just wasn't sure what she was supposed to do now. Exposure to Nick wasn't good for her head or for her heart. He was practically a virus where she was concerned. So . . . a plan.

She shut the door behind her and went to the multi-line phone in the bedroom to call a cab. The dispatcher promised to have a driver there in twenty minutes. *Perfect.*

She walked into the bathroom to grab her clothes, hating the idea of putting on the same thing that she'd worn out of Mexico. But there was no other option, unless wearing Nick's robe worked for her. It didn't.

She was going home to her waterlogged house as soon as possible. If she could leave without fighting with Nick that would be better, but either way she was leaving. She had to regain her balance, and it wasn't going to happen here.

She glanced at the small clock on the bathroom shelf. If she hurried, she had enough time to shower before her cab arrived. Wearing his robe and sleeping all night on his sheets and pillow, enveloped in the familiar smell of him, had done nothing for that elusive stability she was searching for.

Taking a shower would go a long way to reestablishing her center. She hadn't told Nick yet about what had happened all those years ago, and she wasn't going to do it now either. The time for explanations was past.

She'd just stepped out of the shower and was wrapping herself in a towel when the door opened, and Nick stepped inside the bathroom.

She stifled a shriek—barely. "Hey, don't you knock?"

He shook his head. "Not when I know the answer will be *go away.*"

"Well, that's too damn bad. Get out of here. I'll be out in a minute." She would have felt more in control if her voice hadn't cracked.

Making zero effort to leave, Nick leaned into the doorframe and took a good long look, perusing her body to the point where Jennifer imagined the water droplets from her shower were sizzling on her skin. As the heat worked its way from the top of her head to her toes, he turned and stepped back into the bedroom without a word.

She took a deep breath, pissed off and turned on at the same time. *Nope, no equilibrium to be found here.* She was about to pull on the pants and T-shirt she'd worn back from Mexico when there was an actual knock at the door.

"Yes?" she asked, relieved that her voice was steady this time.

Nick held an armful of clothes. "I thought you'd like something clean. Risa, my boss, has some things here for when she can't get home before a job. She said you could use whatever you needed." He held out a stack of yoga pants, sweatshirt, flip-flops, and underwear.

"Thanks, I didn't want to wear those others again." She reached for the clothing.

He left, and she changed. Staring into the mirror, she cursed her cowardice for not having dealt years ago with the problem she currently faced. She'd been fooling herself earlier. She had to tell him. Still, now wasn't the time.

God, she'd thought she was past all this, but she wasn't. And the hell of it was, Nick wasn't to blame. He'd never known.

She'd quit writing to him and broken off all contact, quit keeping in touch. That had hurt them both, and it had been wrong of her. Unfortunately, she hadn't realized *how* wrong until much too late.

She'd met Collin Petersen and had thrown herself into the relationship with an abandon that had more to do with burying sorrow than falling in love. Sadly, she hadn't figured that out either, until well after she was married to him.

What was the point of telling Nick now? It was a bad idea, especially if she wanted to get him out of her life and get herself to Africa. Keeping things to herself seemed a wiser choice.

Maybe she could write him a letter after she was in Niger? No, that wasn't right either. Was she really that big of a coward?

Perhaps in this particular situation she was.

She arrived at that unpleasant realization as she slipped into the borrowed clothes. When she emerged from the bathroom a couple of minutes later, Nick was seated on the bed, staring at his phone and oblivious to her turmoil.

"Hi," she mumbled.

"Hi, yourself."

"I need to get home. I've got a house that's in shambles, plus I've got to make some arrangements for travelling."

"Right. About that—"

She interrupted him. "I've already called a cab, and it should be arriving any minute."

"No, it's not. The front gate called while you were in the shower. I sent the cab away."

"You what?!" She heard the shrillness in her tone and decided she didn't care what he thought anymore.

"I sent them away," he explained, as if he were dealing with someone who wasn't particularly bright. It made her furious. "I'll take you home, or wherever you need to go," he added.

She swallowed an angry retort about his high-handedness. Arguing wasn't going to help this situation. "Can we go now?" She couldn't disguise the fury in her voice, but she'd stay civil as long as possible. He'd come to get her out of Mexico, and she was grateful, no matter how angry he was making her at this point.

"Of course. Let me grab my keys and wallet, and we'll be set."

She waited, stifling the urge to tap her foot as he gathered his things. She followed him downstairs to a sports car she hadn't noticed last night. The sexy, sleek Italian job looked exactly like what she didn't imagine he would drive, and she surprised both of them when she said so.

He didn't seem to take offense. "I like fast toys." He shrugged and helped her into the creamy leather passenger seat.

The smooth manners she remembered from the summer they were lovers still struck an unexpected spot of warmth. It had been a long time since a man who wasn't a valet had helped her into a car. Collin had never been much for formalities, even at the beginning of their relationship. She didn't realize how much she'd missed that feeling of being cared for, of being cherished. Even if, in this case, Nick's manners were just ingrained habit.

They rode in silence until they were out of the neighborhood and on a main thoroughfare. Nick didn't ask questions as he drove south along the North Dallas Tollway.

"You know where I live?"

"Give me some credit, Jenny. I used to work for the CIA."

The acknowledgment took her by surprise. She'd suspected something like that, but to hear Nick put things so starkly was still a shock.

"You mean you don't anymore?" she asked.

"Nope, but no one believes me when I say that."

She shrugged. "I suppose that's understandable."

He didn't elaborate. Instead, he changed the subject. "We need to talk . . . about Africa."

"There's not much to say. I'm going, and I'm delighted. I've been planning the trip for months and thought I'd have to give it up, so this offer from the Russ Foundation is ideal."

"I heard." The disapproval was obvious in his tone.

"You don't have to be so negative about it. This work is extraordinarily important to me."

"Jenny, are you really that naïve? Do you have any idea what's going on over there? Thousands of people are dying because of the political unrest, and no one is paying any attention. Cartels from all over Latin America and Mexico are moving in completely unimpeded by law enforcement."

He had one hand on the steering wheel as they sped down the Tollway. "West Africa has become the new Colombia. Cartels operate side by side with al-Qaeda narco-terrorists moving cocaine across the continent and into Europe by the ton. They've exterminated entire villages that won't cooperate."

She shook her head. No, she could not listen to this. Besides, the alternative—staying here with Nick—was unacceptable.

"You're just trying to scare me. The area of Niger I'm travelling to is perfectly safe. I'll be fine. What gives you the right to have a say in what goes on in my life anyway?

Where I go and what I do is none of your business. Africa has got to be better than staying here where I was kidnapped, shot at, and burned out. We've hired Tuareg guards for the digs. They're excellent at security. I've gotten all the approvals from the Niger authorities."

"Which means you'll be fine unless someone tries to take over the government, which seems to be happening in that country every other month."

Arguing with him was pointless, and the only other option—not going—was unthinkable. She didn't answer as he pulled into the driveway of her small rental house. The pansies she'd planted out front by the porch steps as therapy a week ago were wilting in the unusual Texas December heat, a visual aid for how she felt herself.

Nick turned off the ignition. "I'm not trying to scare you. I'm just trying to show you this situation in a realistic light. The cartels control anything and everything they want over there."

He was out of the car and opening her door before she realized it. How could he argue and display those impeccable manners that melted her at the same time? She grabbed her keys and slung her trashed purse over her shoulder, cross-body style.

He touched her elbow as he stood beside her. "Local governments are too overwhelmed to notice, even if they had the manpower to fight it. The European drug market is exploding, and West Africa supplies over a quarter of the product. Guinea-Bissau, right next to Niger, is openly considered the first narco-state on the continent. It's hell on earth there and certainly not safe."

"Why in the world would they care about me?" She walked away from him, climbing the porch steps and moving to open the front door. "I'm not anyone important."

He sighed. "A person's influence, whether great or small, doesn't matter. You're an American. That makes you newsworthy and a target for robbery, kidnapping, publicity for their 'cause,' or for human trafficking."

She crossed her arms and stood at the front door, glaring at him. She couldn't back down, not now, even if everything he said was true. She'd just be extremely careful. Paleo-Niger and the Foundation had excellent safety protocols in place. She'd be fine.

"I don't want to talk about this anymore. I just want to get inside my house and put on my own clothes. I appreciate your getting me out of Mexico. Really, I do. But your work is done. Go spend the holiday with your family. I don't want you in my life." That seemed harsh. And yes, it was a bald-faced lie, but she was going with it.

"I'm back. I'm home. I'm safe. I'm fine. And I'm leaving, so I won't be any more trouble to you. I'm starting a new life, just like you did when you joined the Navy. We have nothing to do with each other anymore. Can't you let me go?" She hadn't meant to say that last part. Hadn't meant to reveal quite so much.

"No, I can't. I never wanted—" He stopped talking abruptly, as if to keep himself from saying more.

"I still think you're just trying to scare me," she muttered under her breath, deliberately misunderstanding him. She was not having this conversation. She couldn't.

Not now when she was so close to a clean getaway. Talking about this would lead to her telling him everything, when she was moments from never having to tell him anything.

She put her key in the lock, determined to go inside and shut the door behind her. But a key wasn't necessary. The door swung open of its own accord.

Chapter Eleven

NICK RACED INTO the house behind Jenny. In the bedroom he stopped, watching as she took in the extent of the destruction. A cold ball of fear settled in his gut.

All the drawers had been dumped on the floor, the bed stripped, and holes gouged into the mattress. The master closet had been ransacked. Clothing was strewn about and torn, cut with scissors or—more likely—a knife.

This was what he'd been afraid of—even as he'd driven away from the brothel, helped Jennifer clean up at the airstrip, and held her in his bathroom in the AEGIS office.

Was she a target now because she meant something to him?

If they'd found this house, they knew she wasn't his sister-in-law. Were they coming after Jenny because they knew that hurting her would hurt him?

Whether it was Ernesto Vega or Tomas Rivera after him—or someone else entirely—Nick wasn't sure. What he did know was that Jenny couldn't travel anywhere right now unprotected, certainly not to Africa.

No, he'd get someone else to take her. That would keep it completely professional. Bryan could do it. And if Bryan couldn't do it, Marissa would.

Preparing himself to talk with Jenny about the unpleasant and unwelcome idea of an AEGIS bodyguard, he rolled his head from side to side and turned. That's when he saw the wires attached to the bottom of the bedroom door hinge.

The blood froze in his veins as he scanned the door casing and visually followed the wires along the floor to a small pile of clothing in the corner by the doorframe. An innocuous looking digital timer ticked downward from seven seconds.

"Bomb!" he shouted. Instinct took over, and he stepped forward to grab Jenny's arm. He didn't feel his feet touch the floor once as he hauled her through the doorway and pulled her past the living room to spring from the top step. They'd just cleared the porch when the device detonated.

Heat from the force of the blast caught him and Jenny both, shoving them violently through the air. The power was much greater than he'd calculated in those milliseconds before the explosion when he'd vaulted from the porch. He held on to her arm throughout their crazy flight off the stoop, fighting to wrap his body around hers and cushion her fall before they hit the hard ground.

Umph.

Sprawled near the sidewalk with Jenny in his arms and her massive purse smushed between them, his right shoulder was in agony. The bullet wound from less than a month ago wasn't anywhere near ready for this kind of abuse. He wasn't breathing well, but he assumed that had more to do with the bumpy landing and having Jenny sprawled across his chest than anything else.

Other than his shoulder and some inevitable scrapes, he felt okay. But he suspected that shock adrenaline wasn't going to last long. There was a worrying tingle down his side and a dampness from what could only be blood underneath him.

"You alright?" He couldn't hear himself talk and guessed that was a residual effect of the blast force on his eardrums.

How long would he be half deaf?

Everything was unnaturally quiet, but he could smell the smoke and see flames behind them as the house became completely engulfed. Jenny's head was on his shoulder facing him and he glanced down into her eyes. She wasn't answering, but she was conscious, and her expression held that horrifyingly shocked air he'd already seen enough of in the past twelve hours to last a lifetime. Her face was dirty and soot-colored, as if she'd been cleaning a chimney.

She shook her head a couple of times, trying to clear the effects of the blast. Then she was nodding and saying *yes, I'm alright*. At least that's what he guessed she was saying. Her mouth was moving and he was lip-reading.

She pulled her arms from underneath her belly, accidently elbowing him in the process of sitting up. She was still grasping her keychain in one hand as she helped him sit upright, too. Her purse crashed into his hip as he pulled her along with him and crawled away from the house, moving them closer to the sidewalk.

She was talking the whole time, or he assumed she was as he watched her lips continuously moving. Still, he couldn't understand a word she was saying. But some response was called for. So he said, "You're okay. We're alright."

She quit talking then and flung her arms around his waist, holding him in a death grip. Her body shook, and he felt moisture on his shoulder from her tears. Her "silent" crying left him feeling no less helpless than if he could actually hear her gulps and hiccups as she fought to control the evident storm of emotion.

Apparently, she'd been saying more than he'd realized, and he was sorry he'd missed it. He wrapped her in his arms, continuing to murmur soothing words he couldn't hear himself.

After a moment she nodded her head like maybe she believed him anyway. One of her hands rested against his uninjured shoulder, and he was encouraged when he finally heard the faint jangle of those keys next to his ear. Maybe he wasn't going to be deaf after all.

He glanced up. A couple of folks were out of their houses and in the street, making their way toward them. He thought he could hear a siren in the distance and was relieved to know the initial effects of the blast were indeed wearing off, although his ears would most likely be ringing for hours.

Things were about to get completely crazy with cops, firemen and—he winced as he moved to stand—most likely, paramedics, too. He needed to call either Gavin or Bryan and let them know what was happening, but that lack of hearing thing was an issue. He should text instead.

He reached for his phone, even as he continued to hold Jenny with his other arm. She pulled away with a puzzled expression. "Gotta call Gavin or Bryan." His voice still sounded like he was underwater, but she seemed to understand.

God, she could have died if he hadn't been here. Hell, he'd been here, and she'd still almost died. His deepest fears were coming true: not being able to keep the people most important to him safe, or worse, his work putting the people he cared about in danger.

But why? Was this incident related to his involvement with Leland and Anna last month in Mexico? Or was Ernesto Vega exacting some kind of revenge for Nick not getting him the information about Cesar and Carlita's deaths? Neither scenario felt right.

Nick glanced back to the street as a fire truck made its way toward them. He shot a text to Bryan and Gavin both, then waited on reinforcements.

What had just happened? Why would someone be targeting Jennifer? He'd already established that the people who'd planted the bomb knew she wasn't Angela because they'd found this house. And no matter how paranoid he was, no one knew the extent of his and Jenny's former relationship. He'd had zero contact with her for ten years until he'd seen her yesterday at Tomas's brothel.

It made no sense. Cartels targeted family members of people they wanted to coerce all the time, but this was way over the top. To go after an innocent U.S. citizen on U.S. soil called down too much wrath by the authorities. Whoever set the bomb knew Jenny wasn't a member of his family, as evidenced by the fact that they'd struck at her house.

Was she being targeted for another reason?

And just like that, he understood or thought he did. Maybe this had nothing to do with cartel revenge on him for what had happened last month in Mexico. Perhaps Jenny had seen or heard something in Tenancingo that she wasn't supposed to, or someone in that brothel had. Given what he knew now, it was the only thing that made sense.

Was that why all those people had been killed? Why Jenny had been targeted here in the U.S.?

But what had she seen or heard? Chances were she didn't even realize it herself. But he knew one thing for certain. He wasn't letting her out of his sight until he figured this out. He might not be able to protect her on his own without driving both of them crazy, but she now had him "in her life," whether she wanted him or not.

She might be going to Africa, but she wasn't going without him. He'd take Marissa or Bryan with him if necessary, but he was no longer willing to delegate the responsibility of Jenny's safety to someone else. Until the threat was eliminated, she wasn't going *anywhere* without him.

JENNIFER WAS BEYOND exhaustion by the time they got out of the Emergency Room. It was half past ten in the evening, she smelled like a campfire gone wrong, plus she was starving. Too tired to try and figure out why someone had blown up her house, she just wanted to get cleaned up and get some sleep.

While the ER doctor had examined her, Bryan had retrieved Nick's car from what was left of her house and took the vehicle back to AEGIS. Hollywood planned to give them both a ride back to the office in his SUV.

Nick had refused the standard protocol of being rolled out of the hospital in a wheelchair, and he was quiet—too quiet. The orderly had taken one look at his murderous expression and backed way off. Since Nick was too surly to talk, Jennifer focused on Bryan.

"Do you want me to take you to Walmart to get some clothes? A toothbrush?" Bryan asked as they all walked to his car. "We can take Nick to the office, and I'll run you by the store."

Jennifer smiled sadly. "I'd like to say *no*, but I'm afraid Walmart, or its equivalent, will be supplying my entire wardrobe. My budget can't handle much else." Everything she owned had gone up in flames in the explosion, except the contents of her storage unit and her purse.

She was ruminating on that bleak fact when she realized a possible bright spot. "Hey, is my car still at Angela and Drew's house?"

Nick nodded. "It was when I was there yesterday morning."

His left hand was bandaged. He had bruised ribs with abrasions and a couple of stitches on his forehead at his hairline. Jennifer suspected he felt like hell about now. She certainly did, and she hadn't landed on a piece of the roof with someone else on top of her.

"Then I have a suitcase, or I should have. On my way into Drew and Angela's house, I was carrying groceries, so I left my overnight bag in the car. My computer is in the trunk, too!"

Not even remembering how the luggage had come to be left at the Donovan home could dim her enthusiasm. She was giddy at the prospect of having some of her things intact. Life might not be as grim as she'd originally thought.

"Excellent," said Bryan. "We can swing by to pick up your bag and your car on our way back to the office."

"Can't you just drop me at Angela's?" She wasn't squeamish about staying in the place she'd been taken from. The idea of soaking in her friend's garden tub overrode every other consideration. "I'd rather stay there, since I was house-sitting anyway."

She was so delighted over the possibility of having her own makeup and knowing that her favorite yoga pants hadn't gone up in flames, she didn't see the problem.

Bryan stopped beside a late model SUV and unlocked

the doors. "I'm not so sure that's a good idea," he said quietly.

She turned back to ask why, and that's when she saw the thundering scowl on Nick's face. "No way in fucking hell," he muttered. The chill in his tone was arctic. "Are you out of your mind or just trying to get yourself killed?"

Despite his anger, Nick stood by the passenger door prepared to help her inside. She found it stunning that he could demonstrate such flawless cotillion manners while cursing a blue streak and obviously feeling anything but civilized. She tried to ignore his outburst, but a furious Nick was hard to overlook.

Bryan stepped in, attempting to defuse the situation. "Jennifer, I'll give you a ride anywhere you want to go to get clothes and stuff. I'll even pick up your car, but I think you need to stay at the AEGIS office tonight." No doubt he'd dealt with a livid Nick before.

She knew both men were right. She had no business staying at Angela's house alone this evening, but she was itching for an argument, and she loathed being managed. Tired, dirty, and hungry—she was sporting the trifecta for picking a fight.

She ignored Bryan's well-meaning suggestion and turned on Nick. "You don't have to be so nasty. I'd just like to have some of my own things and a place where I feel comfortable. It's not like your house got blown to hell today!"

Nick took a deep breath and said the one thing she wasn't expecting. "I'm sorry. You're right. Let's go get the clothes from your car."

Seemingly unwilling to argue with her after his initial outburst, he put out a hand to help her into the SUV. His sudden bout of reason took the wind completely out of her sails, but she was in no mood to accept an apology or help.

"I can do it myself." Too late she realized that she sounded like a spoiled child as she climbed into the back-seat on her own and silently seethed.

Nick waited until she was settled before shutting the door and climbing into the front passenger seat. No one spoke as Bryan drove them to Angela and Drew's house. Jennifer's car was still where she'd parked it in the drive-way three nights ago. She hopped out before Nick could open her door.

"I'll ride with you, so Bryan doesn't have to drive back to the office before he goes home," he said.

She didn't want to spend any more time with Nick than she had to but realized how bitchy that would sound if she said it out loud. Bryan had to be exhausted, too. It was time for her to pull up her big-girl panties. "Thank you for coming to get us, Bryan. I'm sorry it's been so much trouble."

"No problem. Just glad you're both okay."

She nodded her thanks again and stood in the cool night air, glancing up at the waning moon.

Nick stood beside her a moment. "Want to see if that suitcase is still here?" he asked.

The evening air cooled her temper. She swallowed the last of her exasperation along with her chagrin and slid her hand in her pocket to pop the car's trunk with the key fob. Sure enough, her suitcase and computer were right where she'd left them. Feeling calmer, she was now thoroughly embarrassed by her earlier outburst.

Nick might not want her going to Africa, but she wasn't listening to any more arguments from him. It made her too crazy, and spending any more time with him had the potential to devastate her life just as much as that bomb blast could have. She was going to the Jobaria dig site.

Why would anyone follow her to the middle of the Sahara? Besides, the danger wasn't about her. It was about Nick and what he did. Tomas had as much as said so in Mexico. She assumed the bombing was connected to Nick as well. If she got away from Nick, she should be safe.

All she needed for the trip was her backpack from her storage unit. She was starting over, just like erasing a chalkboard. She would leave and not think about what had happened to her house and her life until she wanted to think about it, maybe four months from now when the Paleo Niger Project was over. If she was running away from home, she was running away from everything.

"Ready to go?" She pulled the resilient key ring from her pocket, feeling as if she and Nick had called an informal truce.

"Yeah," Nick muttered.

"Want to drive?"

He shook his head.

Okay, so he was still pissed. He'd have to get over it— or not. She wasn't going to be in town for much longer.

She popped the locks on her door and slid behind the wheel.

Bryan waited until she'd started her car before backing his SUV out of the driveway.

Obviously exhausted, Nick leaned his head against the passenger seat headrest. She felt a moment of guilt that he was not already in bed. He had to be beyond pain. She'd seen the barely healed scars when the paramedics cut his shirt off in her front yard. Yet he'd stubbornly refused painkillers at the hospital, even ibuprofen. She shook her head. You could lead a man to Advil, but you couldn't make him swallow it.

Since Nick wasn't talking, Jennifer focused on something else. Her earthly possessions were precious few. Tonight she was beyond grateful that when she'd thought her trip to Africa was cancelled, she'd packed up all her work and camping gear and put those supplies back in long-term storage.

The fire from the explosion had taken everything else, so the pesky problem of dealing with her waterlogged house was a moot point. There was absolutely nothing left except the contents of her car and her storage unit. The five by ten foot space held a formal dining room table that had been her aunt's, a file cabinet from her old office in Austin, and the precious dig pack. That was all Jennifer had left in the world.

No matter what Nick had said, she still didn't believe Niger was that dangerous. The smuggling mess he had talked about was on the west coast, and the Paleo-Niger site was several days' travel—even by car—from that chaos. When they got back to the AEGIS office, she'd try explaining it all once more to him from her point of view. If he was still unhappy, at least she would be out of his hair. And Nick could be unhappy from a distance.

Surely it would be all for the best. She could not stay here with him, getting to know him again and opening her emotions and her heart up to him again. That was much more dangerous than anything awaiting her in Africa.

Here, there be dragons.

More than anything she wanted out of Dallas and away from the insanity of the past seventy-two hours. She needed to be as far as possible from this experience and the emotional turmoil of dealing with Nick. Tomorrow she'd fly into New York, then on to Niamey and Ingal. The Paleo-Niger site outside of Ingal was a twelve-hour drive from the nearest commercial airport. No one would want to follow her there, even if they could find her.

She pulled her car up to the security kiosk for the airpark, and Nick told her the code to access the gate. Beyond the five numbers he muttered, he still wasn't speaking to her. It was time she set the record straight, and if that completely alienated him, it might be for the better.

"I'm sorry you are upset by my choices, but this is my life. You don't get a say in it. I didn't howl when you left at the end of that summer ten years ago. You can't dictate my options now. We didn't even stay in contact." She didn't add that she'd been the one to stop returning his emails and phone calls.

Nick clenched his jaw, and she could practically hear his teeth grinding the enamel off his molars.

"What? What is it?" she snapped. Her vow to stay patient was gone.

"I came back, dammit!"

"What?" Jennifer repeated in a whisper.

"I came back and you were gone on a dig. You'd cut me off and quit emailing. Quit returning calls. Quit communicating completely with anyone who'd known you. I came home to see what was wrong." Nick's voice was quiet, but there was no hiding the pain behind his words.

Nick had come back? She struggled to wrap her head around the idea.

"Turns out nothing was wrong. I was just a fucking idiot. I certainly felt like one when I found out later that you'd gotten married. I thought you'd cut me off because you didn't want to have anything to do with me or my tainted family."

No. Nick had come back, and she'd been off with Collin on that dig in China . . . where he'd proposed. Had Nick really thought she'd dumped him because of his father's embezzlement? Nothing could have been farther from the truth. Why had Angela never told her Nick had come home for a visit?

It wasn't her friend's fault. Jennifer had been so flattened by all that had happened, she'd gone through a period where she wasn't talking to Angela. She'd known her friend would tell Drew, Nick's brother, everything they'd discussed. Jennifer wouldn't have expected Angela not to tell.

God, she and Nick had had such a huge miscue all the way around. She was horrified but not surprised. They had been so young and rash; so confident that they each knew best, they never told the other what they really felt. Had she and Nick really known each other at all?

She hadn't realized how messed up the situation could get when they didn't communicate. She'd been so horribly wrong, never understanding the consequences of her actions until it was much too late.

Could she talk to him now?

This was the perfect opportunity. But what would happen once she did? Would he just feel worse?

She was just . . . God, she was tired. And she wanted out of town more than she'd wanted anything in a long time—away from Nick, away from everything. Surely after she told him he'd be so angry, he would let her go.

"Nick, I need to tell you something. It's about—"

He interrupted. "You know, Jennifer, I don't want to hear it right now. I'm exhausted, I'm hostile, and I'm hurting. I know we need to talk about the bombing, too, but I can hardly see straight. I won't take anything you have to say well. Let's just leave it all until tomorrow."

She held up a hand to stop him from saying more. "Fine."

It was settled. The conversation was over. Truly over. She wouldn't be bringing this up again, ever.

She parked her car in the AEGIS driveway and popped the trunk. Despite his claims of exhaustion, Nick pulled her suitcase and computer case out and hauled them both upstairs to the bedroom she'd slept in last night. She didn't object, even though she knew it was his room. He grabbed more clothes from a dresser drawer after putting her bags on the bench at the end of the bed.

"Help yourself to whatever is in the fridge. I'm setting the burglar alarm and going to sleep," he said. "We'll talk in the morning about how the explosion this afternoon will affect your travel schedule."

She didn't like the sound of that. "How do I disarm the security system if I'm up before you?"

He gave her the code, and without another word he closed the door. She stared at the bedroom door a long time after he'd left, twisting the ring on her middle finger. Anger wasn't the way she'd intended for things to end. She'd meant to tell him . . . everything. To explain what she'd been too scared to spell out before, about how she'd ended up engaged to a man she hadn't loved while Nick had been off risking his life for his country.

It was just as well he had stopped her. She couldn't tell him that, especially not now when he couldn't do anything to change it. Knowing would only make him feel like shit.

She showered, washing her hair multiple times to get rid of the smoky smell. Her conscience nudged her. Despite all the reasons she'd just outlined in her head, she should talk to him before she left.

Drying herself with the thick towel, she stared at her shadowy reflection in the steam-fogged mirror and tried to think of how she'd start that unhappy conversation. She was leaving for Africa tomorrow, no matter what Nick said. Would talking help either of them? He already had enough demons on his shoulder. Surely she could save him that pain?

She made the decision to stop torturing herself with the past and checked her email to find the reservation information from Teddy. Her old teaching advisor and friend was delighted that she was coming to Africa. There wasn't nearly as much to do as one would suspect when leaving the country for so long, particularly since her house had been completely destroyed. Everything could be taken care of with relative ease before her flight to New York tomorrow.

She was up for a couple more hours, composing emails and making last minute lists. After a final tug of war with her conscience, she wrote Nick a short note thanking him for his help and explaining that she was going on to Africa despite his objections.

She couldn't be talked out of it or scared out of it either. She knew if she stayed here, there was every chance she'd end up rehashing their past, and that would be disastrous for them both.

The next morning she woke early, grateful she had the alarm code. Without waking Nick, she propped the note to him against the kitchen coffee maker and left, her heart beating a little harder than she would have expected as she shut the door to AEGIS behind her.

She shopped at Walmart and REI, called her landlord, and stopped by the bank, arranging to take care of her finances from out of the country for the next few months. She picked up her dig pack at the storage unit along with her travel documents. After renting a parking slot to store her car onsite, she called a cab from the facility and was at the airport by two PM.

Getting out of Dallas as soon as possible had become paramount to everything else. She changed her late-night flight for New York to an earlier one by flying standby. If she had to, she'd spend the evening in JFK before her one AM Niamey flight tomorrow morning. She half expected Nick to show up and try to stop her from leaving, but she boarded the New York flight without incident. Watching Dallas grow smaller from her first-class window seat, she felt some of the pent-up tension unwind in her body. Had she finally left Nick, and their past, behind?

Chapter Twelve

Monday afternoon
Mexico

THE THREE MEN sat in overstuffed designer furniture on an Italian marble patio in the late afternoon. Ceiling fans spun lazily overhead amid potted palm trees, exotic hothouse flowers, and landscaping in a home that looked like a spread in *Architectural Digest*. A voluptuous woman dressed in a bikini served drinks and cigars and would later be serving whatever else the men wanted.

It had been a long time since they had all sat down together as allies, although now it was more of a forced coalition. Once, they'd been friends and family, only to become bitter enemies. Today they thought they were united in a common goal.

The man who had travelled the farthest for the meeting sipped his drink and looked around at the others. "The woman survived the bombing," he said quietly.

"What?" Tomas Rivera cursed in his seat. He should have been a broken man by now. This exercise was to have been revenge for the murder of a beloved wife, a brother-in-law, and an entire houseful of employees.

Rivera didn't appear to be broken, not yet.

Ernesto Vega sat beside his brother-in-law in silent fury, probably still wondering who had been responsible for his sister's and brother's deaths, in addition to the carnage in Mexico and the bomb in the American woman's house.

Because the attempt to kill Dr. Grayson had failed, no one was going to admit to responsibility for the fiasco. These men wanted to save face and were excellent actors. It would make for an interesting meeting.

"If we do this together, how will you transport the product?" asked Ernesto.

Tomas sipped his drink and shook the ash from his cigar. "I have contacts at the port in Venezuela. The officials have already been paid off. We have additional product on the coast that will be added on the African side. It shouldn't be difficult to include more weight for the port entry, but we need another solution for shipping across country. We won't be able to fly from the west coast of the continent to Constantine with that kind of added weight."

"How will you transport the women?" asked Ernesto, translating weight to people.

Tomas sipped again before answering. "We can always

use trucks. Hire guides and drive across the Sahara. We can carry as much weight as we like then."

The traveller raised an eyebrow. "With that kind of transit time, will the product be viable when it arrives on the Mediterranean?" He didn't particularly care, but it seemed a valid question.

Tomas shrugged. "There'll be some spoilage, but the majority should be fine if the packages are kept hydrated."

Ernesto sipped his drink, seemingly not at all bothered that they were speaking of women as if they were bags of rice or plants. "Very well. We'll add that extra weight in at the entry port."

The men all nodded in agreement. Working together to expand their separate empires should be more profitable. It should also be safer. Spreading the risk would certainly make it safer, particularly as someone seemed out to destroy the Rivera and the Vega cartels.

The question remained: Was the threat coming from outside this group more dangerous than the traitor within it?

Chapter Thirteen

Wednesday afternoon
Niamey, Niger

TWO DAYS LATER Jennifer stood outside customs in Niamey, desperately searching for someone holding a sign with her name on it from the Russ Foundation. Teddy had said he'd have a car and driver waiting for her. So far she'd had no luck spying either.

Perhaps there was a van outside the airport? Teddy didn't like women travelling alone on these digs or taking transit the Foundation had not arranged. Tired, hot, and jet-lagged—all she wanted was a hotel room and a shower. The thought of waiting here for a ride that might never come made her slightly nauseated.

Mosquitos swarmed in clouds through the open-air building as if she were standing beside a body of water. The place smelled like a combo of dirty public restroom and marijuana smoke. There were people everywhere, but no one appeared to be moving. They were all just waiting in this hellacious purgatory. Children were crying, and for a moment Jennifer felt like weeping herself.

The last time she'd been in a bed was in Nick's master bedroom two nights before. She studied her watch, but her mind was too muddled to make out the time differences of the past forty-eight hours in transit. She'd arrived in New York early Monday evening and had waited at the airport because her Niamey flight left so early the following morning. With all the holiday travel going on, that had been a mistake. She was bone-weary before she even got started with the seventeen-hour flight. Then there was the unscheduled layover in Paris. She was cross-eyed from exhaustion, and despite her determination not to be unnerved about travelling alone after all that had happened, she'd been on edge the entire trip.

She knew now she'd been wrong to leave without talking to Nick. She could have claimed it was shock from all that had happened in Mexico and Dallas, but deep down she knew it had been cowardice. To run instead of facing the past and telling him everything was childish. She'd struggled not to call him back from Paris, particularly after the terse message he'd left on her cell phone, reminding her of the danger and asking her to let him know where she was.

He hadn't asked why she'd left without saying goodbye, although the inference was there. A chill shuddered through her despite the 110-degree temperature in the African airport, but she shook it off. Men in various modes of native attire stood beside the line of taxis, vying for customers. Eventually, she spied a sign with her name and *Russ Foundation* written under it.

She hitched her oversized purse and backpack more securely onto her shoulder and moved toward the prearranged driver with her only pieces of luggage. "I'm Dr. Grayson."

The man gave her a toothless smile. "Excellent. Dr. Tedford Lang of the Russ Foundation hired me. I am to take you to your hotel."

Thankful she wouldn't be forced to hang out in the sweltering heat any longer, she nodded and allowed the driver take her backpack and load it in the trunk of a beat-up Mercedes sedan. As limo services went in Africa, it was above average.

According to Teddy, she was staying at the Hotel Gaweye, a four-star luxury hotel. She'd travelled with Teddy enough before to know what to expect of his wildly optimistic description of third world lodgings. She'd also checked online at JFK before she'd boarded and had seen the hotel booking website pictures, so she knew the Gaweye would be a bit more frayed around the edges than one generally expected when discussing four-star hotels. Still, if the room had air-conditioning and a bed, that was all she cared about. Although, hot water would be nice at this point, too.

The driver took off, and she sank back into the seat, ignoring the way her skin stuck to the cracked vinyl and grateful to let someone else be in charge for a bit. They'd ridden out of the airport and had just arrived in town when the driver pulled to a curb and stopped. Immediately, another man stepped off the sidewalk and opened her door, forcing his way into the cab.

Jennifer, startled out of her travel stupor, took one look at the man climbing into the car and scooted across the seat to the other door, intending to get out on the opposite side. That's when she saw the revolver in his hand.

"Dr. Grayson, stay where you are." The black man was big and muscular. The large gun in his left hand was particularly sobering, and it was aimed at her face.

She stopped with her fingers on the door handle. After Nick's dire warnings, she'd read up a bit on Niamey travel tips while she'd been looking at pictures of the Gaweye. Carjackings were quite prevalent in Niamey and considered one of the more typical types of crime in the city, although this appeared to be no common carjacking. The man beside her holding the revolver knew her name. Icy tendrils of fear raced up and down her spine despite the heat in the un-air-conditioned cab.

The driver took off again, but had to stop immediately with all the traffic around them. Too late she realized that this must have been some kind of set up from the beginning.

"What do you want with me?" she asked.

"I've no idea, but my services have been bought and paid for. Sit tight and you'll be fine." His accent was clipped, British. The hulking man smiled, but it looked more like the kind of grin a cat gives a mouse when it's about to pounce. She got the distinct impression he was lying.

She studied the back of the driver's head directly in front of her and called herself all kinds of a fool for ignoring Nick's warnings. The man beside her, whoever he was, had found her with no trouble whatsoever. She'd walked straight to the sign with her name on it.

The cab crept slowly through the city traffic and shot through a small opening. Jennifer tried not to panic. Members of the dig projects had been told what to do if they were ever detained while travelling on behalf of the Foundation.

You cooperated and you waited for the cavalry. She wasn't the least bit surprised to realize that this was much easier to read about and consider academically from the safety of one's office, halfway across the world, than when it was happening to you in real time.

Jennifer didn't plead or beg but sat rigidly in her seat, staring forward. That was why she didn't see the other vehicle coming from the intersection until the last minute. The sound of screeching metal tore through the air as a small pickup truck barreled into them, T-boning the passenger side of the car directly behind the front wheel.

The pickup truck hadn't been going fast, but the Mercedes still spun multiple times. Jennifer was thrown forward then sideways, striking the window and knocking into the man's gun arm next to her. He dropped his revolver as the Mercedes came to rest against the curb on the opposite side of the street about fifteen feet forward from where they'd started.

They were facing in the same direction they'd been travelling, but the driver was slumped over the steering wheel. Blood covered the dash and windshield. The front passenger door was crumpled inward. The gunman scrambled for his weapon, but it was under the driver's seat in front of her and out of the man's reach.

She moved for the door handle again. Blood covered her fingers, and they slipped on the metal. Adrenaline kicked in as she fought for a way to get out of the car. Her forehead bled profusely where she'd hit the window. She grasped the handle, but her door was stuck, thrown out of line somehow in the accident.

She searched the street for the occupant of the pickup and froze when she saw Nick behind the Mercedes, stalking toward the car with a scowling expression and a gun.

Bryan was behind him in the street, and the truck was in the middle of the intersection at a distant right angle to the cab's bumper about twenty feet away. Jenny's breath caught in her throat when she saw both men were pointing their huge handguns directly at her. It took an uncomfortable moment longer than she liked to realize that they weren't pointing the weapons at her, but at the man beside her in the backseat.

The gunman saw Nick and Bryan seconds after she did and quit reaching for his own revolver. Instead, he started trying to open his passenger door on the street side of the cab. His door was jammed shut from the impact.

Her would-be carjacker lifted his hands in the air as Nick approached the Mercedes. Bryan came around to Jenny's door on the curb side while Nick leaned into the opposite window with his gun pointed at the man who'd tried to kidnap her.

"Get out, Jenny," Nick ordered. The pet name wasn't comforting at all right now, perhaps because she didn't recognize the man using it. He stared hard at the blood on her forehead before skewering the gunman with his glare.

"I can't get out, my door's stuck," she said.

Nick nodded, but his gaze was completely focused on the man seated beside her. "Hollywood."

"Got it," said Bryan, slipping his weapon into a shoulder holster and prying open her door.

The damaged metal made another horrific screeching sound. Bryan grabbed her big purse and held out his hand to her. Nick leaned through the window, still staring into the face of the man who'd held her at gunpoint. She was fixated as well. Nick's eyes were dark and expressionless, vastly different from the man she thought she knew.

"Who sent you?" asked Nick.

The gunman shook his head.

"Who sent you?" Nick repeated the question, and his voice was cold—so cold. He said something else under his breath that Jennifer couldn't understand.

The man started talking, then weeping. Bryan grasped Jennifer's hand and pulled her out of the car. She was glad she couldn't see Nick's eyes anymore.

"You okay?" Bryan touched her cheek.

She shook her head. She wasn't okay at all.

"Let's go." He took her arm, and she started to follow him.

"Wait. I need my backpack."

Bryan glanced at Nick and at the people gathering around the accident scene.

"Leave it," said Nick.

"No!" she fairly shouted. Her dig pack held items she couldn't replace here in Africa, plus almost every material thing she had left in the world was in it.

"Nick?" Bryan asked.

He stared at her a long moment. "Dammit. Yes, okay, get it. But hurry. The police will be here soon. They can't stop a drug deal, but a car accident will bring the whole force out in record time."

Bryan moved forward to the driver's window and ignored the dazed cabbie who was just coming to. Hollywood leaned in to grab the car keys from the ignition. He popped the trunk. It opened with surprising ease considering the logistics of the truck's impact.

Bryan immediately had her pack on his shoulder along with the massive purse. He tugged on her arm again. "We have to go, Jennifer."

Sirens sounded in the background. Nick was talking quietly with the man who'd forced his way into her cab. Bryan was helping her into the truck when gunshots rang out. Shoving her to the floor beside the bench seat, Bryan pulled his gun from his shoulder holster. The *pop pop pop* of bullets sounded surreal on the rooftop of the pickup.

Are they shooting at me? The onlookers who'd gathered screamed as more shots were fired. People scattered.

"Nick?" Bryan called out, and Jennifer cowered on the floorboard. She'd seen the Mercedes's window breaking, so very close to Nick's head. Now she could only hear the gunshots. Somehow that was even more frightening.

"Nick?" Bryan shouted again over another volley of gunfire coming from somewhere above them. Bryan ducked behind the truck's open driver's side door, trying to cover Nick and spot the sniper. Still more shots rang out, hitting the bed of the pickup.

"I'm okay," Nick called. "Shooter's on the building in front of the cab, top floor." They might have been talking about the weather for all the emotion that came through in the words.

Jennifer watched Bryan nod, stand, and take four precise shots. From the floorboard she looked through the truck's windshield as a body tumbled off the three-story building on her right. He'd been much closer than she'd realized. She moved up on the seat and watched Nick race from the cover of the back of the cab to the fallen shooter. He bent down, appearing to search the man's pockets.

The sirens were closer. The street was deserted, but it wouldn't be for long, once people realized the shooting had stopped.

"Nick, we gotta go!" Bryan handed Jennifer a T-shirt from off the dash. "Not sure how clean that is, but it should stop the bleeding."

Puzzled, she stared down at the shirt.

"For your head," he said.

She reached up to touch the moisture on her cheek and forehead. She'd forgotten about her cut in all the confusion.

"Nick! Come on, man!"

"Just a minute!"

Bryan sat behind the wheel and shook his head. Jennifer focused on watching Nick flip the shooter over. The broken body was so very limp. She swallowed a lump in her throat and blotted at her forehead. Finally, Nick raced to the truck and climbed in beside her.

Sandwiched between the two men, she felt safer than she had in two days. That was until Nick turned to her. The palpable fury on his face had her shrinking back into Bryan's shoulder as they sped away from the carnage.

Nick stared at her for another long moment, his eyes no longer expressionless and dark but filled with a fire she couldn't name. He took the T-shirt from her hand. His jaw tensed when he cleaned the blood from her cheek and eyebrow.

"I'm so—" she started.

"Don't—" he interrupted. "Not one goddamn word."

She could see that he was fighting to regain his composure, so she kept her mouth shut. Still, his fingers on her face were incredibly gentle as he wiped her cheek. He took a bottle of water from the pocket in the door beside him and wet the T-shirt.

"What the fuck was that, Hollywood?" Nick's hands were steady, but his voice broke on the question.

Bryan shook his head. "No idea."

Nick took a swipe at drops of blood spattered on her arm. "Whoever it was killed the guy in the backseat of the cab before I could get any info. He wasn't carrying ID."

Jennifer sucked in a deep breath. She hadn't seen that.

"Shooter hit this pickup, too," said Bryan.

"Pretty sure the guy was Hispanic. No wallet on him either, but he did have a distinctive scorpion tattoo."

Bryan leaned forward to look around Jennifer. "What kind of tattoo?"

"Scorpion wrapped in barbed wire."

Bryan turned back to the road, his mouth set in a grim line.

"Tell me," said Nick.

If possible, Jennifer felt the tension ratchet up even more in every part of Nick's body that was pressed against hers on the narrow bench seat.

"Each of Ernesto Vega's lieutenants have scorpion tats with a raised tail. Full color in red, blue, and yellow, surrounded by black barbed wire. It's their badge of honor," said Bryan.

"You think they followed her here? Christ. What is going on?" Nick's voice was still ragged, but his hands remained tender as he pulled Jennifer's hair back to wipe away the blood that had dripped down her neck.

He was so close she could feel his breath on her cheek. She shuddered at the contact.

"What did the guy in the cab say?" asked Bryan.

"Not much. He was too scared. The headshot came as he was telling me they'd kill him if he talked." Nick shrugged. "Turns out they shot him anyway."

Bryan drove just under the speed limit through the streets of Niamey, past the Gaweye and the National Museum.

"I have reservations there," Jennifer said as they passed the hotel entrance.

"I know," said Nick. "So does everyone in Niamey, apparently. We're going to a different hotel. Bryan and I have already checked in."

"Oh," she murmured.

How do they know? Why would anyone care? She didn't dare ask either of these questions since this was the first time Nick had spoken to her in the truck without growling.

He reached into the glove box and retrieved a small, red zippered pouch that turned out to be a remarkably well-supplied first-aid kit. Within two minutes he'd disinfected the cut on her forehead and applied a bandage, all without making eye contact.

Afterward, he zipped the pouch and handed the kit to her. "Hang on to that. We'll clean you up better back at the hotel."

He started unbuttoning his shirt. For some reason, that frightened her more than the blood he'd just wiped from her face, and had her asking questions, even though she'd promised herself she wouldn't.

"What are you doing?" she asked.

"You can't walk through the lobby of the Grand Hotel du Niger in a bloody shirt without attracting attention. We'd like to avoid that if possible." He slipped the dark button-down shirt off. He had a black tee on underneath. "Hollywood, drop us a block away."

"Yeah," Bryan said. "I'll dump the truck and get some more transportation. They'll be looking for this."

Moments later Bryan stopped at the side of the road. The hotel was visible in the distance. Nick opened the door and helped her out, his touch as gentle as his look was grim. Helping her put his shirt on over her blouse, he buttoned it for her in a couple of places to cover the blood on her clothing. If she hadn't seen his face, she would have no idea he was furious with her.

"Can I have my backpack and purse?" she asked.

Nick took the first-aid kit from her and slipped it into her purse before lifting both bags out of the truck bed and sliding them onto his own shoulders. "Let's go."

"I'll be back in a couple of hours," said Bryan. "I've got to talk to some people."

"Sounds good. See you in a bit." Nick took Jennifer's hand firmly in his as they walked in silence along the road up to the entrance of the hotel.

She was happy not to talk, particularly as anger still radiated off Nick like the heat rising off the black asphalt. No one was out front, save one security guard smoking a cigarette. Nick nodded to him as they walked inside.

The sliding glass doors led them to an air-conditioned oasis that looked very different from what Jennifer had seen on the dusty street outside. Cool white marble floors, crystal chandeliers, an indoor fountain, and leather couches decorated the lobby. A crowd of businessmen speaking multiple languages stood in line at the front desk.

Nick kept hold of her hand and bypassed them all, walking through more sliding doors and past a massive swimming pool, then down a series of steps leading to the hotel grounds beside the river. His eyes were flat and emotionless. His long strides ate up the path before them. Once beyond the pool he picked up his pace and moved so fast she was out of breath, but he didn't seem to notice or care.

The hotel grounds were massive and spotted with bungalows that spread out from the main building along a paving stone path that wound steadily closer to the water. Jennifer thought it would have been a lovely place to sit and gaze over the landscaping, but Nick didn't appear the least bit interested in the view as he led her to the cottage farthest from the pool and closest to the river. He still wasn't speaking when they climbed the steps onto the porch that ran perpendicular to the water. The bungalow itself was situated sideways beside the river. Without a word, he opened the door and steered her inside.

The living room was small with a leather sofa, a massive window facing the water, and a kitchenette tucked in the corner. Doors on either side of the main living area led to what she assumed were two bedrooms and baths. Nick took her into the room on the right and didn't let go of her hand until he'd shut the door and flipped the thumb latch.

Mosquito netting hung from the ceiling but was drawn back to the headboard of a king-size bed. A fan mounted on the wall lazily stirred the air. He slung her backpack and handbag off his shoulder, setting them on the long dresser with a decided *thwack*.

His not talking was starting to make her a little nervous, but even more than that was his lack of eye contact. She stood in the center of the room trying to catch her breath. Bryan had said he wouldn't be back for a while. It was shaping up to be a long, uncomfortable evening.

Nick turned his back to her after unloading her bags. He didn't appear to be ready to talk yet. She should be relieved, right?

This was crazy. She had to say something. It was past time for one of them to be speaking. But where to start?

Thank him for saving her? Apologize for running away? As much as she hated to admit it, running away was exactly what she'd done in Dallas. Apologizing was the obvious place to start.

She took a breath, and the words came out in a rush. "Nick, I'm sorry. I know I shouldn't have left without talking to you. Thank you for what you did today. I don't know what I would have done if you hadn't—"

She broke off as he turned to her. His gaze held her captive, even though his eyes were no longer filled with smoldering fire. Instead, his expression was awash in misery.

"Dammit, Jenny. Do you have any idea how much you scared me?"

Chapter Fourteen

JENNIFER COULD ONLY stare as Nick's words poured out in a torrent.

"I had no fucking idea where you were. I wouldn't have had a clue how to find you if that man in the cab had succeeded, not to mention the shooter on the roof."

Nick's hands were shaking as he reached for her shoulders and pulled her to him, wrapping his arms around her with a force that took her breath. She had no idea what to say, but words weren't necessary because he wasn't finished talking yet.

"Don't ever do that again. No matter how upset you might be with me, don't ever leave when I've told you it's dangerous. God, I was going crazy till I found you." He buried his face in her hair, the desperation in his voice translating to his entire body.

Her mind was catching up to what was happening here. He wasn't mad, he was just scared spitless for her.

That made sense. It was something like what she'd felt when he'd left after their summer together to join the Navy. Only she hadn't been able to tell him how scared she was for him then or to even object to his leaving.

She hadn't realized how the fear had affected her until it was too late. She'd felt that same terror this afternoon, listening to those gunshots from the floorboard of that pickup truck and wondering if she was going to lose Nick before she got a chance to tell him . . . everything.

She lifted her head from his chest to look up, to explain. Before she could speak, he kissed her and steered her backward toward the bed. She stopped walking when the mattress bumped just above her knees and she sat with an *umph*.

He went down on his knees in front of her. No longer playing things cool, he was frantic as he ran his hands up and down her arms.

"I see," she stuttered.

"Do you? Do you really?" His chest was between her knees and she lifted her hands to his shoulders. He wrapped his arms around her waist and held on. She felt dirty and grubby from her forty-eight-hour trek across the globe, but he was holding her, really holding her, and that was all that mattered.

"God, when I saw you in that car and that man was holding a gun on you." He pulled back to look at her again. "Something died inside me."

He shook his head, and his eyes filled. "Then after . . ."

She touched his hair and brushed over the small bandage covering the stitches on his forehead, wanting to show him she understood. He put his head against her chest and held her as the words tumbled out. "Please, Jenny. Don't ever . . . I can't protect you when you do that kind of crazy shit. I want to just lock you in a room somewhere until this is all figured out. It seems like the only way you'll be safe. Do you understand?" His voice was wild and his hands were everywhere at once.

She nodded, identifying with his fear of losing her because she'd felt the same about losing him. She held the back of his head, wanting to calm him, but he was beyond soothing.

He slid his shirt from her shoulders, then pulled her bloody blouse loose from her waistband. His hands skimmed along her sides. The intensity was even more powerful than she remembered as he kissed her with a determination that had all her resolutions melting away.

She couldn't think about why this was a bad idea, or why she should talk to him about what had happened ten years ago, or why she should wait to have sex with him until they'd discussed it all. Instead, she closed her eyes and concentrated on feeling.

NICK HELD ON to Jenny, not wanting to ever let go. He'd figure out what that meant later because the white-hot panic at seeing a man hold a gun to her head was not subsiding. Fifty years from now, he'd still see it whenever he closed his eyes.

He could feel her heart beating under his cheek as he clasped her to him and breathed in the scent that was uniquely hers, mixed with the dirt, grit, and blood from earlier. She was whispering soft words that he supposed were meant to comfort him, but he wasn't hearing her. He couldn't be nonchalant anymore about what she did to him, and despite all appearances, he wasn't mad. He'd just been so unbelievably frightened for her—on the plane ride over, in the airport, following her in that damned cab.

All he wanted to do was hold her and make love to her. Mark her as his. Show her that he couldn't—wouldn't—let her go, or let her loose in the world. If it made him sound chauvinistic or like a Neanderthal, he was beyond caring. He needed her right now like he needed oxygen.

He stood, and her eyes widened as he drew his T-shirt over his head, pulled the gun from his waistband, and toed off his shoes. She watched with a dumbfounded expression, and he would have laughed in another time, in another place. But nothing about this was remotely amusing. He wanted her so much he could hardly breathe. He hadn't wanted anyone like this, ever.

Only when his hands went to his belt buckle did she seem to register what he intended. Instead of pulling away or shaking her head, she reached forward and helped him with his zipper.

"You're wearing too many clothes," he muttered.

"I'm sure you can take care of that," she answered and slid his pants down to the floor along with his underwear.

"I believe I can." He nodded, while pushing her back to the bed and followed her down to the mattress with one knee between her legs. He recognized that he was still entirely too keyed up, even as he reached for her.

Still, she raised up on an elbow. Meeting him half-way, she nipped at his jaw and reached for him, seemingly ready for whatever he wanted. He stared at her a moment longer, steeping in the frantic beat of his own heart. There was no way he was going to do this with any finesse. He was too far over the edge. He kissed her once more.

"Don't you let me hurt you." He murmured the words, but his voice was rough.

"You won't." She smiled at him as he pulled her shorts and panties off in one motion and skimmed straight to the core of her with his fingers. Her eyes widened again, then closed when she tilted her head back.

He watched her face. The crease between her eyebrows disappeared as she relaxed into the sensation of what he was doing, but she kept her hands on him at the same time. He wanted her so much his own hands were shaking.

She moved her legs and put him exactly where he wanted to be. Pressing against the heat of her, he stopped and mumbled her name. He had to see her, needed to see this was real.

She opened her eyes and stared at him with the faintest of smiles on her face, just like in his dreams. He was inside her so fast, her eyes widened again in pleasure. He raised himself up over the top of her and moved, pushing deeper.

She moaned. The sound of her sighs and the sensation of feeling her surrounding him almost undid him. This was going to be over entirely too soon.

He pulled back and she raised her hips to meet him, slipping her hands down to his ass, pulling him toward her. She moaned again, and he lost all adroitness, pumping like a teenager in a backseat on Friday night. For a moment, he was concerned he was too rough and started to pull away. But she held him to her as she locked her gaze on his and slipped her legs up around his hips.

She smiled, closing her eyes and opening her mouth slightly in a breathy "oh." He felt her clenching and pulsing around him, felt the sensation start at the base of his spine as he pressed into her once more, and then he was diving off a cliff, falling into the orgasm and whispering her name once more.

JENNIFER FELT NICK's body completely relax as his weight pressed her into the mattress. His heartbeat slowed to a normal rhythm against her chest while he nuzzled his face into her neck. She wasn't breathing very well with him on top of her, but she was beyond caring.

She didn't regret making love with Nick, but she was surprised at his intensity. Over the years she'd thought about being with him more than she cared to admit. Sleeping with Collin had never been like it was with Nick.

She moved her hands to his shoulder and he raised his face to study her. The smoothness of his skin was marred by . . . scars? His shoulder blade felt like latticework, and lower down his back there were butterfly bandages.

She'd felt the raised welts and small pits in his skin earlier but had been much too distracted by the lovely things he was doing to her to think about them. She stopped moving her fingers and slid her hands down his side, where she felt more scarring.

"What's this?" she asked, touching the bandages again.

He lowered his head and kissed a spot behind her ear before exhaling and levering himself up on an elbow to look at her again. "I got some stitches out last week, and things reopened when I dove off your porch Sunday. They put on a couple of butterflies at the hospital."

"What happened that you needed so many stitches before my house exploded?"

His open expression changed from relaxed sexy to shadowed wary as if he'd flipped a switch.

"I'm sorry that was nosy. I just—"

He shrugged, but the motion didn't come across as nonchalant. "Yeah?"

"Um . . . I just realized you might not want to talk about this."

He nodded and didn't say anything else.

Okay. So he really didn't want to talk about this.

He started to move away, but she pulled him back to her, not wanting to break their most intimate connection. He dropped another kiss to her cheek and held her close before rolling away and sitting up with his head against the headboard. She wasn't sure what he was going to say. From all appearances, he was thinking very seriously about something.

He touched her hair and stared at the end of the bed a moment longer before speaking. "Are you alright with what just happened? I didn't exactly come dressed for the party. I'm clean. Tested. You don't have anything to worry about."

She held up her hand. What a way to shut down the afterglow. She felt ridiculous for not realizing that not having used a condom would be one of the first things he'd think of.

"Don't worry, I'm fine. All tested here, too."

After discovering Collin's affair, she'd run—not walked—to her doctor to have a full battery of tests for every STD out there. Thankfully everything had come back negative. She didn't want to go into that sordid story now, but she did want Nick to assume that she was on birth control. Under no circumstances did she want to tell him the real reason he didn't have to worry about her getting pregnant.

He nodded. "You're sure everything is okay? Because you could have missed a few days of your pills there in Mexico."

"I'm fine," she repeated, disappointed in herself to hear the edge in her tone.

"Alright." He shrugged. "Look, I just . . . I'm trying to be responsible here and—hey, are you okay?"

Ah, God. She was crying. She had no idea where the tears had come from, but suddenly there they were, burning at the edges of her eyes and overflowing down her cheeks. Trying to hold them back was useless. It was like a running faucet she didn't know how to shut off. She'd already cried on him once. She hadn't wanted to do this again, but there seemed no hope for it.

Her nose ran as he slid back down onto the mattress beside her and pulled her into his arms. "It's okay," he murmured.

A huge sob escaped, and she shook her head. *I have to tell him.* This was about ten years ago, not today. Could she do it? She'd been this close a couple of times. But she *had* to do it now. She clasped her hands in front of her and against his chest.

"I need to talk to you about something."

"Shhh . . ." He shook his head and held her more firmly, but she kept talking before she lost her nerve.

"When you left after that summer. I didn't tell you . . . I . . ."

God, what was she doing? She could feel his slow, steady heartbeat under her palm. She pulled back to look at him, and as she watched, something changed in his eyes. That change scared her more than when the man had held the revolver on her in the cab. She clenched and unclenched her fingers. It was time.

"I-I didn't tell you that I got pregnant that summer." She blurted the words, and in the quiet of their bungalow by the river, it felt as if she'd shouted them.

She stared at him, twisting the ring on her finger as a myriad of emotions crossed his face. At first he appeared stunned, followed by an expression that came and went so quickly she didn't recognize it. Then his eyes went cold as he carefully pulled his hands from her sides.

Chapter Fifteen

NICK SWALLOWED. HIS mind was awash in disbelief and something else he was scared to focus on.

Jenny had been pregnant with his child.

What had happened to it?

She was crying harder, yet his arms loosened at her waist. It might make him an ass, but he moved away from her in the bed, unable to hide his icy demeanor.

"You got pregnant the summer we were together?" He was surprised his voice didn't crack.

She nodded with tears streaming down her face. "I was going to tell you. We were writing back and forth, and you seemed very interested in pursuing—"

"So why didn't I ever get a letter about it? God, you were having a baby." *My baby.* He fought to keep his tone even.

"I was. I mean, I did. Write. The letter was written." She sniffled, and he flooded emotionally, unable to do anything to comfort her or himself.

All too clearly he recalled the hurt and confusion he'd felt when she'd quit communicating. There was no way he could hold her now, as much as she might need him to. Instead, he went cold.

Because no matter what she said, there'd been no letter, no email, no explanation.

He'd been in his own personal hell, dealing with choices about his future and trying to put the ramifications of his parents' death and his dad's disgrace behind him. He'd always thought Jenny had changed her mind about him and just didn't want to deal with all his baggage after that summer. He hadn't been able to blame her for that, even though he'd wanted more. But this news put an entirely different spin on things.

"Why didn't I receive that letter?" he repeated.

She wasn't looking at him anymore. "I had a miscarriage."

At first he wasn't sure his mind was registering the words she said.

"I was at SMU on a full-ride scholarship and five months along." She took a deep breath and inhaled with a soft wheeze. "There were complications. I ended up having a hysterectomy."

His gut clenched as he shook his head from side to side. "And you never told me," he whispered.

Jenny had been pregnant with his baby, and she'd never said a word. The knowledge hit him like a sucker punch. *A baby.*

He couldn't believe it. He felt like he was learning of his father's embezzlement all over again.

"I never told anyone. I was a senior in college with no family, remember? My aunt had died the year before. Having a baby was going to change my entire world. I wouldn't have been able to keep my scholarship and finish school because the money was in place only for full-time students. I felt like I was completely on my own."

Only because you chose to be. I would have been there if I'd known. If you'd told me. But he couldn't say that out loud. He'd already said too many hurtful things that couldn't be taken back.

"Only the doctor and my advisor at school, Teddy Langford, knew. And Teddy didn't know until the week before I lost the baby. I'd finally gone to him for help. He was trying to figure out how to salvage the scholarship situation.

"I didn't even tell my roommate. The miscarriage happened during Christmas break, the day after finals were over in early December. I called Teddy from the hospital. He helped set things up so I could take the next semester off and go to China on a field study and keep the scholarship. I was gone from late January until July."

"You didn't even tell Angela, did you?" He was back in control, for the moment, his iceman persona taking over.

"No, I couldn't. I couldn't tell you either. What could I have said that wouldn't have made you feel horrible? You were starting your life over with a new direction and a new career, still working through all the issues with your parents' accident. In your letters that fall, it sounded like you loved what you were doing. I didn't want you to feel some obligation to me—and you would have—particularly once I was no longer . . ."

"Pregnant," he finished for her.

"I'd convinced myself that we'd had a simple affair, a summer romance."

He'd moved to the far side of the bed and turned away from her in an attempt to escape the painful things she was revealing, but he needed to hear this more than he needed to protect himself. Finally, he turned back to her. She was still wrapped in a sheet and looked almost exactly the same way he remembered the first time they'd slept together.

A stinging regret washed over him, like a breaking wave on the shore filled with broken shells and sand. Overwhelming sorrow engulfed him as he realized all they'd lost by not communicating. Then anger bubbled inside. Where was all this emotion coming from? He tried to push it away, to push it down. But everything spun up together and spilled over in a hot, ugly rush.

"We were friends, Jenny. Friends before we slept together. Did it ever occur to you that I had a right to know? A fucking right to grieve the loss? It was my baby, too."

She swallowed hard but never cowered at his tone. "No. At the time your grief over this didn't enter into my thinking. I was twenty-one, self-absorbed, and focused on my own misery. My own catastrophe. You'd lost your parents six months before and changed the entire direction of your life. You were trying to figure things out. How would knowing this have helped?"

Jesus, if she only knew. He'd been a walking disaster but hadn't wanted anyone to know it. Nick had wanted everyone to think he was thrilled with what he was doing. In reality, he'd been reeling from the loss of his parents. In addition to his father's betrayal, Nick had been trying to pick up the pieces of his own life and support his brother, Drew, who was finishing up his own degree. As much as it burned, he appreciated Jenny's honesty about where her head had been ten years ago.

She swallowed again audibly. "Not telling you has always bothered me. It's the part of all this that I screwed up so badly."

He watched her, unwilling to say anything else because he was concerned for what other hurtful things might pop out of his mouth while he was still reeling from the shock.

"I was broken and a complete mess," she said.

"You married that spring." He heard the accusation in his voice and only mildly regretted it.

As long as he lived he'd never forget that phone call from Drew. It came just before he was scheduled to leave on his first tour in Afghanistan. As they said their good-byes, his brother told him that Jenny had gotten married while studying abroad in China.

Nick had found himself actually struggling to breathe as Drew told him how surprised Angela was at the news but how happy Jennifer seemed. The bottom had dropped out of his world when he belatedly realized the terrible price of not having told Jenny how he really felt.

He'd hung up after hearing that news, boarded the troop transport bound for Kandahar, and never looked back. With Jenny married to someone else, there'd been no reason to look back. He'd gone on to become a SEAL, eventually joining the CIA and NCS. His throat tightened and his chest hurt for everything he'd lost without even knowing it.

Jenny nodded. "I met Collin Petersen on that dig in China. I was trying to forget you, the baby . . . everything. I was trying to feel again. I mistook distraction for attraction, and I said *yes*."

Nick had no idea what to say to that. He completely understood the *not feeling* part. It was the *wanting to feel again* he couldn't get a handle on.

"I recognized the mistake pretty fast, but unfortunately I was already married."

"Right."

"I had no clue what I was doing or what I wanted. I just knew I didn't want to hurt. And honestly, I didn't, not really, not until Collin had his first affair."

Nick didn't want to feel sympathy for her right now, but he did. "Were there others?" he asked.

She nodded. "There was a revolving door on his office sofa. That doesn't even make sense, but you know what I mean. He had several extremely 'attentive' grad students. But I think he's going to marry this last one since she's just . . ." Jenny's voice drifted off.

"She's just what?"

"Collin's girlfriend just had a baby earlier this month."

Without being told, Nick knew that had to be the ultimate betrayal—her husband having an affair and getting the other woman pregnant. It must have been excruciating. He didn't want to give a shit, but he did.

Still, he was mostly numb. Fifteen minutes ago he'd wanted to rip Jenny's clothes off, now he just wanted out of the room and away from her.

"I suppose that was . . . difficult." God, he sounded like a complete ass. No longer able to stay in the bed, he stood up and gathered his discarded clothes and suitcase. "I'm going to clean up."

He never looked back as he closed the door behind him and headed to the other bathroom off the second bedroom. He didn't want to say anything else nasty to her, but he would if he stayed in that room one moment longer. He desperately needed to process everything she'd just told him, and there was no way that was happening if he was lying in bed next to her.

Given the security situation, he couldn't leave her alone in the bungalow either. He needed to wait for Bryan. Hopefully Hollywood would be back before Nick went completely crazy.

He showered and changed because he smelled like Jenny. When he came out of the second bedroom, the master bedroom door was still closed, and he could hear the shower running.

Good. He didn't want to see her. The image of her standing under the shower spray splashed across his brain for a split second. *Shit.*

The sense of betrayal was just as strong now as

it had been a half hour ago when she'd first told him about the miscarriage. The ache of loss was new but old at the same time. And to top it off, he still wanted her. *Christ.* He might need psychiatric help before this was over.

He stalked to the window and peered out the wooden blinds toward the Niger River. Birds that looked like cranes stood at the water's edge, calling to others circling overhead. The sun would slip below the horizon in the next hour.

In the quiet of the bungalow, he heard the shower shut off behind him, and again his mind flashed on Jenny wrapping her damp body in a towel.

Where the hell was Bryan? Nick needed to get out of here, but there was no way he'd leave Jenny unprotected.

At last, there was a knock at the front door.

"It's me."

Thank God. Hollywood was back. Nick stepped on the porch to talk, to breathe.

Bryan took one look at his face and asked, "Everything okay?"

"Yeah, I just need some air. Did you get the transportation settled?"

"Got it. We're all set. The plane will be ready tonight."

"What did you find out?" asked Nick.

"I tried to check in with Gavin, but he didn't answer. I left a voice mail with all the details about the attempted kidnapping at the airport, the shooter, the tattoo, all of it. He or Marissa should pick up the message. I caught Leland real time and gave him the scoop, too. He didn't have much. He hasn't heard anything back from Hosea Alvarez. He did ask if you were still going to let Jennifer go on the dig."

Nick laughed, but it was a bleak sound even to his own ears. "You mean, besides the fact that I don't have a fucking clue how to stop her?" He stretched his neck from side to side and suppressed a moan as the vertebrae popped. "Did Leland have anything else?"

Bryan shook his head.

"How about your informant?"

Bryan took a breath and shrugged. "This is different from my usual contact. I'm not sure . . ."

Hollywood's troubled expression would have worried Nick more if his own plate wasn't so full.

"What exactly are you working on?"

Bryan looked out over the water before he answered. "Elizabeth Yarborough."

"You think the woman is here?"

He shrugged. "I don't know. It's not clear. Hopefully I'll find out more later tonight."

Nick's concern grew. "You do realize we're leaving tonight, don't you?"

"I understand. I'll catch up with you."

Nick started shaking his head. *How would you do that, exactly?* "You didn't mention this to Gavin in your voice mail, did you?"

"What do you think?"

"I think the man would shit monkeys sideways if he found out you were working Yarborough leads here in Africa without backup." Nick leaned against the patio post, relieved to hear about someone else's problems for a change.

"Gavin doesn't have the manpower. Besides, it's the Hail Mary of long shots." The tone in his voice had Nick studying Bryan more closely.

"I won't tell him. I just don't like not being here to help. Make sure someone back at the office knows where you're going and who you're meeting."

Bryan nodded. "I'm being careful."

"Of course, but that situation's really got a hold on you. And believe me, I know how that can screw with one's judgment." Indeed, Nick knew exactly how that felt.

Bryan wouldn't meet his gaze. "I can't give it up."

"What do you have so far?"

Hollywood finally met his stare and exhaled with a heavy sigh. Nick's eyes widened in surprise. Bryan's expression was as bleak as his own. "The human trafficking problem here is out of control."

Nick huffed a laugh. "That's not exactly breaking news."

Bryan put his hand on the doorknob as if to go inside but made no move to enter. Instead, he leaned against the door and looked out over the water again. "I know. Thousands of women and children from Africa are sold into slavery or prostitution each year. The women are promised a job in a larger city, maybe even a position as a nanny in the U.S. or Europe. When they arrive at their destination, they are told they must work off the debt they've incurred from travelling by selling themselves in a brothel. Many are kidnapped into the lifestyle."

Nick felt his stomach twisting. "What do you think this has to do with Elizabeth Yarborough?"

"Mexican cartels are expanding their human trafficking into Africa using the shipping routes they've already established here with their drug trade. They want part of that pie. Since they've got the connections to ship their drugs straight across the Atlantic from Brazil and Venezuela, it wouldn't be a big leap to imagine their adding women to the mix. I don't know the specifics of the routes, but the demand is certainly high enough, and there's no law enforcement once you reach the West African coast."

"But why Elizabeth Yarborough?" asked Nick again, leaning a hip against the porch railing. Something about this was obviously personal to Bryan. Nick just didn't know what it was.

"If Elizabeth was originally taken for prostitution, even by accident, Africa would be the perfect place to 'lose her.' Think about it. There was so much media coverage in the U.S. and Mexico after she disappeared that she'd have been too easily recognized in almost any part of South America."

Nick wasn't so sure, and his queasiness over the entire situation wasn't going away. Still, he had to ask. "It seems an awful lot of trouble for a cartel to go to for one woman. Why not just kill her and be done with it?"

"There's definitely something I'm missing here. It's what I'm hoping to get tonight."

"Who are the players?" asked Nick.

"I keep coming back to Tomas Rivera and his brothel. I know in my gut he had Elizabeth Yarborough there at one time. I just can't prove it. It sounds crazy, but I think Ernesto Vega could be involved, too."

Nick felt the hair rise on the back of his neck and fought the urge to pace back and forth on the patio. "I don't like jumping to conclusions, but given everything happening with both the Vegas and Riveras, it fits. Even though those men aren't known for working or playing well with others, they're the most likely to set aside differences and work together when you consider all that has happened to their families. That said, they could be double-dealing on each other, too."

Bryan smiled, but the expression didn't reach his eyes. "That would certainly keep it interesting. The market for human and drug traffickers here is huge and this continent is the Wild West. The poverty of the area makes it even more lucrative."

Nick stared toward the setting sun on the water and kept mentally poking at the one piece that wasn't fitting into this scenario. "Okay, say the sex trafficking here is connected to the Mexican cartels, and maybe they aren't all playing nice together. What do you think was going on with Jennifer at the airport? I can't make any sense of it. A kidnapping and an assassination attempt at the same time?"

Bryan shrugged. "The shooter was aiming directly for the area of the truck where she was sitting after he took out the guy in the backseat of the cab."

"Do you think we're dealing with the same people who planted the bomb in Dallas?"

"I do now, and I think it's most likely a Vega connection given that scorpion tattoo on the sniper earlier. Otherwise, it's an awful lot of coincidences."

It made sense, but then it didn't. Why would the Vegas be after Jenny? Nick wanted to growl in frustration. "I agree, but there are too many damn holes. As much as I'd like to, it's too easy to hang everything happening on the Riveras and Vegas." He pushed away from the railing. "I've got a bad feeling about all this. You shouldn't go alone tonight." But Nick wasn't about to tell him he couldn't. His own plate was kind of full at the moment.

"The only thing my informant was positive about earlier was that they had no information about the mess with the airport cab," said Bryan.

Of course not. Nick laughed for the first time in what felt like days. It was that or grind his teeth to dust. All they seemed to be getting right now were more questions.

He had to get out of here and clear his head. "I'm going to do a perimeter check of the hotel and grab a bite to eat. I'll bring something back for you and Jenny." He didn't ask if Bryan was okay staying with her.

"Alright. I'll grab a shower while you're gone."

Nick nodded, walked down the steps, and raised his hand in a backward wave, taking his first deep breath since they'd landed in Africa. God, he was tired and so freaked. What in the world did any of this stuff have to do with Jenny? Why would anyone want to kidnap her, shoot her, or blow her up?

He kept circling back to the conclusion he'd reached

while lying on her smoldering lawn after the explosion. The only thing that made sense was a connection to Tenancingo, and now this possible link with Elizabeth Yarborough.

What did Jenny know that someone would kill to keep secret?

Chapter Sixteen

NICK WALKED THE hotel grounds, taking some time before grabbing food. He needed to decompress, but it was next to impossible with all the thoughts swirling around in his head.

What would happen to Jenny if he wasn't around? He couldn't stay with her and stay sane, not when he was still reeling from everything she'd told him about her being pregnant and losing their baby. Just thinking about her was painful, even thinking in terms of how to keep her safe.

The earlier crowd of businessmen from the hotel lobby now sat at the bar. There were signs for some kind of convention going on involving the oil and gas trade in the region. In the sundry shop he grabbed protein bars, several pieces of fruit, a couple of sodas, and a half-dozen bottled waters before starting back to the bungalow.

He decided he would wait for Bryan to get back from

the meeting with his contact tonight before taking Jenny on to Ingal and the dig site. It was going to be entirely too uncomfortable for them to be alone together otherwise. Nick wouldn't be any good to her as a bodyguard if he continued to be this ill at ease with her. His intuition and reflexes would be worthless, and she wouldn't want him around anyway. Bryan would be better as the primary.

Back at the bungalow Hollywood met him on the front porch with a worried expression. "I'm trying to figure something out. Talk me through the shooting again. What did you see?" he asked.

Nick placed the convenience store food in a wicker chair by the door and took his spot on the porch railing again. He didn't want to face Jenny right now. If that made him a coward, so be it. Admitting he wasn't strong enough was better than being eviscerated.

"The shooter was young, Hispanic. He shot the guy in the back of the cab first, then he went for Jenny," said Nick.

"You sure he wasn't shooting at you or me?"

"Pretty sure. You were a clear shot, Hollywood. The guy specifically aimed for the roof of the truck cab. Right where Jenny was sitting. What's the problem?"

Bryan frowned and shook his head. "I heard from a source. There's a contract out on her."

"What? Why?" Nick felt his eyebrows rise. "Someone's after Jenny here?"

Bryan nodded. "Makes no sense, but nothing does. I'm meeting another contact in an hour. Maybe they'll be able to shed some light on the situation."

Nick stared at the bag of food on the chair seat. So

what should he do now? He knew the answer, but he didn't like it. He wasn't going to be able to ask Bryan to take point on Jenny's protection. He wasn't going to be able to stand the thought of leaving her with anyone.

Bryan seemed to read his mind. "Okay, so don't let her out of your sight. You'll be keeping her safe, and she could lead you to whoever is responsible for this."

"A euphemism for 'Someone may try to blow her head off again, and maybe I'll catch them this time'? She won't take kindly to being used as some kind of bait." Nick didn't much care for it himself.

"From what you've said, it sounds like she wants her life back. The quickest way for that to happen is for her to cooperate with us. To get things back to normal in her world, she should stick with you and help us figure out what's going on."

Nick groaned inwardly. That's what he was afraid of, having to be in constant contact with her. He wasn't sure he could do that, even if she did see his sticking with her as the quickest way to get him out of her life. "What will I do with her?" he mumbled under his breath.

Bryan laughed. "Are you seriously asking me what to do with a woman?"

God, no. At least he didn't think he was. Nick knew exactly what he wanted to do with Jenny. That was the problem. He rolled his eyes with a grim laugh. "Fuck you, Hollywood."

Bryan smiled, taking no offense. "I don't really think that's what you had in mind, is it?"

Jesus. Nick shook his head again, but Bryan kept talking. "I don't know. Take her to that dinosaur dig she's so hell-bent on getting to."

"You really think that's a good idea? If whoever is after her knew how to find her at the airport, they'll know about the dig."

Bryan looked toward the pool area and the main building of the hotel. "Maybe, but it'll still be the easiest place to watch her. It's nothing but desert for miles around, and they have guards, right?"

Nick nodded.

"Perfect. You'll notice if someone's coming. Besides, you'll go crazy holed up here in a hotel room trying to watch her *and* trying to keep your hands off her. Not that it's any of my business."

It sure as hell wasn't, but Nick definitely had that coming. He reached for the bag of food and flipped Bryan off good-naturedly even as he said, "You're right."

"You just now figuring that out?"

The door opened, and Jenny stepped out onto the porch wearing a hotel robe. Her hair was wet and slicked back from her face.

"Is that food?" she asked, initially avoiding eye contact with either man before locking her gaze directly on Nick's. "I'm starving."

Bryan vaporized back inside.

Unable to stop himself, Nick stared back at her, losing himself in her eyes. He was so distracted, he bobbled the two canned drinks in his arms, dropping one off the side of the porch. The soda hit the ground at warp speed and rolled ten feet toward the water.

"Hell," he muttered, heading for the stairs still carrying the food.

"I'll be sure not to pick that one." Jenny laughed, trying to lighten the mood.

"Good plan." He stalked down the steps to grab the fallen drink, knowing he might as well get this conversation over with. He had to explain about how he was going with her to the Paleo-Niger dig site, even though neither of them wanted that. What he really wanted was to peel that robe away and take up where they'd left off earlier in the bedroom. In lieu of that, he'd rather go away and lick his wounds. Too bad neither idea was an option.

Jenny wasn't going to be happy, and no amount of joking would fix the grim reality they were facing. Someone here in Africa wanted her dead and had paid money for an assassin. He glanced over his shoulder at her as she gazed out over the water toward the sunset.

"I know what you're thinking," she murmured, looking just as beautiful to him as she always had.

Doubtful, thought Nick. But he didn't say that out loud when he bent over to get the canned soda.

The sun was glinting off the water, and he stared out over the river then back toward the multi-story hotel behind them. That was how he saw the gun. The reflection from the sun must have hit the rifle scope just so. Otherwise, he'd have never seen the suppression barrel pointing out of the upper level room a hundred yards away in the main part of the building. Curtains billowed in the breeze and drifted gently out the window.

He was still ten feet from her when Jennifer turned to say something, but by then he was dropping the food and drinks from his arms, running toward the stairs and yelling.

"Down!" he shouted. "Gun! Get down!"

He pulled his Sig Sauer, even though the range was impossible. He didn't fire. There were too many people in the hotel between him and the shooter. The soft *psfft* of bullets hitting the porch kept time with the rhythm of his feet on the stone walkway.

He landed on the stairs and hit Jenny at a full run, tumbling backward with her in his arms over the railing of the porch in an eerie repeat of their flight off the steps of her home in Dallas days earlier.

He turned as they struck the ground and Jenny landed on his chest with an *umph*, knocking the air out of him. The pain from the fall seventy-two hours ago blossomed once again in his chest, but he ignored it and scrambled out from under her. Bryan opened the bungalow door with his backup Beretta Tomcat and no shirt, staying well behind the threshold for cover.

Still trying to catch his breath, Nick studied Jenny before he stood up. She looked okay—looked more than okay with her robe askew. The sight would have been distracting as hell if someone wasn't trying to blow their heads off. She was hidden from the shooter by the bungalow. Nick was the one most exposed as he peered over the edge of the porch floor, still holding his weapon.

A maid coming up the walk from next door stared at him for about three seconds before she started screaming. She'd obviously seen Nick's Sig and the tumble off the porch. The gun barrel in the hotel window was no longer visible. With the silencer, the only ones who'd heard the shots hitting the porch were Bryan, Jenny, himself, and possibly the maid.

"Y'all okay?" called Bryan over the caterwauling housekeeper.

Jenny glanced at Nick before answering. "Yeah, but we landed in . . . God, I don't know what. Whatever it is, it stinks to high heaven."

Nick noticed the rotten stench of river gunk for the first time. He'd been so scared when he saw the suppression barrel with Jenny fully exposed on the porch that he hadn't been aware of the nasty smell till now. Jenny's voiced sounded strong, and he smiled despite the bleak situation.

"The river can produce some interesting stink here," said Bryan. "No problem. We'll get you into the shower in just a few."

As unreasonable as it was, Nick didn't like hearing Hollywood talk about getting Jenny into a shower. The idiocy of that thought hit him immediately. *Christ.* Had he hit his head in that dive off the porch?

"You okay?" asked Bryan.

Nick finally had his breath and hopefully his wits back when he realized Hollywood was waiting for an answer. "Yeah, I'm getting damn tired of this though."

Bryan snorted a laugh. "I hear you. Did you see the guy?"

"Third floor, west end of the building. Curtains were blowing out the window."

"Okay, yeah, I see it now," said Bryan, stepping out from behind the doorway. "That window just closed."

"You think he's gone?" asked Nick, standing up straight. The maid quit shouting and took refuge in the bungalow she'd just cleaned.

"If he's got any sense he will be." Bryan had to know they were too far away to make a difference in chasing after the shooter, but he took off for the hotel anyway. The man had definitely been a serious runner at one time in his life.

Barefooted and with no shirt, Bryan called back over his shoulder as he ran. "If I'm not back in fifteen minutes, our car is a dark blue Jeep on the west side of the parking lot. Keys are under the floor mat."

Nick shook his head. Bryan wouldn't catch the shooter, but Nick understood he had to try. It wouldn't matter if the would-be assassin wasn't a professional. The Keystone Kops from the hotel would be challenged to figure out what had happened.

Even without the maid's screams echoing across the property, security would be arriving any minute. He and Jenny had to get out of here tonight. If this was the cartel, they seemed to have an extraordinarily clear bead on where she was at all times. They also seemed to be exclusively focused on her.

The shooter had had a clean shot at Nick on the path and hadn't taken it. Bryan's news about the contract on Jenny appeared to be accurate. Still, nothing about this made sense.

"Jenny, go get cleaned up. And gather up your things."

"Do I have time for a shower?"

He looked at the muddy gunk splashed across her robe and legs. There was more river crud under the robe. He knew because he'd had his hands all over her and the wet goop when they'd gone off the porch and landed in the soggy mess. For just a moment his mind flashed to what else was under her robe besides mud, but he immediately shut that train of thought down. "Yeah, just make it snappy. We're about to have company."

"The local police or hotel security?" she asked.

"Only hotel security if we're lucky. I might be taken to police headquarters, but I'll be back soon. Get packed, and be ready to leave. Wait." He looked at her and at the gun he was about to put in his waistband. "Come here." He pulled her to him when she stopped a couple of feet away. He tugged her into a hug before she could protest and pressed the Sig into her hand. "Can you shoot?"

"Depends on how close the target is."

That would have to be good enough.

"Take this." He looked over her shoulder. Security wasn't on their way down to the bungalows yet, but there was a great deal of activity around the pool area as several guards rushed out of the main building. "Security will just confiscate it if I have it. Lock the door and secure the chain behind you. Don't let anyone in except me or Bryan."

She pulled the weapon into the fold of her robe as she pressed herself to him and kissed him with the same abandon she'd had an hour ago. He wasn't sure what that kiss was about, but at least there'd be no argument about his accompanying her to the dig site. Thank God for small favors. He watched the guards as she pulled away and walked toward the porch, never looking back.

All the activity was still up by the pool, but it would be moving this way soon. He had a couple of options. Dumb tourist seemed the most expedient way out, but he was going to need some help to pull that off.

He hit the speed dial on his phone for Marissa Hudson, and she answered on the second ring. "Good Lord, Nick. What the hell? I just talked to Leland a couple of hours ago. You're in Africa?" Her husky-sounding voice was rough with sleep and sounded irritated.

Nick managed to irritate Risa on a regular basis, but she'd still come through for him, even if it was the middle of the night in Texas. He glanced toward the hotel. The guards were moving past the pool area and hustling along the path toward him. He heard the door to the bungalow close. *Good.* Jenny was now safely inside.

"Yeah, I'm here, and I'm pretty sure I'm about to be arrested. Can you work some of your magic from afar?" he asked.

Risa made an unhappy sound on the other end of the line. "Let me see what I can do. I've got a contact at the embassy there in Niamey. Don't you and Bryan remember what flying beneath the radar means? It means you keep our butts out of hot water with the locals."

Nick breathed a sigh of relief. Risa had contacts everywhere, and she knew how to use them. She was the moneyed half of AEGIS with a family that was deeply involved in politics. She'd bitch about it, but she was a master diplomat. And AEGIS needed one, given the messes they made from time to time getting citizens in and out of other countries through extraordinarily unofficial channels.

"Yeah, well. That's why I work for AEGIS. Nobody worries so much about the politics."

She snorted a laugh. "No, *you* just don't worry about the politics. Where's Bryan?"

"He went after the shooter."

"Not the wisest course of action at this point. Gavin told me you were all staying together."

Nope, not with Bryan checking out Yarborough leads. But it wasn't Nick's place to out Bryan on that.

"We'll be okay. I'm taking Jennifer on to Ingal and the dig site."

"What about Bryan?" Risa asked.

The guards were almost to him, and they were all holding RAP-440 handguns. Nick wasn't going to answer Risa's question now. It seemed the easiest way to stay out of trouble. "I'm hanging up and surrendering to the hotel security guys. Get me out this, Risa, 'kay?"

"It'd serve you right if I let you cool your butt in an African jail overnight."

"Yeah, but you won't. You love me too much."

Her whiskey-coated laugh echoed in his ear. "I sure as hell do not. But I don't want Jennifer Grayson to pay for your mistake, so you just cooperate till I can get everything squared away."

"You got it." Nick hit END on the call as the head security guard started shouting.

Chapter Seventeen

Wednesday evening
Niamey airport

TWO HOURS LATER Jenny sat beside Nick in a single-engine airplane looking down the same runway she'd landed on earlier that afternoon coming from New York. The world had taken on a surreal sense, and she'd lost count of how many times someone had tried to kill her in the past week. That, combined with her misery over having told Nick about the miscarriage, made the evening seem like a bad dream she couldn't wake from.

Hotel security had taken Nick away immediately after the shooting. She'd watched out the window of their bungalow as the guards waved guns and shouted at him, but he'd been back less than an hour later. His AEGIS employers must have powerful connections. He said he'd never been taken farther away than the hotel security office before someone had called from the U.S. Embassy. The Grand Hotel du Niger management had even apologized for harassing him and ended up comping the cost of their bungalow.

"What about Bryan?" she had asked when Nick returned and insisted they leave immediately.

"Bryan can take care of himself. Are you packed?" And with that they'd headed back to the Niamey airport. She'd had no idea where they were going, but she'd slipped into the Jeep at the hotel as Nick had directed, staying silent even as he drove to a secluded hangar by the airfield.

"Bryan arranged a private plane for us earlier. I'm flying us out of here." He hauled their luggage out of the back of the vehicle and headed toward a small plane on the runway.

Of course he was piloting the plane. He could do anything apparently. After they'd boarded the four-seater aircraft and settled into their seats, Nick handed her a headset.

"It'll be easier to talk with these. Blocks some of the noise, too," he said.

She put the noise-cancelling headphones on, surprised at the gentle hiss of dead air that sounded as if the volume had been turned down on a television. All kinds of activities were taking place around them, but she heard none of it in the headset.

"Where are we going?" she finally asked.

Nick's lips were moving, but she couldn't hear him. She stared for a moment before realizing he was most likely on another channel talking to the tower. He turned, and suddenly his voice was clear and directed at her. "To the Paleo-Niger Project site."

Jenny raised her eyebrows. "Directly to Ingal?" she asked, peering at him in the dim glow of the cockpit controls. She didn't mean to sound skeptical. She was just so surprised, she didn't know what else to say.

Nick's face was thrown into shadow by the uneven lighting, but she saw him nod. "We could go to Agadez and drive in, but there's a private airstrip in Ingal. It'll be easier this way, although we may have to ride a camel to your dig site."

She smiled before realizing he couldn't see her facial expression in the near darkness. "I know the airstrip in Ingal. I can't believe you're taking me . . ." *Where I want to go,* she thought. Not being able to read his face gave her an odd, disconnected feeling.

"I think your dig site may be the safest place for you right now," he said.

She didn't have a reply to that, and he turned away to attend to the controls of the plane, taxiing down the short runway and taking off.

She was stunned. After everything that had happened, she was going exactly where she wanted to be—the Paleo-Niger Jobaria dig. She was too numb to be excited. Was it really possible?

After they were in the air with the city behind them, Nick's voice sounded in her ear again. "Could you hand me one of the sodas?" It was disconcerting to hear his voice in her ear as if he were whispering to her.

She turned in her seat to reach the cooler he'd bought at the sundry shop on their way out of the hotel. The padded bag held sandwiches and drinks. She handed over the chilled bottle and took a water for herself, then settled in for the flight. She had the distinct impression Nick did not want to be here with her, but they weren't talking about that.

She didn't want to be here with him either. It hurt too much.

"Why are you letting me go?" she asked. "You seemed so against the idea before."

That was putting it mildly. He'd thrown up a multitude of roadblocks until tonight.

"Like I said, it seems the safest place for you to be. Plus, I can see anyone coming, as opposed to where we were in Niamey—or in Dallas, for that matter."

She nodded. That made sense, and the idea of being able to lose herself in the activity at the dig site was a siren song. She'd have welcomed anything that took her mind off of flying bullets and Nick in her bed.

She shuddered.

"You cold?" he asked.

She shook her head, unable to tell him why she'd really shivered. She still couldn't believe they'd had sex after all these years. But she wasn't the least bit sorry, particularly as she was having such frequent reminders about how short and uncertain life really was. Despite his anger, she was relieved Nick knew everything now, even if he never looked at her the same way again.

She needed to try and make it right. "I know I hurt you," she said.

He didn't answer or indicate he'd heard her in any way. The cloud-covered sky was pitch black and eerie, making her feel all alone in the darkness, even though he was seated next to her. She knew she should let the subject drop, but she couldn't.

"I don't blame you for not wanting to talk about that summer," she started.

For a moment the silence was so complete, she wondered if his headset was on a different channel.

"Oh, I wouldn't mind talking about that summer. It's the miscarriage I'm having trouble with." His voice dripped ice. "Why don't you just drop it?"

All right, so she probably deserved that.

"I will, after I say one more thing." The darkness and shadows made her bold. Not being able to see the temper in his eyes that was clearly audible in his voice enabled her to keep going. "Not telling you before was wrong of me and not well done. I'm sorry."

For a moment there was only the gentle hiss of the headphones as a reply.

"Okay. You've said it. I'm not ready to accept your apology yet. I'm not sure when, or if, I'll ever be ready." Nick's tone wasn't as chilly as the one he'd expressed earlier, but it wasn't warm either.

"Fair enough. I just wanted you to know."

"So now I know. Can we please drop it?" His voice was even and steady, but there was something more, something unsettled there. She could feel it.

"What is it? There's more here than you're saying." She was pushing, despite her better judgment.

"No, there's not." The cadence of his speech was no longer smooth.

She couldn't stop herself, even though she knew he might skin her alive with his words. "I don't believe you."

"Dammit. Haven't you done enough, Jenny? Just drop it, for fuck's sake."

Okay. This was definitely not the time to let it go, not if she really wanted to know what the deal was. "No. I won't drop it. There's obviously something else you want to say here."

He reached to flip on an overhead light above them that he hadn't used before. "Yes, you're damn right there is something else I want to say. When I came back that spring after I enlisted, I was coming back for you. I was rethinking that whole new direction I'd taken. I thought I was in love with you, and I was going to ask you to wait for me. To marry me."

The skinning she'd all but asked for had begun. She was beyond speaking and could only stare at him. His eyes were blazing as he gazed unblinking at her and continued telling her exactly what he thought.

"Crazy idea, I know. I didn't figure it out until you'd dropped off the freaking face of the earth. You didn't return emails, letters, phone calls, nothing. I couldn't understand what the hell I'd done wrong. Now I find out you were pregnant, and you didn't tell me. You could have had my baby, and I might never have known."

He'd come back to propose when she was in China? God, she'd been the idiot. It had never occurred to her that he would have wanted to marry her then, *before* he knew that there'd been a baby. Even though he'd told her Sunday night that he'd come back to find out what was wrong, she'd never considered the possibility that he'd come to propose to her as well.

"I would never have done that—not tell you about—" She stopped and stared straight ahead into the night, longing for darkness inside the cockpit again. How could he possibly believe her? Why had she thought pushing this conversation would be a good idea?

"How do I know what you would have done? I don't know who the hell you are anymore or even who you were to begin with. How can I trust you when you kept this from me?"

She swallowed hard. She'd started this, and she'd finish it. Ten years ago she'd had no idea how much she'd hurt him. Tonight she deserved every bit of his ire. He'd wanted to marry her. God, what had she done? The loss of what-could-have-beens washed over her.

Still, she was dry-eyed when she turned to face him.

"I was young, stupid, and scared. I'm sorry." She put her hand on his arm. "Please. We can't keep fighting like this, I shouldn't have brought it up again. Not here. Not now."

Something changed in his eyes when she said that. She wasn't sure what, but she hoped she was getting through. She needed him to believe that they could work through this together, painful as it was.

"I'm going to need time, Jenny. It hurts too much to just let this go." His jaw clenched as he spoke; the tension was obvious. That had cost him to say.

She nodded. "Fair enough."

He kept talking like she hadn't said anything. "But know this. Mad as I am, I'm not going to let anything happen to you. Get some sleep. We'll be landing in a couple of hours." His voice was still gruff, but that cold, icy tone wasn't as arctic.

She touched his arm again, and he glanced at her for a moment before refocusing on the controls and reaching up to turn off the light.

"I trust you," she murmured.

Saying that, even knowing how angry he was with her, wasn't hard. She did trust him. He would protect her to his dying breath. Deep down she'd always known that.

The question was, would he ever be able to trust her?

Thursday, early morning
Ingal, Niger

NICK DIDN'T REALIZE how wiped out he was until they approached for landing in Ingal. The exhaustion was more than physical. The mental strain of the past twenty-four hours was kicking his ass. At five AM it was still dark, but a front had come through, clearing away the clouds that had cloaked them all the way from Niamey. Light from the moon and stars overhead illuminated the flat area of sand that passed for an airstrip and enabled him to land the plane.

He set down with a jarring thud that shook both him and Jennifer in their seats. A private airport didn't necessarily mean a maintained landing strip. He parked the aircraft. Everything felt extraordinarily quiet after the roaring vibration of the engine.

He and Jenny hadn't talked any more after their argument, and Nick was grateful, even though engine racket wasn't the reason. The headphones would have allowed for easy conversation, but he couldn't have handled any more after their gut-wrenching discussion on the flight out of Niamey.

Jenny had slept. She must be as tired as he was, if not more so. He was used to pushing himself like this, she wasn't.

Two flood lights lit the makeshift airport that consisted of dried-mud buildings. In the distance, more lights outlined palm trees surrounding the oasis of Ingal. They were still seventy miles from the Paleo-Niger dig site, and they needed a car, preferably a four-wheel-drive vehicle.

A man wearing the combination veil and turban of the Tuareg walked out of a shack next to the landing strip. Nick prepared to get out and bargain for several things, including a place to rest for a few hours. In the shadows of the light illuminating him from behind, the man had a peculiar gait. Jenny stared as the man made his way toward them with a distinct limp.

"Oh my God. I think I know him. That's Bill." She opened the plane door. "Bill?!" she called.

Bill? "How can you possibly recognize anyone in the dark wearing the *tagelmoust*, the veil?" Nick's throat was dry from the arid extremes of the area. Not having spoken in several hours made his voice crack like a thirteen-year-old's.

She glanced back at him. "The way he walks. Bill had polio as a child."

"Bill?" Nick asked aloud this time.

She shook her head. "That's not really his name. It's Balfama Tamunominini." She said the name with a perfect accent and smiled. It means *'Don't be afraid, God is with you.'* Everyone on the team just calls him Bill."

"I can see where that would be easier." His tone was as dry as the night air.

"Bill runs the supply transport for the Paleo-Niger Project. His job here at the airstrip makes him a perfect fit. He's done it the past two times the group has been at the Jobaria dig with the Russ Foundation. He's one of the only people in the area with a four-wheel-drive truck who is not government or military. Most civilians travel by camel or on foot."

Of course they do, thought Nick. God forbid we be running for our lives in the harshest desert in the world with access to more than one four-wheel-drive vehicle.

Calling out a greeting in French, she hopped out of the plane as Bill limped toward them. The man obviously recognized Jenny as she drew closer, bypassing the formal Nigerien greeting of a handshake and giving her a warm hug instead.

Nick was introduced in a combination of English and rudimentary French. After finding out that they were the most recent strangers arriving in town, Nick left Bill and Jenny to catch up as he gathered their gear. When he came back to the mud shack airport office with their luggage, Jenny was still buzzing.

"Later in the day, Bill is planning to run supplies to the dig site. He says we can rest at his place for now and hitch a ride when he drives out."

"Okay." Finally, some good news. That gave them time to grab some real food and maybe get cleaned up.

Bill put a plastic gallon jug of water on the counter in front of them. "Drink," he said.

Jennifer nodded, took a deep sip, and handed the jug to Nick. He wasn't thirsty, but he took a slug of the lukewarm water anyway. If you waited till you actually felt thirsty to drink in the desert, it was already too late, and you were on your way to being dehydrated. He'd learned that in Afghanistan.

Without a word, Bill took one of the bags Nick was carrying and placed it on his own shoulder along with the jug of water and led them out of the building. He directed them down a dark path into town with a flashlight.

Even in the early morning blackness Nick could see that Ingal was a study in contrasts, with the desert bordering against an oasis.

Bill handed him the jug as they walked, and Nick took another hit of water before passing it on to Jenny. The air was so very dry. It had a different feel from Niamey.

"I imagine this is beautiful in its own way during the day, but God it's harsh," said Nick.

Jenny took a deep sip from the plastic container. "It's a town of nomads. We're in what's known as the Sahel, the transitional space between the Sudanian Savanna of southern Niger and the Sahara. They've been experiencing perpetual drought conditions over the past several years that have pushed the desert farther and farther into this area."

Nick could see that. The streets of Ingal were nothing more than dry sand, but light from the stars overhead and sporadic oil lamps outside various residences showed that the entire area was also filled with surprisingly lush gardens and fruit trees around the houses. Bill's flashlight illuminated the walls of the homes as they walked past.

The houses were built of mud and straw that looked almost like cement or as if the material had baked in the desert sun. He realized it most likely had. Some residences had tents attached and others had mat-like coverings over what would be considered a front porch. There were occasional straw huts as well.

"Why are all the homes built so differently?" asked Nick.

Jenny pointed at one of the baked cement-like walls they passed. "You have permanent residents here who live in the mud huts. That construction material is called *banco*. But the Tuareg and Fulani are nomads and constantly moving, so most Tuareg homes are tents. The Fulani live in collapsible huts made of mats. That makes it much easier to transport their homes with them."

"How many people live here?"

The enthusiasm in Jenny's voice was tangible. "Depends on the time of year. Ingal's population is usually around five hundred, but each September it increases to several thousand. Tuareg and Woodabee nomads arrive for the Cure Salee festival marking the end of the rainy season. Most have left the area now that it's December, and Ingal's just a wide spot in the road on the edge of the Sahara. Still, the oasis and spring make this place very important to the area."

The walk was warm and dusty, even in the early morning. Nick suspected he smelled ripe, but he wanted food and a place to close his eyes more than he wanted to be clean. He wouldn't be any good to Jennifer in the shape he was now.

Bill directed them down a street lined by another *banco* wall and stopped in front of a combo tent-and-mud-hut dwelling. A fruit tree grew in the front yard, shading the roof. He pulled aside the material covering the door and motioned them forward, lighting an oil lamp as they stepped inside.

The room was large and significantly cooler than expected. Desert nights in December were cool, if one considered sixty-eight degrees chilly. Most likely the house would feel like a pizza oven in a few hours when the temperature climbed closer to ninety-five.

Bill set Nick's bag on the ground. "You rest here," he said, pointing to a foam pallet covered with brightly colored material. "I take you to dig soon."

"Merci, mon ami," Jenny said and gave Bill another hug. Thank you, my friend.

The Nigerien spoke with her a few more minutes before leaving them alone in his hut. Nick couldn't understand much. He had never learned French. Farsi, yes, but he was clueless in Paris and Niger.

Jenny turned from the hut's entrance. The light did odd things with her shadow on the wall of the hut.

"He's going to gather the supplies and be back in a couple of hours when it's light. After that he'll take us to the project site," she explained.

Her voice was stronger than it had been when Nick had found her in Niamey. She was a bundle of energy as she paced across the dirt floor. "This is good," she said. "There's water here for washing up. He'll bring us something to eat, too."

Nick sank to the pallet. "Where's his family?"

"They died in the 2010 famine. Our dig was here right after that in the fall. That's when I first met him. He was grieving so. He had a wife and two children. He's never remarried."

Nick sat, calculating how long it had been since he'd slept . . . at least thirty-two hours. "I've got to sleep, or I'm going to be worthless."

"Yes, you should," she said. "I rested on the flight."

"Will you promise not to go anywhere while I'm asleep?" He'd have to trust Bill's word that he and Jenny were the only strangers in town for now. He'd have to trust Jenny as well, to do as he asked her.

After everything he'd learned in the past twelve hours about their shared past, he wasn't so sure he could trust her for much of anything, even for her own safety. But he was out of options. He had to get some shuteye.

She grinned. "How could I get into trouble here?"

"God, don't ask that." He tilted his head back against the dried mud wall. "But if I don't sleep, I won't be able to do anything to help you if you do get into trouble."

"I'll be fine." She sat down beside him. "And I'll stay here. I promise."

Famous last words, he thought, drifting off to sleep.

Chapter Eighteen

Thursday morning
Niamey

BRYAN SAT IN the café, drinking his fourth cup of coffee before nine AM. He'd picked up his luggage from the bellman hours ago at the Grand Hotel du Niger, well after Nick and Jennifer had left. This particular meeting had been postponed once yesterday and again early this morning. Bryan needed the information before he left Niamey, so he'd stayed, even though he didn't like leaving Nick and Jenny on their own.

Reporters. Crap. They screwed things up every time. And this one, freelance and pint-sized, just kept coming at him like a terrier with a bone. She always had.

But Sassy Smith was on to something with the Yarborough case, even if she kept showing up at the most inopportune times. As mad as she made him, the information she delivered was gold. They were meeting across the street from the Gaweye, the hotel Jennifer had originally been booked in.

Bryan was ordering a fifth cup of coffee when Sassy strolled into the café wearing a *khimar* head covering to hide the most obvious of her western features, her strawberry blonde hair. Still, he had a fair idea of what was under the cape-like veil that hung to her waist. He'd seen her in Dallas right after Elizabeth Yarborough disappeared and everything went to hell.

Blue-eyed, big-chested, and beauty-queen gorgeous— how Sassy kept her manicure a perfect fire-engine red and her makeup applied like a fashion model's in this part of the world, Bryan had no idea. Thinking about her curvy figure had kept him awake more nights than he cared to admit. Even the perfume she wore invaded his dreams. And she was wearing it this morning; the floral tones swirled around the spicy notes and screwed with his head.

"What will you give me for this information, Bryan?" She dove in with no introduction or apology for her tardiness. The suggestive tone and double entendre were completely undisguised. Sassy might not be sleeping her way to the top, but she gave the distinct impression that she was open to the idea.

Bryan unclenched his jaw and took a silent gulp of air. "Are we really going to bargain for the intel? Someone tried to kill this woman yesterday, along with my partner."

Sassy stared at him, her midnight-blue eyes raking over his chest. "So you claim. How do I know you're not just pumping me for information?"

He sighed out loud this time and leaned back in his chair, fighting the inclination to beat his head against the tabletop. "Do I really have to say it?"

"Say what?" she asked innocently. Bryan got the impression she was anything but virtuous.

Jesus.

He might as well get this over with. He and Sassy always did a little dance before they got down to exchanging information, or that's what it felt like: a flirtatious sexual sparring that wasn't quite real. And it drove him nuts. He'd dreamed about her and woken up hard in his bed thinking of her for months.

This was so wrong.

And the sad fact was, she'd never believe him, even if he lost his mind and told her exactly what he was thinking. So why not just play the game? Later he'd blame it on the caffeine overload.

He leaned across the table and speared her with his steel gray gaze that ordinarily had men looking for the nearest exit.

"Sassy, if I was pumping you for information, you'd know it."

A tiny smile played around the edges of her lips, and she ran her finger across the top of his fist on the wooden tabletop. "Would I, now?" she whispered.

"You'd fucking feel it," he murmured under his breath, just loud enough for her to hear.

She smiled as if she'd won the lottery, apparently not at all shocked by what he'd said.

But if she wasn't shocked, he sure as hell was. While

Bryan could cuss with the best of them and—more often than not—screamed profanity in his head, he never talked like this in front of a woman unless his cover called for it. His Gran would be spinning in her grave. Sassy Smith brought out the absolute worst in him. Always.

He pulled his fist from under her fingers, and Sassy's grin widened, if possible.

"I can give you an exclusive when we have the client out of the country," he said.

"Give me her real name now," she said.

There wasn't going to be a way around this if he wanted any information from her.

"You cannot use this until she's out and safe, okay?"

Sassy leaned back in the rickety seat to study him. Even though she was only five foot four, the woman gave the impression that she was looking down her nose at him with more than a little disdain. "My word is my word, Hollywood. What kind of nickname is that anyway?"

"It's a long story that we don't have time for today." Bryan sipped his coffee and gave her a final hard stare. The lady's name is Dr. Jennifer Grayson."

Sassy nodded and scribbled notes in her archaic short-hand before speaking again. "See? That didn't hurt so much." She picked up his coffee, turned the cup to where his lips had been on the rim, and took a sip for herself.

Totally oblivious to the effect she was having on him, or perhaps all too aware of it, she kept talking. "Okay. Here's what I know. The Riveras and Vegas are using the same route to traffic women that they've been using for narcotics."

He shrugged and forced a disinterest into his tone he didn't feel. "Human trafficking isn't news. Besides, why would you think the Vegas and Riveras would work together? They normally don't ever do that."

"I have confirmation of the 'partnership' from two other sources," she answered. "It has something to do with Tomas Rivera's wife dying recently. My informant wasn't clear on why it was happening, just that it definitely was."

Bingo. He'd needed that fact confirmed. Maybe this appointment had been worth waiting for after all.

"Does your source have a name?" he asked.

She snorted. "Are you high? I don't give up sources to anyone."

He'd expected that response. "Okay, how do they traffic the women?"

"I have the contacts Ernesto Vega uses in the shipping yards on the west and east coasts here in Africa, as well as his contacts in Venezuela. I also have the names of the officials Tomas Rivera is bribing to get the women through each country on this continent. The route runs along the Sahel and across the Sahara."

Wonder what she had to do to get that information? Bryan felt his eyebrows rise but said nothing as he drank more of his dark coffee, avoiding the lipstick stain she'd left earlier with her pilfered sip.

Sassy studied the people walking past the front of the hotel. "Once in Africa they ship the women in trucks from the west coast inland and across the desert to the Mediterranean. The drivers don't stop for anything until they reach the ocean. Many of the women don't survive the extreme conditions of the drive."

"But there are more where they come from," said Bryan unhappily.

Sassy nodded. Her eyes had lost the saucy sparkle they'd had when she'd first sat down. "Once the trucks reach the Mediterranean coast, they put the women on ships. Sometimes they are put in containers if the boats are large enough, other times they're just crowded onto the deck. Most of the boats are undocumented. Many are less than seaworthy. They sail from multiple ports in Morocco, Tunisia, Algeria, even Libya, smuggling the women into Europe. If they don't die in the desert, scores of women drown in the overcrowded boats that sink."

"Won't they care that such a large number die in transit from dehydration in the desert or from drowning in the ocean?" The coffee in his mouth now tasted like mud.

"The profit margin is so huge for the women in Italy and France, the traffickers feel they can stand the loss. Sixty percent of the prostitutes in Italy are from Nigeria. It's a stunning number. And like you said, there are more where they came from."

Bryan examined the coffee cup once more with its red-hot lip print on the side before looking up to pierce her with his stare again. "What does this have to do with Elizabeth Yarborough?"

Sassy huffed out a sigh. "Well, I don't expect you to find an 'Elizabeth was here' sign, but I think sending her to Africa was a test run for Vega and Rivera's new route. What if they sent her because the original kidnappers, whoever they were, knew they couldn't keep her after they took her, particularly once the world press got the story?"

"That's all conjecture," said Bryan, not bothering to admit that he'd considered the same idea.

Sassy shrugged and kept talking. "Maybe they sold her, traded her, whatever. Somehow she ended up in Rivera's control, but even he couldn't keep her with the *60 Minutes* film crew on site and her picture on CNN 24/7 for weeks. So they got her the hell out of Dodge and killed two birds with one stone."

Bryan shook his head. "That's an interesting theory." No matter what, he wouldn't tell Sassy he'd already considered the same theory with Nick, or she'd never let it go. "The problem is there's no proof that Elizabeth Yarborough was ever held by the Riveras or the Vegas in Mexico, so the idea of her being shipped to Africa is a long shot."

"What if I had a source who swore to me that he brought her to Africa?"

"Do you?" His tone was sharper than he'd intended. "Who was it?"

She rolled her eyes. "I'm *so* not telling you that."

He felt the first real frisson of concern for her. "Be careful, Sassy. You're setting yourself up to be played here. How did they contact you?" Hairs on the back of his neck stood on end when he thought of all the trouble she could get into by trusting the wrong source in this cluster.

"You really don't want to know." Her husky voice was

thick with what Bryan would have thought was regret, if he didn't know her better.

She looked down at her feet and shook her head, shivering slightly. "If you don't trust that information, I doubt you'll trust this either. I can't verify it with multiple sources, but you might find it interesting." Sassy pulled an oversized map from her humongous handbag and unfolded the paper on their table. "It's the route the Vegas and Riveras are using for a shipment this month"

"What?" He leaned forward to get a good look. A dotted line had been drawn in green pencil along with today's date. Bryan followed Sassy's red-tipped index finger across the route marked. "This is current?" he asked.

She nodded and tapped her long nail on a green X penciled on the map. "I got it from the same source that told me about bringing Elizabeth here. See? They're making one stop along the way. That's unusual."

"Fuck," he muttered, standing so fast the coffee cup toppled over.

The X marked the exact spot where the Paleo-Niger dig was located.

Chapter Nineteen

Thursday, late afternoon
Near Paleo-Niger Project site

IN A HYPNOTIC daze, Jennifer watched the road disappear and reappear as Bill drove them through the Sahel toward the project site. Relentless wind blew Saharan sand across the narrow track, completely obscuring the path at times. Without warning the pockmarked road would reappear like a black serpent stretched out in the sun before them. Sun-dried grass, broken and burnt-looking, was sprinkled here and there along with the occasional acacia tree.

The truck's air conditioner struggled to keep up. While sitting between the two men, beads of sweat ran down Jennifer's back as her thighs stuck, then slid on the vinyl seat with a slippery *blech* feeling. Still, she was grateful for the AC and the four-wheel drive. Compared to the nomads they'd seen in the distance travelling by camel, this ancient overheated truck was the height of luxury.

Nick rode beside her in silence, his thigh pressed against hers. He'd slept until right before they left, waking only when Bill had come back to the hut with food for them. Nick had seemed okay with what they were about to do, but he had remained unusually quiet as he'd packed their things into Bill's beat-up Ford.

Jennifer assumed he was just tired. She hoped so. They would be at the camp soon, and she could feel her anticipation growing.

This was going to work out. The dig was where she needed to be to get past everything that had happened in the past six months—hell, the past ten years. She could hardly wait to lose herself in the day-to-day intricacies of field study.

Despite everything that had happened, she grinned. *God, a fully intact Jobaria.* The sauropod dinosaur was an amazing find. Her tummy fluttered at the thought of what it could mean to her career, to her life, to work on the prestigious project.

Her mouth was dry, but that was as much from her excitement as the climate. She reached for the bottle between her and Nick, accidentally brushing his hip with the back of her hand. He tensed, and her awareness of him shot through the truck's rusted roof.

She no longer had difficulty believing she'd slept with him yesterday afternoon. The surprising warmth flooding her body had her fully aware of her response to him as well as acknowledging that she'd gladly go another round, even with their tangled history.

She took a sip of water. That thought was absolute insanity, and the logical part of her brain longed to quiet this "hyperawareness" that was ever present when she was with him. There was no way they were having sex again, not since she'd told him about the miscarriage. That he was sitting beside her without visibly seething was a minor miracle.

She tried to tell herself it was better this way. Being with Nick was too complicated. Even if the sex was amazing, his anger after he had found out everything had hurt like hell—not that she didn't deserve it. Still, she was on the verge of getting her life together. She was not in a good place to deal with him or any of this other madness right now.

There was no way Nick would want to stay at the Paleo-Niger Project with her for months on end. What she'd begun to hope was that he'd stay at the dig site a few days, then get some information on his fancy SAT phone that would send him off to another corner of the globe. For sanity's sake, she needed him to leave her, to go away and allow her to deal with this "new start" alone.

She glanced at her watch again and felt her heart rate bump up in anticipation. They should be arriving at the project site any moment. Nick had let her use the SAT phone to call Teddy and tell him that they were on their way. She hadn't told him about her adventure at the airport or the hotel. She'd do that in person.

Teddy was going to be devastated and feel so responsible. A gentle soul, her mentor was strictly an academic, lost in the world of paleontology. Hearing about the events of the past two days would be just as foreign to him as they had been to her.

Bill slowed the truck. They'd been riding up and down the gentle slope of dunes for several hours. The sun hung low in the sky. Lights in the distance grew steadily brighter. They were almost there. If the smoke was any indication, dinner was cooking.

Jennifer wet her lips and leaned forward in the seat to get a better view of the camp. The scraggly acacia trees were more dead than alive in this area but rose like sentinels beside the road. She was ready to be there now.

Nick made a final call on the SAT phone as they topped the last dune. It sounded as if he was leaving a message. "Hey, it's me. We're here at the Paleo-Niger site. Bryan's still in Niamey but should be joining us soon. I'll touch base with you tomorrow."

He disconnected. The project site was spread out before them. The sun was about to dip below the horizon. The red-tinged light would fade quickly. Around the actual camp were several pop-up shelters to shade workers from the blazing heat during the day.

At the perimeter, armed guards from the Nigerien military stopped the truck for confirmation that Bill, Jennifer, and Nick truly belonged here. Jennifer could tell Nick was surprised by that and felt a small spurt of pride. On behalf of the Russ Foundation, she'd exchanged countless emails and several phone calls with

Niger's Minister of Culture and Tourism, who in turn had negotiated with the local tribesmen arranging security here at the dig site. In years past, the Foundation had employed freelance paramilitary guards, and it had not worked well at all. She could already tell that this was a more secure system.

Bill drove into the middle of the camp and parked beside what she assumed was the cooking tent, the largest of all the others. As workers and students gathered around the truck, she glanced at Nick before they climbed out.

"You ready?" she asked him.

"Yeah. Remember my cover?"

Her throat narrowed, but she nodded anyway. He'd asked her not to tell her colleagues exactly why he was with her. Since everyone here from Dallas had already been on the way to Africa when her house blew up, she hadn't told Teddy anything about it when they spoke on Sunday. She hadn't told him about her misadventures in Mexico either. She preferred to do that all in person, if the topic ever came up.

Given the circumstances, the easiest cover was obvious.

Nick touched her hips and pulled her to him on the seat, lingering longer than was necessary with his fingers practically inside her shorts pocket. She didn't look down at his hands but instead focused on his eyes. He kissed her with a possessiveness she wished was real, but in her heart she knew she'd be safer assuming this was all for show.

As far as the camp was concerned, Nick was an old boyfriend from college with whom she'd just reconnected. They'd been unwilling to spend the holidays apart with Jennifer's last-minute addition to the project, so he'd come to be with her. Naturally, they would be sleeping in the same tent.

She tried not to think about that as they climbed out of the truck, and she introduced Nick to people she knew from the last time she'd been here on the dig. Though professors of paleontology and archaeology were from all over the world, it truly was a very small community. Many of them had received the same birth announcement from Collin and his "baby mama" last week that she had. If there were raised eyebrows at this latest development in her personal life, no one commented.

In addition to the professionals that Jennifer had known for years, there were grad students and some local tribesmen hired to work in the camp. There was a distinctly festive atmosphere. She counted in her head and realized with a shock that Christmas Eve was less than two days away. She'd been so caught up in everything that she'd lost track of time.

Fifteen people had already gathered around the truck when Teddy arrived to wrap Jennifer in a hug. She introduced him to Nick, and if no one else's eyebrows had risen earlier, Teddy's did now. He knew exactly who Nick was, or rather who he had been to her.

Her former professor, who had made sure Jennifer got a spot on the China dig after her miscarriage, had even taken the chance of asking her if she was sure about marrying Collin in a foreign country so soon after all the up-heaval in her life. He'd also been instrumental in helping her find a new job at SMU when she'd left Collin and her old position in Austin at the University of Texas to file for divorce last summer.

Jennifer didn't address any of that history with the others. She simply explained that she and Nick had known each other years before and had just reconnected. During the introductions, Nick slid his arm possessively around her waist, pulling her close. He was taking their cover story quite seriously.

Teddy gave him a hard stare as Nick deliberately took her hand and threaded his fingers through hers. She shot a sideways glance at Nick, but he didn't seem to notice. They walked through the camp on a small tour before moving into the dining tent.

Bill had unloaded the truck and parked it back on the outskirts of the camp before joining the group for dinner. All during the meal Nick played the dutiful, entranced boyfriend, touching Jennifer every chance he got.

Her colleagues were just settling in and recovering from their own jet lag, so work on the latest phase of the dig hadn't started in earnest yet. Things would get cranked up in the next couple of days. Throughout the meal there was talk of papers, projects, and publications, all having to do with this new Jobaria find. Jennifer felt a tangible, bubbling excitement at the prospect of getting into the field again.

Nick listened politely, not participating much. All too soon it was time for bed. They would be sleeping in the same tent, and she had no idea how she was going to handle that. His touches all through dinner had seemed so personal, so real.

"Sleep well," said Teddy, pointing them to their quarters. Her friend hadn't mentioned it, but she was certain it had complicated things to show up with Nick and no warning. Still, she didn't acknowledge the inconvenience. She was becoming quite good at ignoring things that were too difficult to face.

"Thank you, Teddy." Nick shook his hand, never letting go of hers, as they said their good nights. "I appreciate your welcoming me on such short notice."

Nick was still touching her as they made their way through the darkness to their tent, but he was no longer talking. Had all that affection been for show?

Sleeping with him again would be pure insanity. But with each step closer to the tent, Jennifer realized that was exactly what she was about to do, against her better judgment.

NICK HELD JENNY's hand until they reached the tent. There'd been no reason to drop it until they stood at the canvas door. He unzipped the flap and put his hand on her lower back, guiding her inside.

She was driving him completely crazy. He'd barely survived the multi-hour ride in the truck pressed against her, then dinner—sitting beside her with her fingers wrapped around his. If he touched her one more time tonight, he'd be taking her clothes off. He was drowning in her, and he worried about being able to protect her like this.

A lantern burned brightly on a table beside a double-size foam mattress. *Good God*. He wasn't sure if he should be grateful or running from the tent like a scalded dog. He clenched his jaw in frustration. There was nowhere else to sleep but the sand.

Teddy had explained that they'd hired two of the local tribesmen to work as housekeepers for the camp. That kept other locals from showing up and begging for work. It had been a problem in the past. The housemen did everyone's laundry and kept the tents in order, or as orderly as they could with sand floors and limited electricity from their generators.

Nick and Jenny's packs were beside the bed on a small carpet that looked like it had been woven by the Tuaregs. He was standing behind her, sizing up the rug for what kind of mattress it would make, when he saw the bottle of red wine. It was beside the lantern, along with two plastic cups and a note addressed to Jenny.

He stood reading silently over her shoulder and tried to get a grip on himself before he forgot all the reasons why he should sleep on the floor alone instead of pulling her down to that mattress.

Merry Christmas, Jennifer (if a bit early). Sorry this is not a finer vintage. It's good to see you happy. Fondest wishes, Tedford

He blew out a deep breath. So their cover had worked. And why wouldn't it? Much of the story was true. Nick *was* a boyfriend from the past who couldn't stand to be away from Jenny over the holiday. If he liked touching her more than he should, that just made the story look better.

And that carpet was too damn short.

Jenny glanced at him over her shoulder. Her face was partially shadowed in the lantern light. He could smell the hotel shampoo she'd used at the Grand Hotel du Niger along with the wood smoke from the cooking fire they'd just left, plus something else that had him longing to reach for her. She turned back to the table to unscrew the top on the bottle of wine.

"Want some cabernet?" Her voice held a slight tremor.

Was she affected by this scenario as much as he was? He needed to understand what was happening here, what was happening inside him. He had to touch her. Without thinking beyond the next moment, he put his hands on her again, turning her in his arms.

She was shaking her head *no* even as she looked up at him.

"I can't do this, Nick. I don't understand what you want—"

Interrupting her protest, he leaned down and kissed her because he couldn't stand not to anymore. It had been so long since he'd felt anything. When he pressed his lips to hers, she tasted like no other woman ever had. She tasted like . . . home. That thought had his own voice shaking as he pulled back.

Still, he surprised himself when he whispered, "I just want you."

He did want *only* her—despite what she'd told him earlier, despite the betrayal he still felt about their history.

Despite the hurt the past had inflicted on both of them, he wanted her. Here. Now.

But more than anything he wanted her safe.

He ran his hands up and down her arms, pulling her to him as his body hardened. Her hands moved behind his neck and her fingers teased the ends of his hair, like he remembered from that long-ago summer.

She kissed him back, and when he slid his hands to her ass, she made a tiny noise in her throat that completely undid him. It was obvious, but he said it again anyway. "I want you. Today, tomorrow, all the time."

"How—" She pulled away with a wrinkle between her brows.

"Jenny, I've always wanted you."

She smiled, but her eyes were wet.

And damn, if he didn't feel like crying, too. "That summer wasn't some fluke. I wanted you from the moment I met you. I never stopped."

Tears rolled down her cheeks, but he didn't stop talking, knowing he'd never tell her if he didn't do it now. "I still do."

"Even after . . ."

"Yes, even after." He swiped at her tears with his thumb. "I know it's a helluva thing. The choices we made ten years ago haven't stopped me from wanting you, from—"

She interrupted him this time with a kiss, and it was a good thing. He'd been about to say something that couldn't be taken back. Something he wasn't sure he felt yet.

I forgive you. I want to start again.

Did he? Was he there yet? He wasn't sure, but he wanted to be.

He steered her to the bed, sliding her shirt over her head with one hand as he reached for the zipper on her cargo shorts with the other. His fingers ached to touch all of her bare skin.

Is it always going to be like this?

He couldn't get her clothes off fast enough. She pulled at his T-shirt as he went for the clasp on her bra. Soon they were both naked. The night air was cool on his back. The hair lifted along his arms, but he didn't know if it was from the temperature or from wanting her.

She stifled a squeal when he gripped her waist with cool fingers and gently pushed her to the mattress. Following her down to the bed, he pulled a loose blanket up over the top of them. Under the covers he reached for her again, and this time, if his hands weren't steady, at least they were warm.

She touched his face when he stroked his fingers from her throat down the middle of her chest to her stomach and lower. There was a vulnerability in her gaze that hadn't been there yesterday afternoon in the bungalow in Niamey. He wanted her to know it was okay.

She was safe. No matter what happened. No matter how things ended between them in the days to come.

He moved on top of her and sank into her heat, engulfed in the sensation. She closed her eyes as he skimmed his fingertips along her cheek.

"I need to see you," he murmured, balancing his weight on his elbows, careful not to crush her.

JENNY SMILED AND opened her eyes to find herself locked in a laser-like gaze that she wouldn't have been able to tear herself away from unless the tent was on fire. Nick kissed her, and the sensation of it all—his being inside her, the cool air on their feet because the blanket had slipped off, the rasp of his whiskered cheek on her face— had her catching her breath in a deep gulp of air.

She couldn't believe he still wanted her. After everything that had happened, had he forgiven her for not telling him about the miscarriage?

She wasn't sure. But for now, this would be enough.

He set a slow but distinct pace, pulling away then sliding back inside her. It hardly seemed possible, but everything felt more intense than yesterday; maybe because it was all so deliberate. In Niamey, they'd been frantic, and she'd been overwhelmed. Tonight was intentional, as if he was telling her something with his body that neither of them could say with words.

Still, he was holding back. She could feel it when she ran her hands over his shoulders. His muscles strained as she slid her fingers down the center of his back. Stopping at the curve in his lower spine, she moved her palms to pull his hips closer, reveling in his quiet moan as he relaxed then pushed deeper. She didn't want to be treated like she was going to break.

"You're not going to hurt me. If we're doing this, I

need all of you." She hoped he knew she was referring to more than his body.

He nodded and pulled back. Her pulse rate skittered up in expectation. He lowered himself completely on top of her, and she shuddered as if something deep inside her chest had shifted.

She was almost panting, unsure if it was the pace or the sensations overwhelming her emotions. Gasping for air, she spun out of control and shattered into tiny pieces. He came immediately after her with a low groan that no one could hear but her.

His full weight pressed her into the mattress as he kissed the side of her neck and the top of her shoulder. She still couldn't breathe very well but decided on the spot that breathing was overrated. With bone-deep contentment, she took as deep a sip of air as possible.

"I'm crushing you." He rolled, pulling her with him so she was sprawled across the top of him. She tucked her head into his shoulder, feeling a deep sense of peace for the first time in ages.

Nick wanted her and was on the way to, if not forgiving her, at least accepting her apology. She was on a Jo-baria dig site, and she'd just had amazing sex with a man she'd thought of for years. Life was looking better than it had in a very long time. Everything else faded to the background as she drifted off to sleep.

Chapter Twenty

NICK LAY BESIDE Jennifer, her back snuggled to his chest, as reality hit. What in hell was he doing here? What had he just done?

Thoughts swirled in his head but without the familiar feelings of despair to which he'd become so accustomed. Should he ride back to Ingal tomorrow with Bill and head for Niamey to help Bryan? With the government guards on site, Jenny would be safe here, wouldn't she?

He dismissed that fantasy with a quiet snort. The Tuareg guards were marginal at best, so her safety was questionable unless he stayed. Right now Nick didn't trust anyone to protect Jenny, except himself. Still, there was no reason he should be in bed with her, besides the fact that he just wanted to be. At least he wasn't lying to himself anymore.

He hadn't stopped reeling from her story of the miscarriage. The grief was a physical pain, like the healing bullet wound in his shoulder. He understood what had happened, or at least he thought he did. Yet, he wasn't able to let go of the sorrow. He was struggling to forgive her, even as he sympathized with what had brought her to that point.

Leaving himself open to her and to more of that kind of regret and heartache was beyond what he could stand at this point. But he had no business judging her.

His work with the CIA might have all been in the name of national security, but it wasn't as if he'd been feeding starving children. More often than not he'd been killing people. It was what had driven him to quit—wondering what kind of man he was, wondering if he was becoming as unprincipled as his father and riding that same slippery slope downhill, wondering if there was such a thing as redemption.

He was in no position to judge another person's motives about anything, least of all Jenny's. Particularly when he'd just screwed her into oblivion. Was he taking advantage of this situation?

Hell, yes. Although he figured currently they were taking advantage of each other. Conflicting views of their past battered at his conscience, along with the madness of the present situation.

He pulled her closer, sliding his hand just below her ribcage. He wasn't sure what he was feeling, but he knew that he wanted her for more than sex. Despite everything she'd told him, despite the betrayal he'd felt not knowing the truth of their past until yesterday, he still wanted to be part of her life. How that could happen with their painful history, he had no idea.

Yet lying next to her and holding her like this quieted his mind. He wasn't sure what to call it. He hadn't experienced peace in such a long time, he'd forgotten what it felt like.

Whatever this new emotion was, he didn't want to give up the respite. At the moment, he was so freaking grateful to have her back in his life, and back in his arms, that he wasn't going to dwell on whether or not he was taking advantage of her. But he had a feeling that keeping this sense of tranquility would require payment.

He would have to forgive Jenny, and he wasn't sure he was ready to do that. To forgive her would mean he'd have to be open to being hurt again, to feeling again. Was this new serenity worth it?

Besides, wasn't he already feeling again? Being able to turn off his emotions had always been a good thing. For now, there was no need to make a decision about changing that or his relationship with her, one way or the other. The situation was too tenuous, and he was too far from a place where any peace he experienced would be temporary at best.

He turned the LED lantern down to the barest hint of light. Gradually he heard her slip into deep, even breathing beside him. She had the tiniest snore that she'd be mortified to know about, but he found it incredibly sexy. In a weird way, the little snore showed she was trusting him with a vulnerability that wasn't there when she was awake. A vulnerability that made him want her again, not that it would have taken much.

Low voices and laughter carried across the camp. A

night bird's call echoed in the dark. He knew he should sleep, but something wasn't sitting right—that gut feeling he'd learned a long time ago not to ignore. It was too quiet. He slid his arm out from under Jenny's waist and moved to leave the bed.

She stirred, turned toward him, and opened her eyes. "Hey, what's—"

He held a finger to his lips, leaning down to whisper in her ear. "Something's wrong. Get dressed while I check things out."

He was off the mattress and pulling on his clothes as she nodded, her eyes wide. His vision had already adjusted to the darkness. He moved confidently across the floor, grabbing his Sig before heading toward the tent flap. He could hear her moving behind him and decided there was no way he was leaving her, even for a moment. But he needed to look outside and see if he could figure out what was going on.

A cry ripped through the night as he opened the tent flap. The not-so-distant sound was cut off abruptly. He guessed it had come from just outside the camp, but he wasn't sure. Was it a guard or someone out for a stroll?

He stared into the darkness. He could see nothing amiss. The night was deathly quiet again—too quiet, like all the ambient sound was being sucked out of the area.

A shock wave rolled through the camp. Chaos erupted as the dining tent exploded. At the same time—shouts, screams, and gunfire broke out on the opposite side of the dig site.

Nick's mind immediately clicked into combat mode.

What was happening? Was someone after Jenny, or was this just random violence?

The whole country was a tinderbox of seething hostility more often than not. Still, it seemed entirely too coincidental that the camp would be attacked the night they arrived.

He didn't have time to dwell on the specifics. He had to assume the worst. *Someone was after Jenny.* He needed an exit plan—yesterday.

He hadn't seen the entire project site when they arrived, but he had a general idea of how things were set up. He could get her out, if they left immediately and didn't stop for anything.

Another explosion rocked the center of the camp as one of the storage tents burst into flames. It was time to go.

JENNIFER STOOD IN the darkness trying to get her bearings. She felt as if she'd been drifting, and she'd finally gotten to sleep when Nick woke her. She hoped he was just being overly cautious, but she suspected he wasn't. Something was dreadfully wrong.

She pulled on her shirt with no bra and dug for her panties in the covers. She was about to give up and go commando when her hands closed over the thin cotton lace. She slid the underwear on and pulled up her shorts. A scream ripped through the night just before a deafening roar that sounded like Armageddon erupting outside.

The reverberation knocked her to the mattress, but

Nick was there, grabbing her hand and pulling at her arm until she was standing. Light from the explosion danced along the wall of the tent in a macabre display.

He snatched up their backpacks and helped her put hers on before sliding his onto a shoulder, then he was towing her relentlessly across the camp toward the darkness at the edge of the site. Smoke and flames rose in the night behind them. She glanced back and saw bodies on the ground. She'd seen this scene before, and she flashed to her memories of Tenancingo for a moment with the bodies on the lawn there.

This couldn't be happening again.

A gush of warm air blew through the camp, pushing smoke and fiery embers from the conflagration into their backs. Nick never slowed down or looked back as they continued rushing toward the outside of the camp and away from the chaos. The smoky haze cast a surreal sense over the entire area.

If only this was a dream.

Nick pulled her beside him into the shadow of a tent. A man she didn't recognize ran past with a gun. She knew it wasn't one of the guards they'd seen when they drove in because he wasn't in uniform. This man was in tribal dress. He stopped a few feet away in the middle of the pathway and pulled the weapon to his shoulder. She stared in horror as he shot a uniformed guard running toward him.

Thinking this was some kind of accident, students and professors emerged from their tents to see what was happening. The man in tribal dress turned to the first two students and took aim on one before Jennifer could shout a warning. One student fell to the ground, and horror rose inside her as the other raised his hands in surrender. Frozen in place, she was too shocked to scream or even protest.

Then Nick was running again, pulling her behind him and heading toward the truck they'd arrived in with Bill. Nick never stopped tugging her along and never offered aid to anyone they passed.

"Stop! We have to help them!" She tried to slow down, clutching at his arm.

"We can't, Jenny. We're surrounded, and I think they're after you." He pulled her into the darkness cast by another tent.

After me? That couldn't be right. They couldn't be after her. Why would they be?

But something inside her whispered he was right. Too many people had tried to do her harm in the past week for this to be a coincidence.

Two other gunmen in tribal dress ran toward them. Definitely not guards from the project, they were headed for the conflagration and shouting to each other—in Spanish?

Jennifer was so surprised that she stopped running and pulled Nick to a halt beside her. The men spied Nick and Jennifer at the same time. One gunman raised his hand to shoot, but Nick shot first, and the man fell backward.

Oh my God. Had he just killed that guy?

Nick was right. They *were* surrounded. How many

were there? Nick changed direction, and this time Jennifer didn't pull away as gunshots rang out around them.

Screams and shouts echoed in the night air. Bile rose in the back of her throat when she realized the students and professors didn't have weapons and were most likely being hit with every shot fired.

Nick grasped her hand with an unrelenting grip but kept her behind him, using his body to shield hers. Finally, they were beyond the camp, which was now completely engulfed in flames. Another explosion rocked the sand beneath her feet.

At this point, she couldn't tell where the blast had originated. Cans of kerosene, cleaning materials for the fossils, and cooking fuel were all part of their supplies. Those items were typically stored in the center of camp to protect them from thieves who might pilfer from supplies stored at the outer edges of a dig.

The attackers didn't have to set off many explosions after the first few because everything fed on itself. The camp burned and the destruction took care of itself. One deliberate fire set in the right place had been enough to start the chaos. But why? What were they gaining by doing this?

The Spanish spoken by the gunman ruled out marauding nomads. Obviously the tribal dress had been used to hide their identity. The only thing that made sense seemed crazy. Could these be the same men who'd been after her in Dallas, Mexico, and Niamey?

Nick guided her toward the vehicles parked outside the camp. In the firelight she could see the outline of

Bill's truck. Earlier, when they'd been running from the camp, she'd wanted to help people. Now, even though it made her feel like a coward, all she wanted was to be in that vehicle and on her way out of the area. Nick tugged her along behind him, and he was reaching for the door handle on the passenger side when he dropped her hand.

"Nick, what's going . . ." The question died on her lips. Two gunmen in tribal clothing stood with rifles aimed directly at them across the hood of the truck.

"Drop your weapon." The man's voice was heavily accented. God, he sounded like the voice from Angela and Drew's house. How was that even possible?

Jennifer and Nick did as he asked. Another gunman approached from the opposite direction and motioned for them to back away from the truck.

The man with the familiar voice jerked Jennifer away from Nick and held her back pressed to his chest, giving her a sickening sense of déjà vu when his body odor overwhelmed her, just as it had in Dallas. He put his hand low on her belly and jerked her closer. His erection pushed against her butt, making her skin crawl.

Between the moon and the firelight, she could clearly see Nick's expression freeze in place. He was staring at her, but his eyes had gone completely blank. She had no clue what he was thinking.

"Ernesto Vega wants you to know that he is not pleased. He wanted information you have not provided."

"I'm sorry to hear that," said Nick.

"You certainly will be." The man holding the gun on

them seemed to be the one in charge. Jenny was relieved it wasn't the man holding her.

"Take me to him, then." Nick leaned against the truck. "I have the information he wants. We need to talk."

The gunman in charge took aim at Nick's head. "I don't believe you. You're just trying to save yourself."

"I have the name he wanted."

"Give it to me."

"So you can shoot me and rape her?" Nick shook his head and laughed with a dark humor. "I don't think so. I'll talk only to Ernesto."

The leader stared hard at him then back at Jennifer before nodding to "Body Odor." Body Odor moved his hand from her abdomen and took hold of her wrist from behind. He twisted her arm back at an impossible angle and squeezed, while at the same time wrenching her fingers in a painful burst of agony. Gasping in surprise and anguish, she was amazed her wrist didn't snap.

Biting her lip against the pain, she stared straight ahead, even as he let go and smoothed his hand down her body from shoulder to hip. She wanted to vomit when his hand slowed at her breast. Whispering in her ear in Spanish, he rubbed his fingers against her nipples. She was grateful she couldn't understand whatever gutter phrases she was certain he was using.

Nick moved to walk toward them but stopped when the leader shoved a gun in his face. "I still won't give you the name. What do you think Ernesto will do when you give him a 'damaged' woman and then tell him you lost the information he sent you to retrieve? Take me to Ernesto, or at least deliver me along with her. Let your boss decide how best to deal with my impertinence."

"If you insist." The lead gunman nodded.

The third man stepped up from the shadows. With no warning, he struck Nick in the back of the head with the butt of a rifle.

Chapter Twenty-One

Friday evening

NICK GRADUALLY WOKE to darkness. The back of his skull throbbed in mind-numbing agony, even as his face rested on something soft. Fingers brushed his cheek. It took a moment for him to realize his head was in someone's lap. He felt as if he was being rocked by a hyperactive child on a trampoline.

"You awake?" whispered Jenny. Her voice came from above him. There was a slight shifting beneath his head. His neck rested on her thigh.

He breathed the stifling air and took a moment to wish he were somewhere else. It had to be over one hundred degrees in here, wherever *here* was. A mechanical white noise muffled any clue to their location.

"You okay?" she asked, a bit louder this time.

He started to nod and remembered his head at the last

minute, choosing to speak instead. He most likely had a concussion. "Yeah, think so." His mouth was dry as dust, and his lips cracked with his answer.

She touched his face again.

The last thing he remembered was standing beside the truck at the edge of the camp and getting hit from behind. "Where are we? How long have I been out?" He had his suspicions but desperately hoped he was wrong. Now that he was acclimating, he could hear others in the darkness.

"They put us both in the back of an SUV and drove into the desert to meet a two-and-a-half-ton truck. You've been out almost a day. Scared me to death."

"How long exactly?" His voice was stronger this time.

Jenny picked up his wrist and looked at his digital watch. "Maybe eighteen, nineteen hours? It felt like forever."

He figured it had been a while, if his bladder was any indication. Eighteen hours meant it was now Friday night. "How many men are up front?" he asked.

"I saw three," she said. "They stopped a few hours ago and gave everyone water."

"I need you to be sure."

She blew out a quick breath.

"It's definitely three," another woman said from the other side of Nick.

He started to turn his head and stopped himself. "How many people are in here with us?" he asked.

"Twenty." The same voice answered.

"You think it's that many?" asked Jenny.

"I counted heads before they put me on. It was light when I was loaded. We're all very cozy here." The woman speaking, whoever she was, had an accent like Leland's. She sounded like she was from the deep South—Alabama, Mississippi, or Georgia—definitely not Texas. "Although how many of them are still alive is questionable. Some of these girls have been in transit for over a month."

"Where are they from?" asked Nick.

"Benin, Mali, Nigeria, Venezuela, and Mexico. The ones from overseas have been travelling the longest and are in the worst shape."

"What about you? How long have you been here?" asked Nick.

"I joined the party a few hours before you two did."

"Who are you?" Jenny asked.

"I might ask you the same thing. You're not the usual cargo, I can tell. They made a special stop for you."

"My name's Jennifer Grayson." She volunteered the information before Nick could stop her.

The woman paused a beat before replying, as if the news had startled her. "Nice to meet you. My name's Sassy, Sassy Smith."

Smith? Nick tried to focus on figuring out if he'd ever heard of a Sassy Smith, but his head was so muddled he wasn't sure if the name rang a bell or not. His gut said the woman knew more than she was telling.

But his own bell had been rung so hard earlier, he didn't trust his own judgment. He smiled before realizing that his head injury might be somewhat serious if he considered that idea amusing.

"How did you end up here, Sassy?" Jenny's voice was calm and low.

"That's a long story." Sassy's answer was vaguely reminiscent of Bryan Fisher's when he didn't want to talk about something.

"It appears we have time," said Nick.

"Who are you?" asked Sassy.

"My name's Nick."

"Well, Nick, do you have a last name, or is that a one-name moniker like Prince or Cher or Lassie?"

Nick snorted a laugh along with Jenny. He was surprised when she answered for him. "Oh, he's definitely a rock star."

Sassy chuckled with them both.

"How'd you end up here?" Nick repeated Jenny's question.

"I'm a freelance reporter. A contact mentioned some trouble Dr. Grayson was having."

Dr. Grayson. How did Sassy know that Jenny was a doctor? He got the impression the two women hadn't spoken much before now since Jenny didn't appear to know Sassy's history.

"What are you doing here in Africa?" he asked.

"I've been working on a story about the crossover between drug and human trafficking in Mexico." Sassy paused a minute before continuing. "I think I may have stepped on some toes."

"What makes you think that?" Nick couldn't get a bead on Sassy Smith. Something about her seemed off.

"As soon as I talked to my source, I was busted. And

for the record, all your questions make this feel like an inquisition."

"Who was your source?" Jenny asked.

"Did you two practice this beforehand?" Sassy muttered. "I'm a reporter. I don't share sources."

Nick sighed, frustrated he wasn't thinking clearly enough to recognize all the implications of what Sassy was telling them. Something was right here in front of him, and he couldn't see it.

"Why do you think this has something to do with your story?" he asked, ignoring Sassy's snide comments.

"Ever since I started asking questions about a drug and trafficking crossover, even before I got here, someone's been following me."

"Who?" Jenny asked.

"I don't know. But it's not the cartel," said Sassy. "It's too . . . smooth. They wouldn't bother hiding their tracks like this."

"Do you think it's government?" asked Nick, intensely curious with a growing feeling of dread as pieces of the puzzle started coming together.

"Maybe," said Sassy. Something in her voice still sounded wrong. He didn't know a thing about her, but he didn't like it. "I can't be su—"

"Why are you telling us this?" interrupted Nick. "You don't know us or a thing about us."

"Actually, I do know about you. You're back here and not riding up front. I figure that means you aren't one of the bad guys."

"You're a reporter. You don't strike me as someone

that naïve," said Nick. "Why are you really telling us this?"

There was a long silence before she spoke again. "Because you're Bryan Fisher's partner, right? You work for AEGIS?"

Finally, Nick got it, the thing he hadn't been able to grasp. Bryan was how Sassy had known Jenny was a doctor.

"I met with Bryan yesterday at a café in Niamey. We traded information, and he left in a hurry. He wouldn't tell me why, just said he had to talk to someone right away. I think maybe he was coming for you."

Not likely, thought Nick. Instead he asked, "So, what happened?"

Sassy leaned forward as she spoke, directing her voice toward him. "I headed back to my hotel after the meeting, but I was picked up on the street in a van before I got there. They blindfolded me. I was on a plane for a while before I was put on this truck, then you two joined us."

"What did you tell Bryan?" asked Nick.

"I consider him a source."

Of course she did. Nick gritted his teeth and counted to ten, twenty, then fifty, before speaking. "I know you don't want to share that information with me, but if we stand a snowball's chance in hell of getting out of this, I need to know what's going on."

There was a long moment of silence, broken only by the white noise of the truck's engine and the occasional mutter or moan from other women in the truck.

"I told Bryan that the Vegas and Riveras were definitely working together smuggling drugs and women across Africa. I showed him a map that I'd gotten from a source outlining the cartel's trafficking routes. There was a stop at a place near Ingal. Bryan got fairly torqued when he saw it."

Nick thought through the attack on the dig site. While several people had known they were headed there, no one had known the exact timing.

Shit. Just like that, things that had been out of focus and fuzzy started to crystallize. Nick had been blind.

As much as he hated to consider the possibilities, he had to. Could Ernesto Vega's suspicions about government and AEGIS involvement in last month's attack on the Rivera compound and the vet clinic be true?

There wasn't any way to know for certain at this point. Nick sure as hell didn't like to think about it, but he'd be foolish not to consider the possibility that someone within AEGIS or close to their organization was dirty.

Could it have been Bryan? Maybe. Maybe not.

It certainly was more than a possibility if Hollywood was telling reporters about them. God, he didn't want to believe that. Why would the man have given up Jenny's name? Nick supposed there could have been any number of reasons, but he couldn't think of one that didn't have unpleasant implications.

The only way anyone could have known about Nick and Jenny being at the Paleo-Niger dig at that particular time was if someone with an inside track to AEGIS had told them. Just like the only way anyone could have known about Nick and Jenny being at the hotel in Niamey was if they were being fed information by someone privy to their plans. Could it have been the same with the brothel in Tenancingo?

Nick had left a message via the SAT phone as they'd arrived at the dig site. But Bryan had checked in with Gavin and Leland both when they arrived at the hotel in Niamey. Nick had called as they'd landed in Mexico before going into the brothel in Tenancingo.

Indisputably someone at AEGIS, or someone with access to AEGIS information, was selling them out.

But who was it?

Bryan? Leland? Gavin? Marissa? Someone else with a connection to AEGIS? It seemed impossible and unthinkable on all counts. Still, cartels could offer too much money to assume anyone was incorruptible.

Whoever it was, Nick had to discover who was dirty now, or at least eliminate possibilities before he reached out for help again.

JENNIFER COULD FEEL Nick's tension ratcheting up as Sassy spoke quietly beside her. She was zip-tied at her wrists and chained to the truck wall behind her with about two feet of steel. Her fingers were on Nick's cheek, but she couldn't get as close as she wanted with Sassy's head bent over her lap. It was hard to hear over the truck's engine and the woman was whispering, bowing forward by Nick's face. Eventually, Sassy tilted back, done with her part of the conversation.

Jennifer leaned down to Nick and lowered her voice. "What did she say? What's going on?"

"I don't know." He tried to sit up but couldn't.

Jennifer wasn't sure if it was getting hit in the head that had him so out of it or if it was what Sassy had told him that kept his head in her lap. He wasn't chained to the side of the truck like she was; he was simply handcuffed with zip ties, but he seemed almost incapacitated.

He reached for her hand and held it to his lips, despite his shackled wrists. She drifted down as close to his face as possible. "What's going to happen to us?" she asked.

"I don't know." He kept hold of her palm and kissed her fingertips again.

"Is it okay for me to be scared?"

She felt his smile against her hand. "I'd think you were a little crazy if you weren't scared," he said.

"Where do you think they're taking us?"

"Not sure. Could be Algeria. I imagine they want to deliver these women first. They're going to need a port for that or a cargo plane and a secluded airstrip."

"I'd say we have the secluded part down." She squeezed his hand.

"We'll have to travel through the Hoggar if they're headed for Algeria. I'm not sure what the closest port would be. Algiers is over thirteen hundred miles from where we were at the dig site."

"We've been travelling for almost a day. Surely it'll be less than that now, unless we're riding in the opposite direction?"

He nodded against her hands in the darkness. "If Algiers is where we're headed, it's still not exactly a Sunday drive."

"Do you think they'll take us all the way to wherever they're going?" she asked.

His laughter vibrated against her thighs, but his voice didn't sound cheerful. "As opposed to dropping us in the desert?" he asked. "I think we'd just as soon ride in the truck, darlin'."

Darlin'? Did that mean anything?

She was too keyed up to dwell on the thought, but for a moment it made her feel less frightened. Still, the words were no sooner out of his mouth than she felt the downshift of the truck's engine, and they rolled to a stop.

"Or maybe not," he muttered.

The cloth doorway of the two-and-a-half-ton truck was pulled to the side, and a flashlight shone in their eyes. Two men in stained white T-shirts pulled Nick out of Jennifer's lap despite her protest.

Another man pulled himself inside the truck bed and began to unfasten the chains that tethered her in, but he didn't unfasten her wrists. *What is he going to do?*

Outside Nick was propped up between the other two men. His head hung down as if he wasn't able to hold himself upright. She hadn't realized he was so weak. They shuffled him off to the side where she could no longer see him.

The man dealing with her chain had to climb farther in to release her, and a couple of the women seated in the darkness inside started moaning, almost keening. The eerie sound echoed all around her.

The man managed to touch Jennifer's breasts and squeeze her butt from the side as he moved closer to unlock her chain. She knew without being told that this was to be expected. Wherever he was about to take her, it wouldn't be pleasant.

The other women's reactions seemed to confirm it. Ambient light from the stars overhead reflected off the sand outside and revealed the man holding part of her chain wrapped around his own wrist, pulling the slack out of the way in an effort to get to the lock behind her.

She heard rather than saw what happened next: an *oomph* and a cry from outside the truck was cut short. Light from a flashlight threw zigzag shadows across the canvas at the back of the vehicle. The man dealing with her turned as Nick burst around the corner with his wrists still in zip ties.

One of the other men grabbed Nick around the waist from behind, and he disappeared from view again. She heard another short cry. A gunshot tore through the night.

Jennifer screamed as she jerked hard on the chain holding her by the waist. The man dealing with her tripped inside at her feet. Sassy came forward, clobbering him in the head with both hands over and over again, holding what looked like a wedge-heeled shoe between her bound wrists.

"Having to wear heels all the time has to be good for something," the petite woman muttered.

Where was Nick?

Jennifer pulled at her chains, but she was still attached to the truck bed. Her line of sight was blocked by the canvas side of the truck. She was powerless to help or even see what had happened until she was free.

Sassy came up with the keys to the chain from the now unconscious man's pocket and unlocked Jennifer, before moving to loosen the chain that ran between each woman and the sides of the truck. The freed women found a knife on the prone guard and started cutting the others' plastic cuffs.

Jennifer slipped to the edge of the tailgate, still in her zip ties, searching the darkness for Nick. One moment there was nothing but empty space and the dim light from the stars, the next he stood before her. She stifled her own squeal, all but tumbling off the back and into his chest.

His heart raced against her cheek as his arms came around her waist. His nose was bloody, the zip tie was broken off from his hands, and his wrists were bleeding. But he was holding a gun with a competence that made her feel infinitely safer.

"Are you okay? God, I thought . . ." She couldn't finish. The frightening thoughts about what could have happened rose inside her like a hot angry tide, clawing to get out.

He pulled her closer and pressed a kiss to the top of her head. "Yeah. I'm alright now."

She swallowed hard against the panic and looked around, still processing it all. The man Sassy had hit with her shoe was out cold, and the other women from the back of the truck were free. The two men who'd had Nick were on the ground alongside the truck. She wondered if they were dead or just wounded. She was surprised that she didn't care if they were indeed dead.

This area didn't appear as bleak as Jennifer had first assumed. It wasn't a true desert, but rather the edge of another oasis settlement. Beyond the front of the truck, lights shone in the distance, illuminating palm trees and homes constructed of *banco* outlined by moonlight. The men had definitely been stopping here for some "recreation" before heading into the town.

Jennifer turned her head back into Nick's chest. "What do we do now?" she asked.

At her question his body tensed up completely in her arms. "Stand perfectly still," he said.

"What?" She tried to pull away.

He tightened his hold. "We've got company."

Three more men, much better dressed than the ones who'd been driving the truck, stepped around the canvas side of the vehicle. All held scary-looking weapons pointed directly at them.

Jennifer turned and watched as Sassy froze, then sank to her seat in the truck. One of the three gunmen moved to the tailgate and directed all the newly freed women to sit back down. The second man began cuffing and chaining them again.

The other gunman took Nick's weapon and directed him and Jennifer to the front of the truck. They stepped from relative darkness into the blue white beams of headlights from both the canvas-topped truck and a four-door Mercedes parked beside it.

"Hello, Mr. Donovan." The accented voice came from the shadows. "It seems I had to find you rather than the other way around. I'm not sure I believe you are that good at what you do after all."

Chapter Twenty-Two

SHIT. NICK RECOGNIZED the voice immediately.

"What is it?" whispered Jennifer.

He didn't answer but pulled her behind him as Ernesto Vega stepped from the shadows.

"I was told you had information for me," said the cartel leader.

Nick shrugged. He'd lied at the camp about having a name for Ernesto. Saving Jennifer from being assaulted and sparing his own life had seemed worth the risk.

If Vega's fantastic accusations were true about a drone attack on the Rivera compound and the vet clinic, Nick leaned toward believing there was a U.S. government connection. And after his conversation with Sassy, he had to consider that someone in AEGIS could be involved as well. But he wasn't ready to share his theories with anyone yet, much less Ernesto Vega.

"You ignored my request. I don't take disobedience

well." Ernesto motioned for another man to come forward who'd been watching from the shadows beside the sedan. The man looked vaguely familiar.

"You should get used to disappointment. It builds character," said Nick.

Ernesto sighed, and his two men stepped closer. One patted Nick down a second time for weapons. Without warning, the other punched Nick in the back at his kidney. As Nick reeled to the side, "Pat Down Guy" hit him with an upper cut to the jaw.

Combined with the lick to his head he'd received earlier, Nick wasn't surprised that he came to on the sand. He was out only a few seconds, but his brain felt like a scrambled egg.

The headlights illuminated his immediate surroundings perfectly. Jenny's face blanched, and tears shimmered in her eyes as the two men pulled him roughly to his feet.

The man who'd hit him in the kidney grabbed Jenny and pulled her into his body, wrapping his hand possessively around her waist. He whispered something in her ear, and she bit her lip. A lone tear broke free and slid down her cheek.

"What do you want with me?" Nick's mouth was bleeding, among other things. But he wanted their attention on him, not on Jenny.

Ernesto moved closer and got in Nick's face. "I thought I made that perfectly clear a week ago. I want to know who killed my brother and my sister. Surely you've been able to figure that out by now. Is it someone at AEGIS?" The man's words were clipped, his eyes wild and unfocused.

Nick shrugged with an air of nonchalance he didn't feel. "I've been trying to find out, but it seems your family is into some sketchy stuff."

Pat Down Guy shoved the butt of a Heckler & Koch MP5 into Nick's abdomen—once, twice, three times before Ernesto held up his hand to stop. Ernesto pulled a .357 Magnum from his own shoulder holster and pressed the barrel against Nick's forehead.

"I could shoot you. There's no reason I can think of as to why you should live." Ernesto stared into Nick's eyes; his own were cold and devoid of emotion.

Nick knew that look. He'd worn it himself in the past. And that particular weapon he was holding would more than get the job done. At point-blank range the revolver would practically take his head off.

Undaunted, Nick stared back. If he blinked, he was dead. And Jenny was dead, or worse.

Ernesto seemed to read his mind and turned his attention to her, swinging the gun around to Jenny's chest. The other man still had his arm around her waist.

Nick tried to move toward her but was held back.

"I would think you would know how this feels. You're the one whose . . ." Ernesto stopped talking and studied Nick in the white beams of the multiple head lights. The look in his eyes was coldly calculating, even as the man seemed to lose interest in Jenny. Nick fought not to respond to the relief coursing through his body.

"Reese Donovan was a conflicted man," said Ernesto.

The sudden chill in Nick's chest at hearing Vega mention his father made the pain from the punches thrown earlier feel insignificant. "How do you know my father's name?"

"Know thy enemy and all that shit." Ernesto smiled with a grim insincerity. "Don't you ever wonder what really happened to him?" He lowered the .357, but Nick had gone completely cold—the way you did when you knew you were about to hear something you didn't want to know.

"I have information for you, even though you've brought me nothing." Ernesto's laugh sounded liked a crow's cackle. "I'm a giver that way." He turned to the man holding Jenny. "Juan, put Dr. Grayson in the truck."

Ernesto pivoted back to Nick. "Yes, I did learn her real name, no thanks to you, Mr. Donovan. Santos, take the shipment and all the other men with you, except Félix. The women must be in Constantine by seven AM."

Juan Santos nodded and started for the back of the truck, dragging a struggling Jenny along with him. Something caught the man's attention out of sight of the others, and he stopped at the edge of the vehicle's hood. "Mario's dead," he called, looking toward the back of the truck where Nick knew he'd left two bodies.

"Happens to us all eventually," said Vega.

Nick heard Jenny gasp in what sounded like pain. He strained against Ernesto's last man, trying to see what Juan was doing to her. But Félix, aka Pat Down Guy, was ready for him, and Nick couldn't get away. He heard

Jenny shout, then the sound of a hand striking flesh, then nothing.

Moments later Santos was climbing behind the wheel of the canvas-sided truck along with the other men who'd been securing the women earlier in the back. Apparently, the one who'd been laid out cold by Sassy was remaining in the truck bed.

Without a word the men drove into the darkness with Jenny, Sassy, and the other women—leaving Nick alone with Ernesto and Félix. Nick watched the truck's progress, and his stomach churned.

Once these women were shipped from the coast, they'd never get away from the traffickers. They'd be turning tricks on the streets of Milan or Paris until they were dead either from drugs, AIDS, or some overzealous john or pimp.

He could taste the bitterness in the back of his throat. As the taillights disappeared in the darkness, Nick studied Ernesto. This was about to get very ugly. He strove for a disinterested expression but doubted he was selling it too well.

He assumed Ernesto was planning to kill him and leave his body here in the desert. But what was he going to do with Jenny? Her fate wouldn't be much brighter than Nick's unless he did something right away.

He shifted on his feet, desperately trying to detach from the conversation, from the situation. Where was his iceman persona now? He had to ignore the danger to Jenny and to all those women, or he'd never regain control.

"What, no interest in your father?" asked Ernesto. "And here I thought you were such a family guy."

Nick took a deep, silent breath. "What can you possibly tell me about Reese Donovan that matters? My parents have been dead for a long time." He'd prefer to know what was happening with Jenny, and why Ernesto had been after her to begin with.

It was Ernesto's turn to shrug. "You never know. You might learn something."

Nick clenched his jaw. He was on the edge of losing control and didn't want to hear anything about his father. There'd been such a sense of betrayal when the news broke about Reese Donovan's embezzlement. It was why Nick had changed his plan for law school, wanting nothing to do with anything resembling his father's career path.

Ernesto sensed Nick's discomfort and absolutely reveled in it. "I can't tell you everything, but you should know by now that the past, as well as the present, isn't always what we think it is."

The flash of anger was there instantly, and Nick couldn't stop himself from snarling, "What the hell kind of mumbo jumbo is that? I don't give a damn about my father. I want to know why you've been targeting Jennifer."

Ernesto laughed, true humor in his tone at last. "This has never been about Dr. Grayson. This was always about you, Mr. Donovan. You and your family. It was personal."

Nick shook his head. What did his family have to do with this? It didn't make sense.

Ernesto studied Nick a moment, and the look in his eyes was one of genuine pity. "You think your father and mother died in a simple car accident?"

Nick cocked his head to the side, a growing ball of *something*—he wasn't sure what to call it—in his chest. He'd never wanted to believe it. Not really.

Had his father missed that curve on purpose and gone off the embankment to avoid embezzlement charges?

Nick had certainly never wanted to hear that out loud. Still, the vague suspicion had settled in the back of his mind years ago in the aftermath of the accident, amid whispers and insinuations from police investigators and insurance companies.

Ernesto smiled and nodded. "That's right. Everything is not always as it appears—"

A muffled sound, like a loud champagne cork popping, interrupted him. Nick recognized the true source almost instantaneously and ducked, even as Félix held his arms. The sniper's silenced shot had come from the shadows beyond the Mercedes and struck Ernesto Vega squarely between the eyes. Vega was dead before he hit the ground.

Félix hesitated a moment too long, caught in the surreal scene of watching his boss die so quickly. The hesitation cost him everything. The man was dead and sprawled beside Ernesto as Nick dove to the sand beside both bodies. Ernesto's gun had fallen too far away to be retrieved, but Nick pulled Félix's MP5 along with him as he army crawled across the ground to the Mercedes. Ignoring the pain in his ribs, he moved on pure adrenaline.

The keys were in the ignition. *Thank God*. The shots whizzed by his head, indiscriminately coming from the shadows in a quiet-but-lethal barrage. That wasn't anyone from AEGIS out there, at least no one who wanted to help Nick get out of this alive.

He crawled into the driver's seat and made a plan at the same time. His ice-like calm was back. First, he had to catch up to that truck and get to Jenny. He had no clue what else Ernesto had been talking about, so the mystery of how this involved his family would have to wait.

Everything is not always as it appears.

That wasn't exactly a news flash. But the idea of someone Nick trusted being involved in all this was frightening and brought up the same feelings of betrayal he'd experienced over ten years ago when his father died, and Nick's life imploded.

He turned the ignition key and pressed his foot down on the accelerator. The road before him was half-covered with sand, but he could see well enough. The back window shattered, and the car fishtailed. Then he was out of range of the sniper.

Saturday, early morning
Algeria

NICK DROVE WITH one hand on the wheel and an eye on the rearview mirror. To find Jenny he was going to need help locating the truck. If Ernesto was to be believed, she and the others were on their way to Constantine—but that was a city of well over 400,000 people. His options were extraordinarily limited unless he used AEGIS resources.

It was almost a certainty that someone he worked with or who had access to those he worked with had tried to kill him and Jenny. The kicker was that he needed AEGIS to locate her, so he was going to have to choose someone there to trust. And he was going to have to do it now.

Rather than evaluating the muddy information currently at his disposal, he'd probably have better luck discovering the traitor by closing his eyes, spinning around, and picking someone in what would amount to a game of pin the tail on the rat. In this particular situation his gut was no help, and he was out of time.

It wasn't as if Nick had never had to consider someone betraying him before. He'd experienced similar scenarios in his work with the CIA. But then the betrayal had been somewhat expected. Not trusting those around you was part of the job. At AEGIS, it had never been a consideration. Nick's naiveté in his current situation surprised the hell out of him because he'd never seen it coming.

Gavin, Leland, Marissa, Bryan. Who was the least likely to be involved with the cartel? None of them was likely, and Nick didn't want to consider any of them, but he had to.

Leland had the most to lose with his new "instant family." He also had the least contact with the office since he was still out with his leg in a cast from his own misadventures last month. Even though this had all started when Leland first arrived on the scene at AEGIS, the man had saved Nick's ass in Mexico at considerable risk to himself. He'd worked at AEGIS the least amount of time, too.

Trusting Leland wouldn't mean Nick thought anyone else there was guilty. Instead, he would just be acknowledging that Leland was the least likely of the four to be involved. Jesus, what was he thinking? Did he really believe any of them were involved?

Enough. He was playing mind games with himself. It was time to do this.

Félix's MP5 had a full clip, so life wasn't as bleak as it could have been. Still, Nick's SAT phone was long gone. Thankfully a cell phone rested in a cradle on the dash of the Mercedes. It must have belonged to Félix or Ernesto. None of the men who'd driven off in the truck would have left their phones behind.

Nick clicked the dialing mechanism on the steering wheel and got an open line without needing a password. Thank God for drug dealers who didn't believe in password-protected phones.

He was about to put Jenny's life into someone else's hands. Could he do this? Moments later Leland's voice flowed over the line, and the time for decision-making and second-guessing was past. Nick quashed any lingering doubts about the man's loyalties and dove in. He had to trust someone now.

"It's me, Leland. It's Nick."

"Are you okay?"

"Define 'okay.'" Nick huffed a bleak laugh and summarized the events of the past twenty-four hours, including the truck leaving with Jenny, Ernesto's death, and—after a short pause—his suspicions about someone possibly playing both sides within AEGIS.

"Damn," Leland breathed. "I'm not sure where to start. I thought you were just going to tell me you needed to arrange transport out of the country. Who at AEGIS would do this?"

Nick kept his eyes on the road ahead as he listened carefully for any inflection or tone that didn't ring true. "I have no idea. I only know it's not you, and it's not me. So I'm starting there and moving forward. Fill in any gaps you heard when I described the—"

"Wait a minute," interrupted Leland. "Not that I'm arguing, but how do you know it's not me?"

"If you were on the other side of this, you'd have left me bleeding in Tomas Rivera's driveway last month. No one would have blamed you. If I was dirty, it's what I would have done. I sure as hell wouldn't have jumped out of that Hummer and taken a bullet getting me out of there."

The hiss on the phone was soft but definitely audible as Leland took a minute to absorb that. It was the closest Nick would come to saying he trusted the man.

"Of course, I'm not sure how straight I'm really thinking. I'm practically seeing double at this point. I could have it all wrong."

"Ah, fuck you," said Leland, without any real heat.

"You're cute, but not my type. Now, fill in any gaps you heard earlier when I described the situation," Nick repeated.

"You mentioned a guy that Ernesto referred to as Santos. Most likely that's Juan Santos. Watch out for that fucker. He's a nasty piece of work. He'd just as soon sell someone out as work for them. He's been on the payroll for both sides of the Rivera-Vega feud from time to time. He's all about whoever pays more."

"Surprises me they'd keep using him," said Nick.

"As opposed to just killing him? I agree, but apparently he comes in handy from time to time. Santos has got such a reputation as a liar, no one ever knows if what he's saying is true or not. So the disloyalty can work in the employer's favor if they're trying to spread disinformation. Still, I believe the man has a very short shelf life."

"Understood." Nick thought about how Santos had held Jenny, and for a frightening moment he flashed on what would happen to her if he didn't find her soon. He forced himself to loosen his grip on the wheel.

"What else do you need?" asked Leland.

"I put a GPS tracker in the pocket of Jenny's shorts as we got to the dig site. She didn't realize I was doing it. After she flew to Niamey alone, I swore I wasn't letting her out of my sight again until this was over. A GPS app for the tracker was running on the AEGIS server and my phone, but I don't have the phone anymore. I think she's somewhere on the road to Constantine. Can you look it up on your computer and give me the exact coordinates?"

"I'm opening my laptop now."

Nick exhaled. He'd made the right call. "Once I have eyes on her, I'll give my contact in the embassy at Algiers a call. I should be able to access some resources to get the women out. I figure Marissa can help me if I can't get through on my own." He'd known Risa a long time, and he was going to have to trust her, at least for her contacts within the embassy. He didn't mention that he would share as little as possible with his boss until he knew what was going on within AEGIS. That was understood.

"That's probably not a good idea," said Leland.

Nick could tell he was typing as they talked. "I understand it's a risk with all the unknowns. And I hate having to call in the cavalry, but I'm out of options here. The State Department won't get involved for those other women, but Sassy and Jenny are both U.S. citizens kidnapped on foreign soil. I've got a concussion, one weapon, and no backup. I need help."

"I understand, but that's not the issue." Leland sounded extremely unhappy. Something in his tone had warning bells going off.

"What's going on there?" The calm Nick thought he'd regained evaporated like raindrops on a hot sidewalk.

The AEGIS relationship with the U.S. State Department was a refuge of last resort. Nonetheless, it was a relationship that was extraordinarily valuable. It could mean the difference between getting out of a foreign country safely with a client or rotting in a third-world jail cell for several months, or even years, while diplomatic avenues were pursued.

AEGIS was known for their results and being able to step in when U.S. officials' hands were tied by diplomacy. Gavin's group left a mess sometimes, but his and Marissa's contacts within the embassies and consulates around the world were worth their weight in gold. The families of AEGIS's clients would argue that a diplomatic headache was a small price to pay for having their loved ones back home.

Without those embassy contacts, AEGIS operatives were on their own. In some cases that was preferable, in others it was impossible, like now. Nick wasn't fool enough to think he could rescue twenty-plus women on his own with his current lack of resources.

"It's complicated," said Leland, "particularly in light of what you just told me."

"Dammit, I'm not four years old. 'It's complicated' is not an answer."

"You're not going to like this," said Leland.

There was a long pause, and for a few seconds Nick thought they'd been disconnected.

"It's Gavin," said Leland. "There's a warrant out for his arrest."

Chapter Twenty-Three

"Arrest? For what?" The fear Nick had been trying to ignore since the conversation in the truck with Sassy came roaring to the forefront of his mind. "Christ, talk about burying the lead. Why didn't you tell me this first?"

"Chill the hell out, Nick. You and I both know it's bullshit."

Immediately, Nick's unnatural icy calm was back. Betrayal had that effect on him. "Tell me what's going on. Now."

"Gavin is suspected of collaborating with the cartels. DEA and FBI agents have been crawling all over the AEGIS office for the past two hours."

The same AEGIS office that had been Nick's home for the past year. "I sure as hell hope it's bullshit," Nick muttered, but Ernesto's words echoed in his head. *"Everything is not always as it appears—"*

Did Gavin sell them out?

Leland's sigh was long and heavy. "I realize the evidence looks bad, but I think Gavin's being set up."

"Even after what we just talked about?"

"Yes, I'm sure. I'd bet my life on it," said Leland.

"Well, I wouldn't." Blind loyalty could get you killed. Nick knew that from experience, but he wasn't going to argue the point. Leland knew it, too. He wasn't a stupid man.

"What's the evidence against Gavin? Do you know?" asked Nick.

"Yeah, I know. My old boss, Ford Johnson, is in charge of the investigation. There's an obscene amount of money in an offshore account in Gavin's name. And he's disappeared with no explanation."

"You do realize he's been in a bad place since Kat—"

"Yes, of course I know that," snapped Leland. "But I don't think losing his wife to cancer would have driven him to this. They grieved together for months before she died. I won't believe he's lost it so completely now."

Nick hated this, hated suspecting someone who was a friend. He'd known Gavin for six years. They'd worked together on several operations when Nick was with the NCS and Gavin was still with the DEA. Gavin had had his back multiple times.

Could it be true? Ernesto's words and Nick's own growing suspicions were toxic.

Leland's voice pulled him from the miserable direction his thoughts were taking. "The only reason they didn't bring me in was because I'm so new to AEGIS. And the DEA just finished investigating me thoroughly before the Colton trial last month."

"What's everyone else doing? Where's Marissa?" asked Nick.

"Risa's gone to ground, or that's what I assume. I haven't heard from her in several hours. Until we know what's going on, there don't seem to be many other options, unless everyone else wants to end up in jail, too."

Leland's frustration made his Southern accent thicker, if that was possible. "I'm pretty sure she's working another angle. She wouldn't go into it with me when we spoke. Hell, for all I know she could be with Gavin."

The sound of Leland's voice became muffled, as if he was putting his hand over the receiver and speaking to someone else. *"Anna, I'll help get the meds together for Zach in just a minute. Go ahead and get your things packed."*

The line went quiet. When Leland spoke again, his voice was calmer. "It's gotten crazy. The evidence they have on Gavin looks so damn bad. I don't believe it, but I'm not taking any chances with the cartels involved. I'm checking Anna and Zach into a hotel for a few days."

Nick sped through the night. It was suddenly easier to talk this through than to chase the conflicting thoughts around in his head. "I think that's an excellent idea. For all we know Gavin was set up. Ernesto wanted answers about his brother's and sister's deaths, and he wouldn't have cared who he ruined in the process of getting them."

Static over the phone buzzed. "Things are much more likely to get worse before they get better, aren't they?" asked Leland. He was closer to Gavin than Nick was.

The evidence must have been fairly damning for Leland to be so shaken. Still, Nick was relieved to hear the man was moving his family to a hotel. He would bet money Leland wasn't telling anyone at AEGIS where that hotel was, either. The people he cared about most were at too big a risk to ignore the possibility of what Gavin's alleged betrayal could mean. Staying off the radar meant keeping everyone safe.

"You need to keep a low profile." Leland voiced Nick's own thoughts. "So, no showing up at the embassy in Algiers. I'm concerned they'd arrest you as soon as look at you. Then Jennifer Grayson will be completely on her own. I'm into the backdoor access with the AEGIS server now. I don't know how long I'll be able to stay on before the investigative team at the office notices and takes it down, but I'll give you everything I can for as long as I can. Give me the ID for the tracker."

Nick recited the first five numbers of the ID code for the device. He'd known losing his phone could strand him with no way to trace her, so he'd memorized the GPS bug's opening identification sequence before slipping it into Jenny's pocket at the Paleo-Niger camp. Kissing her in front of everyone on their arrival had seemed as good a way as any to establish their cover and to distract her from what his hands were really doing in her shorts pocket.

"I've got the GPS coordinates," said Leland.

Nick scrambled for a pen in the console and wrote them on his arm as Leland read them. "Got it. I'll contact you when I know more. Keep GPS text coordinates coming as long as you can. Perhaps every thirty minutes or so?"

"Will do," said Leland. "Look, I know you don't really like him, but Hosea Alvarez is in Africa. He's still working with Ernesto Vega."

"Hosea from Tenancingo?"

"That's right. He called me the day before yesterday. Ernesto hired him to go with him to Africa. Do you want me to reach out to him? Hosea could help you."

Nick wasn't so sure the confidential informant would be much help. He was fairly certain Hosea wasn't one of the dead men back by the oasis, but that didn't mean Leland's CI was still alive or could be trusted if he was. Hell, Hosea Alvarez could have been the shooter at the oasis for all Nick knew. But Hosea was the only resource in the country Nick had, and beggars couldn't be choosers.

"Alright, Leland, call him. You really trust this guy, don't you?" Immediately a text pinged on Nick's "borrowed" phone with Alvarez's contact information.

"I do," said Leland. "He won't sell you out. At least not till he shakes me down for money first."

"Well, that's just comforting as hell." Nick smiled, feeling the tension loosen ever so slightly along his jaw.

"Seriously, Hosea has excellent contacts. Vega has had him setting up the cartel's network over the northern portion of the continent, particularly East Africa, for the trafficking and smuggling. Hosea knows where all the players are."

Okay, so maybe Hosea wasn't the man who shot Vega. Still, Nick wasn't entirely comfortable putting his and Jenny's safety into a confidential informant's hands, no matter what kind of recommendation Leland gave him.

Right now it was a moot point, since Nick didn't know where Jenny was or where Hosea was for that matter. And if push came to shove, there might be no other option but to trust the man.

"I realize this is not ideal," said Leland. "Particularly with the cartel on your ass."

"No shit, it's not ideal. Quit trying to cheer me up. You sound like Gavin with his flair for the understatement." Nick typed GPS coordinates into a map app that was already installed on the "borrowed" phone.

Leland laughed. "Stay in touch. And watch your six."

"You do the same. I'll keep you posted." Nick disconnected the call and pressed down on the accelerator as he gathered his thoughts to formulate a plan. He had a full tank of gas and could drive for several hours if needed.

Examining the situation from every angle, he could think of only one way to do it. The idea was insanity, but he was going for it. The GPS location he'd plugged in pinged on the phone's map. The two-and-a-half-ton truck carrying Jenny and the other women appeared to be headed straight for Constantine.

The ancient Algerian city was fifty miles inland from the Mediterranean and located on the Rhumel River in the mountains. Surrounded by bridges, Constantine was a stunning change from what one thought of as the usual African topography.

Ernesto had said that they had to be inside the city by seven AM. Something was definitely happening there.

He glanced down at the map, and his mind raced. What if he used the mess with the State Department, instead of avoiding them all together? The closest embassy to Constantine was in Algiers, over two hundred miles away. This might not even work. He stared ahead for a moment thinking through his options.

It wouldn't help Gavin, but saving Jenny and the women on that truck was his primary concern. He'd use what he had. He googled the number for the U.S. Embassy on his "borrowed" phone and made the call.

THREE HOURS LATER, as the truck rolled to a halt, Jennifer squeezed Sassy's hand and that of the woman beside her, Maria. The other women around them started moaning in an eerie, keening wail. They all knew nothing good happened when the truck stopped.

"What's going to happen to us?" asked Maria over the weeping. "Where are we?"

Sassy shook her head.

"I don't know," said Jennifer. The plastic cuffs dug into her wrists, and she was frightened—much more so than when she'd been in Tenancingo. Nick was dead or beyond being able to help her. If she thought about that too long, she'd completely shut down. But the reality was there was no one coming this time. She would have to help herself.

The women continued to keen as the back flap was opened, and light poured in. The truck was parked inside what appeared to be a warehouse. The two men who'd locked their chains earlier at the oasis stepped back up to unlock the women's waists from the side panel of the truck, but they didn't remove anyone's zip ties.

"*¡Venga, arranca!*" Get a move on! The man Jennifer had dubbed Body Odor stood glaring at them all. One of the other men addressed him as Juan and discussed the time frame they were dealing with.

The unchained women stood slowly. They'd been sitting for so long, it was impossible to move quickly. Maria, the woman chained next to Jennifer, shook with fear.

Jennifer had learned that she was from a farm in Venezuela and had been lured to what she thought was a good job in the city over a month ago. Maria had not been allowed to contact her family when she'd changed her mind about taking the new "job"; instead, she'd been assaulted. She couldn't be more than fifteen.

Juan didn't help the other men but continued to watch the women being unloaded, impatience obvious in his gaze. Maria moved too slowly for him. When he began to shout, the girl cowered and slipped to the ground.

He laughed at that and immediately pulled off his belt, snapping it like a whip. Jenny pulled at the chain around her own waist, anxious to help Maria get up, but she could only watch in horror. The young girl screamed as the leather struck her across the back.

At last, Jennifer was unlocked from her waist chains. She hurried to Maria's side just as Juan swung the belt back to strike her again. Jennifer threw herself forward, covering Maria's body with her own. The belt struck her instead. The sting was shocking, but the adrenaline rush it provoked dulled the pain.

Juan reached out to pry Jennifer away from the younger girl. He wasn't smiling anymore. He cursed her in Spanish, spitting the words in her face with breath as foul as the rest of him. Maria scrambled forward and out of his way. His vehemence seemed extreme for what had happened.

"You'll pay," he shouted.

Sassy grabbed Jennifer's other arm, pulling her away from him. But Juan shook his head and stared directly at Jennifer.

"No, you're not going with the others. You're staying with me." He smiled and turned away, snapping the belt in the air again with a cracking *pop*.

"I don't want to leave you," whispered Sassy.

She clung to Jennifer's cold fingers with her bound wrists, and they leaned into each other, giving a semblance of a hug, before they were pulled apart. Jennifer bit her lip to keep the tears at bay, even as fear flooded her system and threatened to paralyze her entire body.

"I'll be okay," she lied, hating the way her voice shook. "They'll bring me later."

Sassy's blue eyes filled with tears, but she nodded and smiled with tremulous lips. What they would do between now and later was the part Jennifer didn't want to consider.

Chapter Twenty-Four

Saturday morning
Constantine, Algeria

AFTER DRIVING A circuit around the secluded building, Nick rolled to a stop beside a Dumpster and used it to hide the Mercedes as best he could. Leland had kept up the GPS texts from Jennifer's bug over the past three hours. The last two texts had held the same coordinates, so it stood to reason that Jenny was here.

The warehouse appeared abandoned. It was located just outside the city of Constantine. If this worked, and especially if it didn't, Nick would need that car again. The hangar-like structure had two huge openings on opposite ends of the building, almost like vastly oversized garage doors. A side entrance near the Dumpster stood wide open.

That didn't look good.

Before he exited the vehicle, Nick checked the semiautomatic rifle one last time. He'd found a tactical knife in the center console earlier and clipped the serrated folding blade onto his jeans. Creeping toward the side door, he slipped the MP5 over his shoulder.

When he neared the warehouse, a scream rent the air. He fought the urge to rush inside. He wouldn't do anyone any good if he got himself shot before he entered the building.

Instead, he crept through the side entrance. Even with the two openings at each end, the air was stifling. Almost immediately sweat began to roll down his back and forehead, blurring his vision further as he studied the warehouse layout.

The two-and-a-half-ton truck was parked in the middle of the space, several hundred feet away. Women were being unloaded from the canvas-topped vehicle and shuffled into a different, hard-sided truck, like a moving van but smaller.

Two women were sprawled on the floor. *And Christ, one of them was Jenny.* He recognized her hair immediately. He was so far away that he could only watch in seething rage as the man who'd driven the truck, Juan Santos, struck her with a belt.

Sliding behind a row of shelving, he balled his fists and swallowed hard against the nausea. He had to be patient, even if his plan included tearing Juan apart.

The man hit Jenny once, then Sassy was there. The two women hugged each other as best they could with their hands bound together in front of them. Another man pulled them apart, leaving Jenny with Juan. Juan immediately shoved her into the back of the canvas-sided truck, where Nick could no longer see her.

Juan stood at the tailgate and watched as Sassy and the women were loaded into the other vehicle. The women weren't chained at the waist this time, but they were all still cuffed with the zip ties. One of the other two men closed the back of the new truck, and the second man climbed into the driver's seat waiting for his partner to finish securing the door. Soon after, the truck rolled out of the back exit, leaving Juan and Jenny behind.

Nick watched in agonized frustration. There was no GPS on the hard-sided vehicle. He'd never find those women again if he didn't follow that truck. He had to make a decision now. But there really was no decision.

He couldn't leave Jenny. Not here, not ever.

He waited to move forward, staying out of Juan's line of sight as the man climbed into the back of the canvas-sided truck and moved to the back, toward Jenny. As much as Nick wanted to, he couldn't shoot the son of a bitch before he knew where those other women were being taken. His one chance for finding them lay in keeping Juan alive, at least for a little while.

Nick hurried toward the truck as quietly as possible. Juan was too caught up in what he was doing to notice. That was a good thing because there was a lot a ground to cover. The sound of a zipper lowering echoed in the empty warehouse and gave Nick an adrenaline spike that roared through his veins like molten lava.

"No!" Jenny's voice sounded panicked.

When Nick heard her scream, he rushed the back of the truck. By the time he reached it, she was in a corner. Her T-shirt had been ripped open, and Juan loomed over her with his pants loosened, twisting her hands viciously above her head in those damn zip ties.

Nick took aim on the man's back. "Stop, or I'll shoot."

Juan froze, still holding Jenny's fingers at what had to be a painful angle.

"Let her go, and turn around," Nick ordered. "And don't give me a reason to pull this trigger. God knows I want to."

Juan dropped Jenny's wrist, but before he could turn toward Nick, Jenny slammed her knee into the man's groin. The high, wheezing noise he made sounded like a balloon deflating. Cupping himself and doubling over, Juan shuffled around to face Nick and his MP5.

Nick took grim pleasure in the look of pain crossing the scumbag's face and in the very vulnerable state the man was in with his pants around his knees and his boxers sliding off his hips. It would have been funny if they didn't need to get the hell out of here—*right now*.

"Hands on your head. Knees on the ground," Nick ordered.

Juan put one hand behind his head and started to reach for his pants with the other.

"No," said Nick. "Touch those pants, and I'll let her kick your nuts into your nasal cavity."

Nick lowered his rifle slightly, taking deliberate aim on Juan's crotch. Juan put his other hand behind his neck and scrambled to kneel on the floor of the truck. There was a handgun propped against the tailgate.

The idiot had left his Glock on the floor when he'd scrambled in the truck to attack Jenny. Nick bent down to retrieve the gun and tucked it in his own waistband. A bag of zip ties were busted open beside Juan's knees. Several of the heavy-duty plastic cable ties were scattered all over the floor.

Jenny still stood in the corner, watching everything unfold. Her ripped T-shirt revealed scratches all across her chest. Her eyes held a horrified vacancy.

"Jenny, honey, come here," said Nick.

Hearing her name seemed to bring her back from whatever place she'd gone. She hurried to Nick's side, and he slid an arm around her waist.

"You okay?" he asked.

She nodded but didn't speak. She wouldn't look at him, either. Was she going into shock? He looked at her hands and reached for the knife clipped to his pocket. That bastard had hurt her. Her wrists were raw and bleeding, and a couple of her fingers were already swelling.

"I need to get those cuffs off you." Nick sawed through the plastic with the serrated blade while keeping an eye on Juan. "I want to shoot you so bad, you son of a bitch. Twitch, just once. That's all it'll take."

Juan was barely breathing and kept his eyes on the space in front of him as Nick bent down to retrieve a pair of loose zip ties.

"Can you hold a gun?" Nick asked Jenny. "I need to secure him."

She nodded, and he handed over the Heckler & Koch. Nick pulled Juan to his feet but had him tug his pants up before frisking him. There were no more weapons. Nick pulled Juan's arms behind his waist and slid the zip ties on his wrists. He slipped a second pair on him as well, in case the man was an escape artist.

"Where are they taking those women?" Nick asked.

Juan shrugged. "What will you give me if I tell you?" His accent was heavy, but his English was perfect.

"I won't kill you." Nick pulled the second set of zip ties much tighter than necessary.

Juan winced. "They're going to Algiers."

The capital city of Algiers was two hundred miles from Constantine, on the coast of the Mediterranean. "That doesn't make sense. Why did you stop here in Constantine?"

Nick pushed him forward out of the truck but avoided passing too close to Jenny. He took very little care to be gentle with Juan and basically shoved him out of the back of the truck.

Juan stumbled and fell. "Algiers is a failsafe for the route," he answered from the ground.

Nick left him on the concrete as he helped Jenny down from the truck. "Where in Algiers?" he asked, pulling Juan up by the shoulders.

"If I tell you where, are you going to let me go?"

They both knew he wasn't.

Now it was Nick's turn to shrug. "We'll see, when we get to Algiers."

Nick felt a slight breeze as they made their way across the massive warehouse to "his" Mercedes outside by the Dumpster. The day was going to be a scorcher. Still, he felt no remorse for what he was about to do, particularly after Juan had driven those women through the desert in such torturous conditions. He opened the trunk and pointed. "Get in."

"What?" Juan's voice cracked.

"Get in. I'm not taking you on a fucking road trip. Get in the trunk, or I'll drag your ass behind."

Juan realized arguing was pointless and climbed in the trunk. Nick helped Jenny into the front passenger seat, hurried behind the steering wheel, and peeled out of the car's hiding place.

"We need to catch up to the truck if we can," he explained to her. "They'll be headed through Constantine. Maybe we can catch them there. I don't know how I'll find them otherwise."

Jenny had been staring straight ahead, scaring him a little with her lack of responsiveness. Finally, she spoke up. "I don't understand. How did you find me?" She turned to him.

"I slipped a tracker in your shorts pocket before we got out of the truck at the dig."

"When you kissed me?"

He nodded. "I was lucky you didn't change clothes."

She was looking at him, but she didn't say anything. He needed to explain. God, he'd gone about this all wrong. The past week had been a lesson in what not to do when trying to win back the woman you loved.

The woman he loved.

It hadn't dawned on him until now, of all times. As tangled up as his feelings still were about the miscarriage and the past, he was in love with Jenny. He had been for ten years.

He wanted to protect her. To cherish her. To be part of her life and to spend his with her. Those feelings overwhelmed him.

He struggled to get the words out. "I know it makes me sound like some kind of stalker, but I was scared of losing you again, like I did when you flew out of Dallas to Niamey. That's why I didn't tell you about it. I didn't want to make you mad."

Despite the dire circumstances or maybe because of them, he laughed at himself. That sounded fairly ridiculous. People had been trying to kill them since they'd landed in Africa, and he'd been worried she'd be mad over a GPS tracker.

"You didn't want to make me mad?" Her eyes widened, but she smiled. "My God, you saved my life. Why would I be mad?"

He glanced away from asphalt ahead of them and was lost in her gaze a moment before he hit a pothole and jerked his eyes back to the road.

"Should I be concerned about your stalkerish tendencies?" Her tone was light and that reassured him given the vacancy he'd seen in her eyes earlier "Are there other women you keep these kinds of tabs on?"

"Nope, you're the only one." He took a deep breath. "You've always been the only one," he whispered loud enough for her to hear but focused his gaze on the bridge ahead.

I can't lose you again. I won't.

He needed to say that last part out loud before he lost his nerve. If he looked at her right now, he'd stall. He kept his eyes on the potholed road, but he wanted to tell her everything. He reached for her hand and, avoiding her hurt fingers, carefully threaded his fingers through hers, while keeping his other hand on the wheel.

"What are you saying?" she asked, unaware of the revelation he'd just had and the emotional overload he was experiencing.

For the first time, he knew exactly what he wanted and who he wanted to trust with these "new" feelings. He only had to say it out loud to make it real. "I want . . ."

A BMW sedan passed them as he pulled onto the main road. *Damn*. He hoped that wasn't anyone looking for them, but the odds were not in their favor. He should have stolen another vehicle. There hadn't been time.

Disheartened, he watched in the rearview mirror as everything he'd been about to say was relegated to a back burner. He gently squeezed her palm before letting go. The BMW slowed, stopped, and turned around to chase after them.

Shit.

There was no way to be sure who it was after the phone calls he'd made to the embassy. He floored the Mercedes anyway and shot down the main thoroughfare, headed for the Sidi M'Cid. If he could make it across the narrow 164-meter suspension bridge, one of several leading into Constantine, they'd escape into the anonymity of the almost half a million people who lived there.

The early morning traffic was minimal. But they were being chased by a BMW, so it wasn't as if Nick could leave them in the dust. He barreled around the sweeping mountainous curves.

He could see the Sidi M'Cid in the distance. The BMW was two hundred yards behind and gaining. He shot through a short tunnel carved from the mountain, then out into the light again.

Egg-shaped cars from the city's urban gondola system hung suspended from cables moving steadily over the gorge connecting the mountainous terrain of the city. The suspension bridge grew larger as they swerved around rocky curves.

Once the highest bridge in the world and a true architectural wonder, the Sidi M'Cid was only one lane with sidewalks on either side. Any other time it would have been fascinating to look up at the brick towers, but the BMW was on their tail. When Nick looked ahead to the other side of the bridge leading into the city near the Casbah, the exit was blocked by what appeared to be official police vehicles.

Whoever was doing this had connections that ran deep. He slammed on the brakes, forcing the car behind him to stop about seventy feet from his bumper in the middle of the span.

They were blocked in from both sides with no way off the bridge but over the side.

"What do we do now?" Jenny asked. Her voice was stronger than he would have expected given the circumstances. Unfortunately her thoughts echoed his exactly, and he didn't have an answer.

WHAT DO WE *do* now? Jenny watched in her side-view mirror as three men exited the BMW that had been chasing them and started toward the Mercedes with guns drawn.

"I'm not sure what's going to happen here," said Nick. We're outnumbered. Stay low and follow my lead."

She nodded and scooted farther down in the seat as her heart rate ticked upward.

"I'm sorry, Jenny."

She felt the sting at the corner of her eyelids. "Don't say that," she whispered.

You saved me.

He'd come for her. Multiple times. He'd gotten her away from the horror in Mexico, the kidnapper in Niamey, the sniper at the hotel, the massacre at the dig, away from Juan and what was sure to have been a vicious rape. For the past nine days Nick had been relentless in coming after her.

Even when she'd run away and told him she didn't want him anymore. When she'd lied. Because she did want him. Despite all the running, she wanted him desperately. She'd been running away from Nick Donovan for ten years, and he just kept coming after her.

Who did that? Why did Nick do it?

She looked at him and saw the answer in his eyes, before he turned back to watch the three men draw closer in the rearview mirror. It was a hell of a place to figure things out, to finally know what she wanted and to have found it.

The men were even with the back of the vehicle when Juan started beating on the trunk lid. His shouts echoed through the busted window. Jenny couldn't understand much of what he was saying, but she knew enough Spanish to recognize impressive profanity.

One gunman came forward on the passenger side window, another on the driver's side, while the third remained at the rear of the car. The driver's side gunman shouted to be heard over Juan. His English was perfect.

"Put your hands on the wheel. Throw all your weapons out of the window. Use one hand only. Screw with me, and I shoot the woman."

Nick nodded and did as the man asked. The rifle, knife, and pistol made softer sounds than she would have thought when they landed on the steel and concrete. Jenny placed her hands on the dashboard. The heat from the morning sun was already warming the black surface. Her fingers, which had been so achy and cold earlier, now felt clammy.

The driver's side gunman kicked the weapons under the car, pulled Nick from the vehicle, frisked him, then popped the trunk at the dash before dragging Nick to the rear of the Mercedes. Jenny knew Nick wasn't fighting back for fear of her being harmed.

She continued watching in the rearview mirror as Juan burst out of the trunk with the snarling grace of a cat who'd fallen in a commode. He was spitting mad and all but crawled into Nick's face.

She was still studying Juan's temper tantrum, grateful he didn't have a weapon yet, when the gunman on her side of the car spoke. "Dr. Grayson."

She looked up. Her breath caught in her lungs. "Ohmygod," she whispered. "It's you."

Chapter Twenty-Five

NICK STRUGGLED TO keep up with Juan and Jenny at the same time. Head down, Jenny walked in front of a man toward the BMW that had chased them onto the bridge. Juan stood in front of Nick, practically foaming at the mouth he was so angry. The third gunman who'd remained at the rear of the vehicle came forward to help secure Nick's hands behind his back.

At the same time, Juan sucker punched Nick once more in what felt like a repeat from the oasis—first a shot to the kidney, then another to the face. Warm blood dripped from his nose as he was shoved from the back end of the car toward the edge of the bridge.

He kept watch on Jenny. She was stuffed into the front passenger seat of the BMW with a great deal more restraint than Nick would have suspected. Still, she put up a good fight. He heard the car's engine rev.

What were they going to do to her?

"I see you're confused," said Juan, moving to block Nick's view of the BMW and taking a Beretta 9mm from one of the two men with him. "It's complicated."

He turned to the man who'd cuffed Nick. "Go tell them at the city end of the bridge to keep the barricades up for the next ten minutes. This won't take long."

Nick bit his tongue against a smart-ass comment and a quick trip over the side of the bridge.

Juan brandished the gun a bit. "My boss would have liked to have been here, but now, he just wants you dead."

"Why? What is this about?" Nick kept his tone even, despite the dire outlook. Staying calm was all he had going for him at this point.

"You wouldn't believe me if I told you." Juan shook his head. "I'm almost sorry it's going to end this way for you. Hell, I would be sorry if you hadn't crammed me into that damn trunk earlier. It's ironic though. Shit, it's practically prophetic."

"What are you talking about?" Nick's head swam as more blood ran down his chin and neck, but there was nothing he could do to stop it.

"Your father."

"What about my father?" The cold feeling Nick had had when talking to Ernesto Vega at the oasis earlier washed over him once again.

"It's interesting. Your father didn't quite see it coming either." Juan laughed and stared into Nick's eyes. "No one's ever told you, have they? And you've never suspected?"

Nick felt his brow furrow. "Suspected what?"

Juan stepped closer now that Nick was completely secured. "Your father's car didn't go off that embankment accidentally."

"What are you saying?" At last, Nick would hear the truth spelled out whether he wanted to or not.

"He was helped."

Nick shook his head. "What are you saying? Who *helped?*"

"Your father wouldn't go along with the program. He worked for my employer, but he didn't realize that my boss worked for a cartel. Things were set up through a series of shell companies, and Reese Donovan managed those holdings in the U.S. Even though the scheme wasn't terribly complicated, he didn't realize until too late that he was being used to launder cash."

Nick shook his head again, but Juan kept talking.

"Donovan examined things too closely, asked too many questions about the holdings, the partners. Car accidents are ridiculously easy to arrange. I should know." Juan smiled, but his expression was cold.

Something clicked as Nick listened. This bastard was confessing to the murder of his parents. The thought took Nick's breath, and he fought to regain his equilibrium.

"My father never worked for a cartel," said Nick, but the words lacked conviction. With Juan's declaration, so much about Reese Donovan's embezzlement that hadn't made sense before, suddenly did. Paperwork that had been confusing, even when Nick thought he knew all the details. Papers he had looked at just a few days ago.

Juan raised an eyebrow. "Technically, that's true. Your father never worked for a cartel. But the evidence showed he was embezzling funds from his law firm's clients. In reality, he was working for someone else within your U.S. government, trying to figure out who was behind all the shell companies. When my superiors found out, they wanted Reese Donovan dead."

Nick fought against the turmoil in his gut as his thoughts raced.

"And they had orders," Juan added.

"Orders from whom?"

Juan shrugged. Now he was the one who shook his head. "It doesn't matter any longer. I think I've proven that I can make anyone look guilty."

Nick just bet he could. He swallowed the anger and moved slightly to focus on Jenny in the BMW.

Juan followed his gaze. "If you want to make this easier on her, you'll do as I say." He and the other gunman herded Nick ever closer to the edge of the bridge but never came near enough for Nick to disarm them.

"Sidi M'Cid is beautiful. It's also known for its suicides." The other man's Glock was pointed toward Nick's face as Juan kept talking. Both men had their backs to the BMW. "You're going to jump. Now. No one will question it. You've been acting so erratically lately. You've been depressed, recovering from painful injuries. It's understandable."

"You're insane." Nick didn't plan on jumping, no matter what Juan said. The man was certifiable.

"If you jump without a fight, we won't rape the woman before we kill her." Juan slipped the Beretta into his waistband at his back. He seemed to like inflicting pain, and Nick braced for what he knew had to be coming. Juan was now close enough for Nick to touch, but the other guy was still pointing a Glock at his head.

"Fuck you," Nick mumbled, and got another shot to the kidney from Juan. If he survived this, he'd be peeing blood for a week. He straightened and took a shallow breath. "Why would I do that?" he asked.

"My word is good, even to you. You're going over the side, whether you jump or we put a bullet in your chest and push you over the edge."

Nick shook his head then stopped for a moment, at least giving the impression he was considering the option. It wasn't hard to fake devastation. He must look like hell with all the blood on his face. His vision was blurry from the headshots he'd taken earlier, his nose felt swollen to twice its normal size, and every breath was painful.

God, this was it. He and Jenny were well and truly screwed. No cavalry was going to ride in. He'd been set up from the beginning. He still didn't know by whom, but despaired to think it could have been someone at AEGIS. For about two seconds he considered doing as Juan asked, but there was just no way. He wouldn't give up, even if it would save Jenny pain at the very end.

"Not going to take me up on it?" Juan pulled the Beretta from his waistband. "That was how I got your father to cooperate. I promised not to hurt your mother before I killed her. No one could blame a man for wanting the woman he loves to have a painless death, if death is truly inevitable."

Nick had thought he'd heard every revelation about his parents' deaths, but the hits just kept coming, and this last blindsided him. He tried to take a deep sip of air but couldn't breathe beyond a shallow gasp. The overwhelming rage made him dizzy.

This scum-sucking son of a bitch had killed his parents and was now boasting of how he'd done it? If Nick focused on that, he wouldn't be able to function. He had to think.

He tried breathing through his nose but couldn't get any air past the blood. He wasn't sure if it was the knowledge of what his parents' last moments had been that had him so shattered or if he had a broken rib.

What would it be like to know you were about to die with the person you loved most in the world? To look into their face for the last time. Would you be sorry you'd loved them to begin with?

No, you'd only be longing to have had more time.

He turned his face toward Jenny again. *Dammit.* This was not going to be the last time he looked at her.

"Why her?" Stalling for time, Nick motioned to the BMW with his head.

Juan smiled but didn't turn around. "This was never about her. It was always about you. She just ended up in the wrong place at the wrong time. And after that, there was no escape."

It was always about you.

Nick wanted to howl, even as he felt the stonework of the bridge at his hip. Ernesto had said that, too, but Nick hadn't picked up on it at the time. He should have known. Putting the people he cared about in danger was always his biggest fear.

Juan and his gunman stood side by side, again both aiming their weapons from point-blank range at Nick's head. Nick stared down the barrel of the Glock, then the Beretta. Strangely, he felt no fear, only regret for the time he wouldn't have with Jenny. For the danger he'd put her in without realizing it.

He gazed out over the gorge and took another step backward along the edge of the railing. Juan had the expectant look of a child on Christmas morning.

Nick looked to Jenny one last time. He loved her. He knew that now.

He'd wanted a lifetime with her. He wasn't giving up and quitting. He'd done that once before when he'd thought he'd lost her. Giving up then had been the biggest mistake of his life.

He gathered himself, preparing to wade into the two men and the bullets. Seventy feet down the bridge from Juan and his gunman, the BMW engine revved again, louder this time. Before they could react, the front bumper was ramming into both men at an angle.

It happened in less than five seconds, but the world took on a surreal, slow-motion camera effect as Nick stumbled backward beside the railing and fell to his knees on the concrete. The side of the car's grill hit the bridge's steel-and-iron wall, forcing the railing to give way. The two men were catapulted in what seemed like a circus stunt, up and over the side of the railing into the empty space below.

It was several hundred feet to the bottom of the gorge. One of the men screamed all the way down, but Nick couldn't have said which one it was. When it was quiet again, he tried to stand, but he couldn't with his hands cuffed behind him. All those shots to the head and body had slowed him down to the point where he still wasn't clear on exactly what had happened.

The sides of the bridge were shoulder-height, but the car had practically scooped Juan and the other man over the edge.

The bumper was crumpled and one of the front wheels hung precariously off the bridge, but the BMW still looked drivable. The man who'd taken Jenny to the car earlier slid out of the vehicle shouting at her. Ignoring him, Jenny hopped out on the passenger side and ran toward Nick.

"What the hell, woman? You can't just put your foot over mine on the accelerator. We could have gone over the damn edge!"

Who was that? The voice sounded so familiar.

"But we didn't, Hosea."

Nick heard Jenny's voice clearly and stared, unsure he'd understood correctly. *Jenny had saved him?* Who was this man with the cigar in the side of his mouth?

Jenny's hands were on Nick's face, then at his elbows, pulling him up from the concrete.

"Get in the car." The man motioned to Nick, even though he stood alongside the broken railing as if he were rooted to the spot. "I've got to get you and your crazy *chica* out of here."

The man Nick assumed was Hosea pointed to the other men racing from the barricades on the city side of the bridge. "They'll be here soon."

Jenny pulled Nick away from the broken railing toward the BMW's backseat. Her eyes were huge. He was still in a little shock himself that she'd driven into Juan and sent both men tumbling over the edge.

Nick hustled into the backseat, wincing as he sat down. Jenny climbed in beside him and sawed through his plastic cuffs with a pocketknife from the empty front passenger seat. Hosea raced to and from Nick's abandoned Mercedes to the driver's side of the BMW. He held two key fobs in his grasp.

"That should slow them down," Hosea muttered, sliding behind the steering wheel.

The Mercedes Nick had driven onto the bridge was blocking the narrow roadway, and with no keys the vehicle was likely to be there for a while; hotwiring it would be next to impossible without a lot of time.

"You're Leland's contact," said Nick, still feeling as though he was playing catch up.

"Hosea Alvarez. We've spoken on the phone." The man nodded his introduction and slammed the BMW into reverse. "We'll shoot the shit when I get us out of here."

Nick snorted a laugh and grimaced at the painful sensation breathing caused in his chest. It made sense this smartass would be a friend of Leland's. One scary three-point turn later, Hosea was zooming off the bridge and headed for the hills outside Constantine.

Chapter Twenty-Six

"YOU OKAY?" ASKED Jenny.

Nick stared at her, unsure how to answer. His family history had just been rewritten. He was no longer the son of a man who had driven off a hundred-foot embankment and embezzled from his clients. His parents had been murdered. His father was most likely set up to take the fall for something Nick didn't yet understand.

When those truths sank in, Nick's thinking about a lot of things would change. He still had questions, the first one being: Who had ordered his parents' deaths?

If Juan was to be believed—and that was a big "if"— Reese Donovan had been working for someone within the government. According to Leland, Nick shouldn't trust anything Juan Santos had said, but why would the man have lied if he'd thought Nick was about to die on that bridge? It made no sense to tell a lie when the truth would do.

For Nick, knowing his father was innocent of embezzlement would affect how he saw himself and his future, even in the uncertainty of this moment. He could already feel the change starting inside.

So he said the only thing he could in answering Jenny's question. "I feel good."

She took in his battered face and body, looking at him as if she feared for his sanity. "Are you sure you're not overstating the 'good' part?"

Nick shook his head. "Nah. I'm really . . . I'm gonna be okay." And he meant it, for the first time in a long time.

He had no idea where they were headed, and his head was still reeling from the turn of events and the pot shots Juan and his men had taken at him on the bridge. He was trusting a man he'd never met, a man who was the confidential informant of another man he probably shouldn't be trusting—but was—to get them to safety. There were no other options right now. He leaned back in the seat and realized he wasn't breathing too well.

"Where are we going, Hosea?" They were a long way from being home free. "Leland claims you can walk on water with your contacts here. Can you get us out of the country and back home, or at least into Europe?"

Hosea caught Nick's glance in the rearview mirror and grinned. "Absolutely. That I can do. If you don't mind me saying, you're not looking so good. Would you like me to find you a doctor first?"

Nick sighed, and *damn*, it hurt. He definitely had a cracked rib or two. "If you can do that, I'll tell everyone about your miraculous abilities."

"Prepare to be amazed." Hosea laughed and moved the unlit cigar to the other side of his mouth. "But keep the accolades to yourself."

"You got it."

The rocky sides of the mountain walls flashed by. Hosea was driving fast, putting as much distance as possible between them and Constantine.

"Where are we headed?" Nick asked again.

"The coast. It's about sixty miles from here. Skikda, specifically," said Hosea.

Nick leaned his head back against the seat, happy to let someone else be in charge for the moment. His head was swimming. Now that the adrenaline rush was over, he was well and truly wiped.

Jenny grabbed a bottle of water from a cup holder and prepared to clean his face.

"Just a minute." Nick had one more thing to do before he shut down, even though he was still bleeding onto his shirt. He pulled his "borrowed" phone from his pocket and texted Leland.

Have Jenny. With Alvarez. Lost the other women and their trail in Constantine.

That last weighed heavy, but there was nothing he could do. Even if he knew where the women were, he was in no shape to help them.

A text pinged back. *Are you okay?* He quashed down the irritation that everyone was asking him that. He was fine. It was all relative.

Yes. Any word from Hollywood?

Not yet.

"Enough, you're bleeding everywhere," scolded Jenny, gently pushing his head back to the seat. "Lean back." She started wiping the blood away using a pile of napkins from the pocket on the seat in front of her.

Damn. It stung like a bitch, but he kept his mouth shut and dropped the phone to his lap. For now, he was content to let Jenny fuss over him and to let Hosea drive as everything else buzzed in his head. His eyes closed when her hands drifted over his face and chest.

The phone signaled an incoming call, and he realized he'd dozed off for a moment. He scooped the cell up, hoping it was Leland with an update, but the caller ID read *Tomas Rivera.* Ernesto must have had the man's number in his contact information.

Nick stared down at the screen. *WTF?* He held the phone up so Jenny could see the name. She froze and leaned back, giving him room to take the call.

It made sense Rivera would have Ernesto's number. Still, it was creepy. He opened the line on the third ring but said nothing.

"Mr. Donovan. This is Tomas Rivera. We need to meet."

"Why would I want to do that? You've been trying to kill me for the past week."

Rivera didn't deny it. "I'm thinking you have questions about all you have learned recently. You'll want to know who you can trust in this 'brave new world,' yes? And I suddenly have need of answers myself—answers only you can provide."

That was certainly intriguing.

At this point, Nick trusted the people in this car, and that was about it. "Where do you want to meet?" he asked.

"You're on your way to Skikda." Rivera was making a statement, not asking a question. With startling clarity, Nick knew the man was either tracking this phone or the car they were riding in.

Again, there was nothing to be done about it. Hell, even now the Algerian army could be headed their way, and the road they were travelling had no detours or turn offs for another thirty miles. They were stuck until they reached the coast.

"Where do you want to meet?" Nick repeated.

"Don't worry. I'll find you." The line went dead.

Saturday afternoon
Skikda, Algeria

TWO HOURS LATER they were in Skikda. Not knowing which item was being tracked by Rivera, Nick had tossed Ernesto Vega's phone a couple of miles from town. They'd left the BMW parked on a side street as soon as they hit the city limits. If Rivera was going to find them, he was going to have to work for it.

Once on foot, they'd grabbed a cab to an out-of-the-way clinic that Hosea knew. There Nick had received stitches in his cheek, pain killers for his ribs, and a clean shirt, so he didn't look like an extra from a horror movie. They'd taped up Jenny's fingers from the incident with Juan and cleaned up her forehead from the cab in Niamey as well. She and Nick now had matching butterfly bandages. After settling them at an outdoor café, Hosea had left him and Jenny to arrange for transportation out of Algeria. The plan was to leave that evening if at all possible.

In the meantime, Nick and Jenny were eating a real meal for the first time since dinner at the Paleo-Niger Project site almost two days ago. Nick was polishing off a second entrée and contemplating dessert as he watched the crowded street in front of their table.

Despite Algeria's large Muslim population, the holiday shoppers were busy. The fact that today was Christmas Eve seemed just as surreal as what Nick had learned on the bridge in Constantine.

"Juan Santos admitted that he murdered my parents."

Jenny tried to stifle a gasp but couldn't. "Why? I don't understand."

"I don't either, at least not yet. But there's more. Dad wasn't embezzling. He didn't kill himself or Mom."

"My God, Nick. No one ever said that your dad killed himself on purpose, did they?"

"Not to you. But plenty did to me. The police intimated, the newspapers hinted, and the life insurance company flat out refused to pay the death benefit initially. Only after a friend at Dad's law firm threatened to sue the bastards did they back down. Hell, I wondered at times myself."

"But why would someone kill your parents?" she asked.

"Santos was making bizarre claims that Dad was really working for someone within the government and that he had orders."

"Do you believe it?" She took a sip of her bottled water.

"I don't know. Why would Santos lie to me when he thought I was about to die? Why mention it at all?"

"I still don't understand why you need to meet with Tomas Rivera," said Jenny, keeping her voice low. "It's too dangerous here. Why can't we just get on a boat and get out of the country?"

It might be crazy to open himself up to Rivera, but Nick had to meet with him. He needed answers only Rivera could provide. He did not, however, want Jenny anywhere near the meeting.

"I've got to know what's going on. Why have the cartels been after you and me?" He cracked the cap on the third bottle of water he'd asked the waiter to bring.

"When this started six weeks ago in that clinic, Cesar said they were already after me. Why? As shocking as finding out about my parents has been, I don't see what it has to do with the past nine days. Why come after me now, after so many years? It doesn't feel right. Something else is going on."

Jenny watched him with concern in her eyes. "Do you have to know? Can't it just be over? At least for now? I can't argue with you, and I know I don't have a claim on you, but I don't want anything to happen to you." She slid her hand across the table to touch his. "When I saw you on the edge of that bridge . . ." Her voice faded.

Twenty-four hours ago Nick wouldn't have spoken. But today had shown him how precious every moment was. Not one should be wasted. "You're wrong, Jenny. You do have a claim on me. I realized it standing on the Sidi M'Cid. What I wanted. What I want more than anything. I want to—"

A shadow fell across the table. They both looked up to see Tomas Rivera standing beside them with a bodyguard at his shoulder.

"May I join your tête-à-tête?" asked Rivera, as if this were an everyday meeting.

Jenny's face paled in surprise. *Damn.* Nick had been so engrossed in what he wanted to tell her, he'd never seen Tomas coming. This was the last place Nick wanted Jenny to be, but he smiled grimly. There was no reaching for the Ruger LCP Hosea had loaned him earlier.

"Before you refuse, you should know I have a sniper across the street with his rifle trained on Dr. Grayson. Any threatening moves or a signal from me, and he pulls the trigger."

If possible, Jenny's cheeks blanched even whiter.

"By all means, join us," said Nick.

A waiter started over to their table, but Tomas's bodyguard stopped him.

"I know you have questions," began Rivera.

"That would be one way of putting it."

Tomas tipped his head. "You want to know why all this happened and who to trust now that your organization is a shambles?"

"Naturally, I'm curious," said Nick.

"I would hope that you are more than just curious."

Nick shrugged. Under the table Jenny gripped his fingers before letting them go to take a sip of her water.

Tomas's attention caught for a moment on her bandage, and something in his eyes changed as he stared at her hand. "But that's not the most important question today," he said.

"Alright. How about this one? Do you know who ordered my parents' murder?"

Tomas didn't answer right away, but he didn't look surprised that Nick was asking. "Yes, I do know. I will only say that it wasn't me. And again, that's not the question you need to be asking."

Nick swallowed an angry retort and thought back to his conversation on the bridge with Juan. To keep Jenny safe, Nick needed to know beyond a shadow of a doubt if Juan Santos had been telling the truth or lying. "Were you after Jennifer all this time or after me?"

Tomas nodded his approval and leaned back in his chair, staring at Jennifer's hand until she slid it back under the table.

"Since it's the Christmas season, I'm going to give you a gift, Mr. Donovan. Those who know me would tell you that doesn't happen often, so listen well. I was never after Dr. Grayson, specifically. This was always about revenge, plain and simple. I wanted to hurt you for what I thought you had done to my wife, my employees, and my home. I know from personal experience that hurting a man's woman and family hurts more than anything else that can be done to him."

"But if that's the case, not all of those attacks make sense." Jenny's voice shook with anger. "At the brothel and at the Paleo-Niger dig site, there were so many others hurt. You killed people who had nothing to do with Nick or with me. People who had nothing to do with any of this."

Despite her sprained fingers, she gripped Nick's hand so tightly under the table, he expected there'd be indentions from her fingertips when this was over.

"I had nothing to do with either of those regrettable incidents. It has recently come to my attention that another was responsible for the attack on my compound and on the vet clinic. I suspect they had a part in those heinous events you mention as well. Someone I trusted betrayed me."

Cold fury burned in Rivera's eyes when he focused again on Nick. "This matter no longer concerns you. If you go home and stay out of Mexico, I will no longer pursue you or those you care for."

"After all that's happened, you'd stop? Why should I believe you?" asked Nick.

"You truly no longer work for the government, do you?" Tomas's smile was wintry, the fury still there behind his expression. "Believe me or not, it is your choice. You are, as they say, off my radar. Ignore my advice at your and Dr. Grayson's peril."

Jenny looked from Nick to Tomas with a dumbfounded expression.

"Just like that?" Nick asked, still holding her hand under the table. Had all this shit happened because people believed he still worked for the CIA? Dammit, he'd quit a year ago. He'd like nothing better than to wrap his hands around Rivera's neck right now, but the threat of the sniper across the street made that fantasy impossible.

"Just like that," repeated Tomas. "Although if my sources are correct, I believe your organization currently has enough trouble of its own, particularly your fearless leader." Sarcasm dripped from Rivera's statement.

"Juan Santos said he could make anyone look guilty. Did you have anything to do with—" Nick stopped himself. Of course Tomas had set Gavin up, or the cartel leader knew who had.

Tomas smiled, genuine warmth in his eyes this time. "Ah, Juan Santos will be missed. Talent comes in all forms. Gavin Bartholomew is in for a difficult time. I'll give you a final word of advice, even though you haven't asked. Consider this a Christmas bonus. You want to know who you can trust in this new world? The answer is complicated and simple at the same time. Trust no one, absolutely no one."

With those enigmatic words Tomas stood, waved a hand signal to the unknown sniper, and left as quickly as he had arrived. Nick and Jenny watched in silence. The waiter returned to take an order for coffee while the cartel leader disappeared with his bodyguard into the street crowd.

Chapter Twenty-Seven

"I'M NOT SURE what to say to all that," Jenny shook her head and turned to Nick. "What do we do now?"

He took a deep sip of water, glad he finally had an answer to that question. "We get the hell out of Africa. I don't think this is over by any stretch of the imagination, but I'm not ignoring Rivera's advice. We're going home, and I'm stashing you somewhere safe."

He reached for her hand again and looked out over the busy street before carefully tightening his grip on her palm. Bryan walked toward the café from the opposite direction Tomas Rivera had taken.

Nick felt uneasy, as if they'd hung out a "we are here" sign. How in hell had Bryan found them?

Jenny recognized Hollywood and stood to hug him when he drew close to the table. "My God, Bryan. How'd you find us? Are you okay?"

Hollywood shook his head. He looked exhausted.

Nick's eyes narrowed as he took everything in. He didn't like this one little bit.

Bryan caught Nick studying him, and his face went completely blank. "I'm alright, Jennifer. How about you?" He reached up, brushed at the bandage on her face, and sat down. "I went to the dig site and—"

"What did you find?" She grabbed for his hand. "It was burning to the ground when they took us away."

Bryan shook his head. "I'm sorry, I don't have good news. The camp was destroyed. The Nigerien authorities were on site when I got there. Mopping up. They're calling it a tribal uprising."

"That's bullshit," said Nick.

Bryan nodded. "Yeah, but they can call it that because no foreigners died. Only Tuareg guards and a professor from Abdou Moumouni University were killed. Several foreign students from the project were hurt but none seriously. It's rather remarkable, considering. I don't know what kind of shape the actual dig site is in, but the government won't knock themselves out investigating what really happened."

Jenny shook her head. "That's awful and wrong and . . . so senseless. Sadly, I doubt the Russ Foundation will put up that big of a stink either. They'll want to be invited back once the dust clears."

Nick remained silent as she told Bryan what had happened since he'd run out of the hotel in Niamey. Her abbreviated explanation didn't include everything. She left out the part about Juan's attack in the warehouse and meeting Sassy.

Nick was still trying to figure out how Bryan had located them when Hollywood said, "I think I saw the women from that truck outside Constantine on the way here."

Jenny's eyes widened in surprise. "Where did you see them?"

Bryan raised an eyebrow and glanced at Nick before answering. "There was a huge road block and a lot of military folks, U.S. and Algerian together. They were unloading about twenty women as I drove past. I imagine the Algerian government has them now." Bryan looked pointedly at Nick. "Any idea how that happened?"

Nick shrugged. "Anonymous tip, perhaps?"

This time Bryan was the one to narrow his eyes. "How'd you manage that?" he asked.

"After I got away from Ernesto's shoot-out at the oasis, I called the U.S. Embassy in Algiers and told them Gavin Bartholomew was travelling with a shipment of women being smuggled out of Constantine. I wasn't sure I was going to catch up with you in time, and I figured the only way to get help with some kind of military involvement was to dangle AEGIS in front of them. Leland had warned me off calling any of my contacts in the U.S. Embassy here. I assumed that meant they already knew Gavin was wanted in a DEA investigation. Given how our rep has recently gone to hell, I didn't figure one more ding would matter."

"So that's why you stayed in the warehouse and came after me, instead of going after the other women?" Jenny asked.

Nick frowned. "No, that's not the reason I came after you." *I couldn't leave you.* But he wouldn't say that here in front of Bryan.

"I didn't think using Gavin's name could hurt his reputation any more than it already has been. And in this case, even Gavin would have said it was worth the price."

"That was a good plan," said Bryan, reluctant praise in his voice.

"Do you believe Gavin was set up?" asked Nick, keeping his own tone carefully neutral.

A pained expression crossed Hollywood's face. "I want to. What do you think?"

Nick shrugged. "I think we can believe whatever we want. It's what we can prove that will matter."

As much as he might wish to, Nick wouldn't swear undying loyalty to Gavin until he could talk to the man in person. Someone else's life depended on his being right, and Nick wouldn't risk Jenny for his boss.

"Did you see Sassy on the truck?" Jenny asked.

Bryan stared at her, the shock slowly spreading over his face. "Sassy Smith? She was with you . . . on the truck?" His low voice cracked, and Nick watched as the man visibly freaked, then pulled himself back together, all in less than seven seconds.

Jenny nodded and explained how they'd met Sassy. "Juan Santos's men put her on the other truck just before it left the warehouse outside Constantine. I have no idea what happened after that."

"She wasn't with the group of women I saw at the military roadblock. I watched them take everyone off that truck." Bryan gazed at the people carrying brightly wrapped packages down the dusty street in front of the café. "I had no idea," he mumbled. "I was so sure she was still in Niamey."

"Do you suppose she could have gotten out of the truck before the roadblock stopped them?" Jenny asked.

Bryan shook his head and shrugged, but Nick knew Hollywood wasn't saying what he was really thinking.

Could something have happened to Sassy along the way to the roadblock? Did one of those idiots driving the truck pull her out of the back and take her for a "test drive"? Had something gone horribly wrong? Was she lying in a ditch somewhere outside of Constantine?

Instead Bryan said, "I didn't get close enough to talk to any of the women. They were all in the custody of the Algerians."

"What are you going to do?" asked Jenny.

"Keep looking." Bryan studied her concerned face. "Don't worry, I'll find her. The woman's a reporter, and she's like a cat. Always lands on her feet." He smiled, but it wasn't a genuine look of happiness.

"Who is she?" asked Nick.

Bryan stared down at the table a moment before answering. "A freelance reporter."

"Who is she to you?" asked Nick, remembering being asked a similar question less than a week ago. For a moment he didn't think Hollywood was going to answer.

"Sassy is the younger sister of Trey Smith."

Of course. Nick had known Sassy's name sounded familiar when they met on the truck, but he'd gotten stuck on the *Smith* part and dismissed the idea that he'd heard it before.

"Who's Trey Smith?" asked Jenny, reaching for Nick's hand.

"Elizabeth Yarborough's boyfriend," answered Nick.

"The Peace Corps girl who disappeared earlier this year?" asked Jenny. It wasn't surprising that she knew who Elizabeth Yarborough was. The young woman's disappearance had filled the world's airwaves, front pages, and social media output for weeks last summer. Everyone with access to a television, computer, or radio had heard about Elizabeth's disappearance, suspected murder, and the subsequent arrest of her boyfriend in Mexico.

"Trey Smith is the boyfriend who's in jail in Mexico, right?" said Jenny.

"The very one," said Bryan glumly. "I've known Trey for years. We grew up in the same neighborhood."

"So that's why you've been all over hell's half acre looking for Elizabeth Yarborough." Nick wondered if Hollywood had ever told any of the operatives at AEGIS his real connection to the Yarborough case. He'd assumed Bryan had a connection to the woman, not the boyfriend. *Did Gavin even know the truth?*

Trust no one, absolutely no one.

Nick's discomfort grew as he thought of Tomas's ominous advice, combined with the relative ease with which people seemed to be able to track him and Jenny anywhere right now. The waiter brought their coffee, and Jenny talked with the man about dessert and another coffee cup for Bryan.

"Why did you tell Sassy Smith Jenny's name?" Nick needed to know if he could believe anything Hollywood told him.

"Sassy's been helping me with the Yarborough case. To pay for the travel, she has to be able to write stories she can sell to the Associated Press. She was working on the human trafficking angle when she heard about the contract on Jennifer from one of her sources. She was trying to confirm who the target was, but she didn't know Jennifer's name. I made her promise not to use any of it in a story until Jennifer was home safe." Bryan never broke eye contact with Nick during the explanation.

Finally, it occurred to him how Hollywood had found them.

"The GPS in Jenny's shorts, right?"

Bryan leaned forward so she couldn't hear them and rolled his eyes. "Yes, you idiot. I talked to Leland before I got here. He can't get in touch with you, by the way. He's going nuts. What did you think, I was dirty?"

"Right now, I'm thinking everyone is dirty until proven otherwise."

"Then why trust me?" asked Bryan.

"Because you've proven otherwise."

Something changed in Bryan's face when Nick said that. He was reminded again that Hollywood was experienced beyond his years with those old man's eyes that had seen so very much.

Nick caught Bryan up to what had happened with Tomas Rivera, ending with their plan to get out of the country as soon as possible. The waiter returned with an extra coffee cup.

"No thanks, I'm headed out," Bryan said, standing to leave. "I just wanted to check in with you two."

"You're going after Sassy, aren't you?" she asked.

He nodded and pulled Jenny to her feet to give her a hug. Nick suppressed the urge to tell Hollywood to get his own woman. Bryan was working on that, whether he realized it himself or not.

"Do you know where you'll start looking?" asked Nick, rising from his chair as well.

"Not yet. I'll figure it out."

"Call if you need help."

Bryan took in Nick's battered appearance as the two men shook hands. "I wouldn't be that cruel. You need a vacation in a bad way. Besides, it's Christmas."

Jenny gave Bryan a final hug. "Thank you, for everything," she said. "I know you'll find her."

He kissed her on the cheek and walked away, melting into the crowd like Rivera had, only in the opposite direction.

Jenny sat back down, staring into the street. "What do we do now?"

"That's a question you've asked a lot lately." Nick felt a flutter of nerves as he leaned back in his seat and watched the people in the street hurrying by. Every time he'd tried talking with her about this, they'd been interrupted.

"You really want to know? Because I have some ideas." He waggled his eyebrows.

She grinned. "Absolutely, I want to know. That sounds kind of naughty."

The waiter chose that moment to set a regional dessert between them and left. Nick felt his jaw tense at the intrusion.

"Well?" Jenny gave him a saucy smile and picked up her fork to dig in.

He took a shallow sip of air. It was time. He'd promised himself on that bridge that if he got the chance, he'd do something with it.

"Sitting here with you is where I've always wanted to be." He leaned forward and carefully took her hand. "I don't ever want to let you out of my sight."

"Is this like that stalker thing we talked about earlier?" She wrinkled her brow, but her tone was sunny and teasing.

"No." Without warning, he felt the hot pricking sensation of tears at the corners of his eyes. He was exposed and raw with the kind of emotion that hadn't been at the surface for him in longer than he could remember. But at the same time, he felt . . . peace. "I think we should get married."

"What?!" Her green eyes rounded in stunned surprise, and she stared at him open-mouthed a moment before she spoke. "My God. You're serious. You want to marry me?"

A burst of panic flared in his chest, but he reached for her other hand instead of stopping. "Okay, I didn't mean to just blurt it out like that. But every time we've been on the verge of talking about this, we've been interrupted."

She stared at him with color deepening in her cheeks by the second. "You now have my undivided attention, I assure you."

Her eyes never left his as he took a breath and started talking. "I love you, Jenny. I've loved you for ten years, and I want to spend the rest of my life with you. I want you to be my family, and I want to be yours. I know we've got things to work through, but I'm willing to work hard. Start over with me."

Her eyes filled as he spoke. "You do realize I just got a divorce?"

He nodded. "Yeah, I know. But that's because you didn't marry the right guy."

She leaned forward against the table, shaking her head in disbelief. "And you're sure that you're the right guy?"

He smiled. "I've never been more sure of anything in my life." And he was . . . absolutely positive. "I can make you happy. I know it. Let me."

"I don't know what to say," she murmured.

"Sure you do." He gently pulled her hand to his lips and kissed the back of her knuckles. "Say yes."

Acknowledgments

SO MANY PEOPLE have helped and inspired me in writing this story.

Thank you to my agent, Helen Breitwieser of Cornerstone Literary, for her continued belief in me and my work.

Thank you to my editor, Erika Tsang, who helped make Nick's story its very best and pushed me to write my very best as well. And to all the folks at HarperCollins who continue to make this a lovely experience—Chelsey Emmelhainz, Heidi Richter, Pam Spengler-Jaffee, and the absolutely amazing cover artists who work hard on my behalf.

Thank you to my friend Dr. Alisa Winkler, for taking me on an extended tour of SMU's Paleontology department and for sharing her fascinating experiences in the field with me.

Thank you to my friend Doug, for sharing his unique perspective on Africa and what it is like to live there.

Thank you to my awesome beta reader and friend, Joyce Ann McLaughlin, for always being enthusiastic about my work.

Thanks especially to the "Bulletproof Babes" for their help and encouragement in promoting my stories and to my "Writer Foxes"—Addison Fox, Lorraine Heath, Tracy Garrett, Jane Graves, Jo Davis, Suzanne Ferrell, Sandy Blair, Julie Benson, and Allie Burton. These ladies keep me sane and smiling.

Thank you to my parents, Gran and Te Daddy, for their continued excitement about my writing and for telling me when I was younger that I could do anything I set my mind to.

Thank you to my daughter, Michelle, for always being excited to read what I've written and for picking really good wine. And thank you to my son, Russ, for loving dinosaurs when he was younger and for understanding now that he still can't knock on my office door when it's closed, unless there is smoke or blood involved.

And finally, to my husband, Tom. Thank you for being the real inspiration for all my heroes. None of this could happen without your support or your mad laundry skills. You make all the difference in my world.

June 2014

Can't get enough of Kay Thomas's Elite Ops team?
Keep reading for an excerpt from Book One,

HARD TARGET

Available now from Avon Books.

An Excerpt from

HARD TARGET

"COULD YOU HAND me my top, please?"

Leland bent down to retrieve Anna's shirt and turned away, staring at the floor in front of him to give her privacy. What the hell was he doing? At least he'd given the room a cursory inspection to rule out cameras or bugs before he'd practically screwed her against the bedroom wall.

What he'd really wanted to tell her, before they'd gotten sidetracked with the birth control issue, was the same thing he'd wanted to tell her last night. She didn't have to do him to get Zach back. Whether or not they had sex had no bearing on whether he'd help find her son.

Not that he didn't want her. He did. So much so that his teeth ached.

He hadn't known her long, but what he knew fascinated him. To have dealt with everything she had in the past year and to still be so strong. That inner strength captivated him.

It was important she not think he expected sex in exchange for his help. Sex wasn't some kind of payoff. He needed to clarify that right away.

Besides, neither of them was going to be able to sleep now. He sighed, zipped his cargo shorts, and pulled on his T-shirt and shoulder holster with the Ruger. He shoved the larger Glock into his backpack. This was going to be a long evening.

The night breeze had shifted the shabby curtain to the side, leaving an unobscured view into the room. He turned to face her, wondering if anyone on the street had just gotten an eyeful.

A red laser dot reflected off the wide shoulder strap of her tank top. Recognizing the threat, he dove for her, shouting, "Down. Get down!"

Leland tackled Anna around the waist and pulled her to the floor. A bullet hit the wall with a *sphlift* right where she'd been standing a half second earlier.

He climbed on top of her, his heart rate skyrocketing, and covered her completely with his body. His boot was awkward. His knee came down between her legs, trapping her in the skirt. More shots slapped the stucco, but they were all hitting above his head.

The gunman must be using a silencer. A loud car engine revved in the street. Voices shouted and bullets flew through the window, no longer silenced.

How many shooters were there?

A flaming bottle whooshed through the window.

Breaking on impact, the fire spread rapidly across the dry plywood floor. The pop of more bullets against the wall sounded deceptively benign.

"What's happening?" Anna's lips were at his ear.

Her warm breath would have felt seductive if not for the shots flying overhead and fire licking at his ass. He was crushing her with his body weight but it was the only way to protect her from the onslaught.

"Why are they shooting at us?" Her voice was thin, like she was having trouble breathing.

He raised up on his elbows to take his weight off of her chest but kept his head down next to hers. "They want the money."

"How do they know about the ransom?" she asked.

"Everyone within a hundred miles knows about it." He raised his head cautiously.

They were nose to nose, but he ignored the intimacy of the position. They had to get out of the smoke-filled room. In here, even with just half the money, they were sitting ducks.

He needed his bag. It held all his ammunition and the Glock 17. And they couldn't leave the cash, not now anyway. Having the money might be the only thing to keep them alive when they got out of here.

"Come on." He rolled to the side and tugged Anna's hand to pull her along with him. "But don't raise your head."

Another bullet hit the wall where she had been moments earlier. God, how many men were there? Knowing that could make a difference in getting out of this alive.

About the Author

Kay Thomas didn't grow up burning to be a writer. She wasn't even much of a reader until fourth grade. That's when her sister read *The Black Stallion* aloud to her. For hours Kay was enthralled—shipwrecked and riding an untamed horse across desert sand. Then tragedy struck. Her sister lost her voice. But Kay couldn't wait to hear what happened in the story—so she picked up that book, finished reading it herself, and went in search of more adventures at the local library.

Today Kay lives in Dallas with her husband, two children, and a shockingly spoiled Boston terrier. Her award-winning novels have been published internationally.

Visit www.AuthorTracker.com for exclusive information on your favorite HarperCollins authors.

Give in to your impulses . . .
Read on for a sneak peek at five brand-new
e-book original tales of romance
from Avon Books.
Available now wherever e-books are sold.

**WHITE COLLARED
PART ONE: MERCY**
By Shelly Bell

WINNING MISS WAKEFIELD
THE WALLFLOWER WEDDING SERIES
By Vivienne Lorret

INTOXICATED
A BILLIONAIRE BACHELORS CLUB NOVELLA
By Monica Murphy

ONCE UPON A HIGHLAND AUTUMN
By Lecia Cornwall

THE GUNSLINGER
By Lorraine Heath

An Excerpt from

WHITE COLLARED
PART ONE: MERCY

by Shelly Bell

In Shelly Bell's four-part serialized erotic
thriller, a young law student enters a world of
dark secrets and seductive fantasies when she
goes undercover at an exclusive sex club in order
to prove her client is not guilty of murder.

After three hours of computer research on piercing the corporate veil, Kate's vision blurred, the words on the screen bleeding into one another until they resembled a giant Rorschach inkblot. She lowered her mug of lukewarm coffee to her cubicle's mahogany tabletop and rubbed her tired eyes.

Without warning, the door to the interns' windowless office flew open, banging against the wall. Light streamed into the dim room, casting the elongated shadow of her boss, Nicholas Trenton, on the beige carpet.

"Ms. Martin, take your jacket and come with me." He didn't wait for a response, simply issued his command and strode down the hall.

Jumping to her feet, she teetered on her secondhand heels and grabbed her suit jacket from the back of her chair. As Mr. Trenton's intern for the year, she'd follow him off the edge of a cliff. She had no choice in the matter if she wanted a junior associate position at Detroit's most prestigious law firm, Joseph and Long, after graduation. Because of the fierce competition for an internship and because several qualified lackeys waited patiently in the wings for an opening, one minor screwup would result in termination.

Most of the other interns ignored the interruption, but

her best friend Hannah took a second to raise an arched eyebrow. Kate shrugged, having no idea what her boss required. He hadn't spoken to her since her initial interview a few months earlier.

She collected her briefcase, her heart pounding. As far as she knew, she hadn't made a mistake since starting two months ago. Other than class time, she'd spent virtually every waking moment at this firm, a schedule her boyfriend, Tom, resented.

She raced as fast as she could down the hallway and found her boss pacing and talking on his cell phone in the marbled lobby. He frowned and pointedly looked at his watch, demonstrating his displeasure at her delay. Still on the phone, he stalked out of the firm and headed toward the elevator. She chased him, cursing her short legs as she remained a step or two behind until catching up with him on the elevator.

When the doors slid shut, he ended his call and slipped his cell into the pocket of his Armani jacket. She risked a quick glance at him to ascertain his mood, careful not to visually suggest anything more than casual regard.

He was an extremely handsome man whose picture frequently appeared in local magazines and papers beside prominent judges and legislative officials. But photos couldn't do him justice, film lacking the capability of capturing his commanding presence. Often she'd had to fight her instinct to look directly into his blue eyes. At the office, his every move, his every word overshadowed anyone and everything around her.

Standing close to him in the claustrophobic space, she inhaled the musky scent of his aftershave, felt his radiating heat.

Mr. Trenton spoke, fracturing the quiet of the small space with his deep and powerful voice. "This morning, our firm's biggest client, Jaxon Deveroux, arrived home from his business trip and found his wife dead from multiple stab wounds."

Once the elevator doors opened, they stepped out into the bustling main floor lobby, and she fought to match Mr. Trenton's brisk pace as they headed toward the parking garage. "While typically I would refer my clients to Jeffrey Reaver, the head of our criminal division, Mr. Deveroux and I have been friends for many years, and he requested me personally. Jaxon's a very private man, but those who are in his circle are aware of certain . . . proclivities that may come up in the police's line of questioning."

What sort of proclivities?

An Excerpt from

WINNING MISS WAKEFIELD
The Wallflower Wedding Series

by Vivienne Lorret

When her betrothed suddenly announces his plans
to marry another, Merribeth Wakefield knows
only a bold move will bring him back and restore
her tattered reputation: She must take a lesson
in seduction from a master of the art. But when
the dark and brooding rake, Lord Knightswold,
takes her under his wing, her education quickly
goes from theory to hands-on practice, and her
heart is given a crash course in true desire!

"Now, give back my handkerchief," Lord Knightswold said, holding out his hand as he returned to her side. "You're the sort to keep it as a memento. I cannot bear the thought of my handkerchief being worshipped by a forlorn Miss by moonlight or tucked away with mawkish reverence beneath a pillow."

The portrait he painted was so laughable that she smiled, heedless of exposing her flaw. "You flatter yourself. Here." She dropped it into his hand as she swept past him, prepared to leave. "I have no desire to touch it a moment longer. I will leave you to your pretense of sociability."

" 'Tis no pretense. I have kept good company this evening." Either the brandy had gone to her head, impairing her hearing, or he actually sounded sincere.

She paused and rested her hands on the carved rosewood filigree edging the top of the sofa. "Much to my own folly. I never should have listened to Lady Eve Sterling. It was her lark that sent me here."

He feigned surprise. "Oh? How so?"

If it weren't for the brandy, she would have left by now. Merribeth rarely had patience for such games, and she knew his question was part of a game he must have concocted with

Eve. However, his company had turned out to be exactly the diversion she'd needed, and she was willing to linger. "She claimed to have forgotten her reticule and sent me here to fetch it—no doubt wanting me to find you."

He looked at her as if confused.

"I've no mind to explain it to you. After all, you were abetting her plot, lying in wait, here on this very sofa." She brushed her fingers over the smooth fabric, thinking of him lying there in the dark. "Not that I blame you. Lady Eve is difficult to say no to. However, I will conceal the truth from her, and we can carry on as if her plan had come to fruition. It would hardly have served its purpose anyway."

He moved toward her, his broad shoulders outlined by the distant torchlight filtering in through the window behind him. "Refresh my memory then. What was it I was supposed to do whilst in her employ?"

She blushed again. Was he going to make her say the words aloud? No gentleman would.

So of course *he* would. She decided to get it over with as quickly as possible. "She professed that a kiss from a rake could instill confidence and mend a broken heart."

He stopped, impeded by the sofa between them. His brow lifted in curiosity. "Have you a broken heart in need of mending?"

The deep murmur of his voice, the heated intensity in his gaze—and quite possibly the brandy—all worked against her better sense and sent those tingles dancing in a pagan circle again.

Oh, yes, the thought as she looked up at him. *Yes, Lord Knightswold. Mend my broken heart.*

However, her mouth intervened. "I don't believe so." She gasped at the realization. "I should, you know. After five years, my heart should be in shreds. Shouldn't it?"

He turned before she could read his expression and then sat down on the sofa, affording her a view of the top of his head. "I know nothing of broken hearts, or their mending."

"Pity," she said, distracted by the dark silken locks that unexpectedly brushed her fingers. "Neither do I."

However accidental the touch of his hair had been, now her fingers threaded through the fine strands with untamed curiosity and blatant disregard for propriety.

Lord Knightswold let his head fall back, permitting—perhaps even encouraging—her to continue. She did, without thought to right, wrong, who he was, or who she was supposed to be. Running both hands through his hair, massaging his scalp, she watched his eyes drift closed.

Then, Merribeth Wakefield did something she never intended to do.

She kissed a rake.

An Excerpt from

INTOXICATED
A Billionaire Bachelors Club Novella
by Monica Murphy

It's Gage and Marina's wedding day, but wedded
bliss seems a long way off: Ivy's just gone into labor,
Marina's missing her matron of honor, and Bryn's
giving Matt the silent treatment. It's up to Archer,
Gage, and Matt to make sure this day goes off
without a hitch. But between brides and babies,
there's the not-so-little issue of the million-dollar
bet to attend to. If only they can figure out who
won . . . and who's paying up. Is everyone a winner?
Or will someone leave broke   and brokenhearted?

Gage

I'm a freaking mess.

"Calm down, dude," Matt whispers out of the side of his mouth. We're standing so close our shoulders are practically touching. Wonder whether he'd catch me if I fell. "You look like you're gonna drop."

"I *feel* like I'm gonna drop," I tell him, sounding like an idiot but not really caring. He's my new best man, so I need him to step it up. If I pass out, it's on him.

"Your girl is going to make her appearance at any minute." Matt nods toward the beginning of the aisle, where no one stands. Where are the girls? We already made our walk down the aisle, Matt taking Marina's mom to her seat, me leading my mother.

"Hope she shows up soon," I mutter, meaning it. I feel antsy. My suit is too tight. My throat is dry. I'm dying for a drink. Preferably booze.

Probably not a good idea.

The flower girl suddenly struts down the aisle, cute as can be in a white lacy gown. Louisa is one of Marina's cousins. She has about a bazillion of them.

Almost all of them are sitting in the crowd, watching me. Probably pissed because Marina and I both agreed that we didn't want a huge, ridiculous wedding party. We blew their chance to wear bridesmaids' gowns.

Then Bryn appears, a freaking vision in pale yellow. She walks down the aisle slowly, a coy smile on her face as she shoots me a glance, then trains her gaze on Matt. As her smile disappears, her eyes widen, and I look at Matt, who's staring at Bryn like she's the most beautiful creature he's ever seen in his life.

Poor dude is straight up in love with Bryn. Like, a complete and total goner. I get what he's feeling.

The music fades, and a new song starts, a low, melodic tune played to perfection by the small group of musicians set up off to the right. I straighten my spine, clasp my hands behind my back as I wait for my bride to make her appearance.

And then . . . there she is. Her arm curls around her father's, he looking respectably intimidating in his tuxedo. A frothy veil covers her face, and the skirt of her gown is wide, nearly as wide as the aisle they're walking down.

Tears threaten, and I blink once. Hard. Damn it, I'm not going to cry. I'm happy, not sad. But I'm also overwhelmed, filled with love for this woman who's about to become my partner in life.

They approach and stop just before us, turning to each other so her father can lift the veil, revealing her face to me for the first time. He leans in and kisses her cheek as the minister asks who gives this woman to this man, just as we rehearsed yesterday. Her father says, *I do,* his deep voice a little shaky and my sympathy goes out to him.

I'm still feeling pretty shaky myself.

Marina steps up to stand beside me and I take her hand, unable to stop from leaning in and brushing a quick kiss against her cheek. "You look beautiful," I murmur, my voice just as unsteady as her dad's.

But I don't care. I have no shame. I'm getting married, damn it. I'm allowed to cry. To smile. To laugh. I'm making this woman mine.

Forever.

An Excerpt from

ONCE UPON A HIGHLAND AUTUMN

by Lecia Cornwall

Legends say a curse lurks among the shattered
stones of Glen Dorian Castle. Will the love
that is beginning to grow between Megan and
Kit be able to withstand fate? For only the
living, those with bold hearts and true love,
can restore peace to Glen Dorian at last.

Megan scanned the valley once more and ignored her sister. "I'm just saying goodbye to Glenlorne. At least for now."

"Better to say farewell to people than places," Sorcha said. "I've already been to the village, telling folk I'll be back come spring." She grinned mischievously at her sister. "You won't, though—you'll be in London, bothered by the attentions of all those daft English lairds at your first Season."

Megan felt a rush of irritation. "Lords, Sorcha, not lairds—and stop teasing," she commanded, and flounced down the steep path that led back to the castle.

Sorcha picked a flower and skipped beside her sister like a mountain goat. One by one, she plucked at the petals. "How many English *lords* will Megan McNabb kiss?" she asked, dancing around her sister. "One . . . two . . . three . . ."

"Stop it," Megan said, and snatched the flower away. She wouldn't kiss anyone but Eachann. But her sister picked another flower.

"How many English lords will come and ask Alec for Meggy's delicate hand in marriage?" she mused, but Megan snatched that blossom too, before Sorcha could begin counting again.

"I shan't go to London, and I will never marry an English lord," she said fiercely.

"We'll see what mama says to that," Sorcha replied. "And Muira would say never is a very long time indeed."

Megan stopped. "What exactly did Muira say?" she asked. Old Muira had the sight, or so it was said.

Sorcha grinned like a pirate and rubbed a dusty hand over her face, leaving a dark smudge. "I thought you didn't believe in the old ways."

Megan rolled her eyes, let her gaze travel up the smooth green slopes of the hills to their rocky crests, and thought of the legends and tales, the old stories, the belief that magic made its home in the glen.

Of course she believed.

She believed so much that she'd decided to become the keeper of the old tales when Glenlorne's ancient *seannachaidh* had died the previous winter without leaving a successor. She loved to hear the old stories, and she planned to write them down so they'd never be lost. But for now, in Sorcha's annoying company, she raised her chin. Now was hardly the time to be fanciful. "Of course I don't believe in magic. I think being sensible is far more likely to get you what you want— not counting flower petals or relying on the seeings of an old woman."

"Muira foresaw an Englishman, and a treasure," Sorcha said, not deterred one whit by talk of sense. "Right there in the smoke of the fire, clear as day."

Megan felt her mouth dry. "For me?" she asked through stiff lips.

"She didn't know that. For one of us, surely."

Megan let out a sigh of relief. Perhaps she was safe. If only Muira had seen Eachann, riding home, his heart light, his purse heavy, with a fine gold ring in his pocket. "That's the trouble with Muira's premonitions. She sees things but can't say what they mean."

"Still, a treasure would be nice," Sorcha chirped. "A chest of gold, or a cache of pearls and rubies—"

"Not if it comes with an Englishman attached," Megan muttered.

An Excerpt from

THE GUNSLINGER
by *Lorraine Heath*

(A version of this work originally appeared in
the print anthology *To Tame a Texan*, under
the title "Long Stretch of Lonesome")

Chance Wilder never wanted to be a hero. That
is, until a young boy offers Chance everything he
owns to rescue his sister from a couple of thugs.
But after he saves her, Lillian Madison awakens
in him long-buried dreams and possibilities.
Facing the demons of his past, Chance is forced to
question his next move. Dare he risk everything
by following his heart . . . and trust that the
road to redemption begins with Lillian?

"Why do you want me in the house?"

"As payment," she blurted, the heat flaming her face. "Payment for your kindness to Toby . . . and for saving me. I hate that you killed the man—". Tears burned the backs of her eyes. She despised the weakness that made her sink to the porch. She wrapped her arms around herself and rocked back and forth, memories of the glittering lust and hatred burning in Wade's eyes assailing her. "He was going . . . going to . . . no one would have stopped him."

Strong arms embraced her, and she pressed her head against the warm, sturdy chest. She heard the constant thudding of his heart.

"No one wants you here. Why don't you leave?" he asked in a low rumble.

She shook her head. "This place was the only gift Jack Ward ever gave me. It's special to me."

"You loved him?" he asked quietly.

She nodded her head jerkily. "I shouldn't have. God knows I should have despised him, but I could never bring myself to hate him. Even now, when his gift brings me such pain, I can't overlook the fact that he gave it to me out of love."

"Have you ever talked with John Ward, tried to settle the differences?"

"No. John came here one night with an army of men. He told me to pack up and get, then threatened to kill me as a trespasser if I ever set foot on his land. Delivered his message and rode out. Makes it hard to reason with a man when you can't get near him."

"It's even harder to reason with him if he's dead."

Lillian's heart slammed against her ribs. Trembling, she clutched Wilder's shirt and lifted her gaze to his, trying to see into the depths of his silver eyes. But his eyes were only shadows hidden by the night. His embrace was steady, secure, his hands slowly trailing up and down her back. "Promise me you won't kill him," she demanded.

A silence stretched between them, as though he was weighing the promise against the offer that he'd cloaked as a simple statement. "If he's dead, you and the boy will be safe."

She tightened her fingers around his shirt and gave him a small shake. "I don't want the blood of Jack Ward's son on my hands. Give me your word that you won't kill him."

His hands stilled. "What are you willing to pay me to keep me from killing him?"

Her stomach knotted, and her chest ached with a tightness that threatened to suffocate her. Even though she couldn't see it clearly, she felt the intensity of his perusal. She had no money, nothing to offer him—nothing to offer a killer except herself. And she knew he was aware of that fact.

Had she actually begun to feel sympathy for this man whose solitary life gave him no roots, allowed him no love? He was worse than Wade because at least Wade had barreled into her, announcing loudly and clearly what he wanted of her. The killer wanted the same thing, but he'd lured her into caring for him and trusting him, catching her heart unawares.

The pain of betrayal ripped through her, and she thought she might actually understand why one man would kill another. Tiny shudders coursed through her body, and tears stung her eyes as she answered hoarsely, "Anything."

Beneath her clutched hand, his heart increased its tempo, pounding harder and faster. He cradled her face between his powerful hands. "Anything?" he whispered. "Even if I want all a woman can offer?"

She nodded jerkily. "I don't want John Ward killed." How could she warn the man when approaching him meant her certain death?

Wilder leaned closer to her. His warm breath fanned her face. He shifted his thumbs and gently stroked the corners of her mouth. "Give you my word that I'll let the bastard live."

He pressed his mouth to hers, demanding, claiming all that she'd offered to willingly pay: her body, her heart, her soul. She could not give one without giving the others.